Molly Moon Stops the World

Georgia Byng

Molly Moon Stops the World

DISCARD

 HarperCollinsPublishers

The Academy Awards ceremony depicted in this novel is fictional
and should not be confused with any actual ceremony.

Molly Moon Stops the World
Copyright © 2003 by Georgia Byng
Printed in the United States of America. For information address
HarperCollins Children's Books, a division of HarperCollins
Publishers, 1350 Avenue of the Americas, New York, NY 10019.
www.harperchildrens.com

Library of Congress Cataloging-in-Publication Data
Byng, Georgia.
   Molly Moon stops the world / Georgia Byng.— 1st American
ed.
      p. cm.
   Sequel to: Molly Moon's incredible book of hypnotism.
   Summary: Believing that she has been sent to Los Angeles by
her librarian friend, Lucy Logan, to stop an evil plot by the
wealthy Primo Cell, Molly Moon and her friend Rocky,
orphans with unusual hypnotic powers, find themselves in
danger from an unsuspected source.
   ISBN 0-06-051410-8 — ISBN 0-06-051413-2 (lib. bdg.)
   [1. Hypnotism—Fiction. 2. Orphans—Fiction. 3. Los
Angeles (Calif.)—Fiction.] I. Title.
PZ7.B9887Mo 2003   2003012485
[Fic]—dc22   CIP
                                                    AC

Typography by Amy Ryan
5   6   7   8   9   10
❖
First American Edition
First published in Britain by
Macmillan Children's Books, 2003

To Tiger,
for being such a
brilliant ray of sunshine

One

Davina Nuttel sat in the back of her chauffeur-driven limousine, reading about herself in a celebrity magazine. Her chubby face, surrounded by posters of all the films and shows she'd already starred in, smiled out from the page.

"*Child superstar Davina Nuttel,*" she read, "*is back on Broadway in the hit show* Stars on Mars. *After surprise newcomer Molly Moon quit the part and left New York, Miss Nuttel was the obvious choice for the lead.*" Davina fumed. She was sick of Molly Moon's name being mentioned in the same sentence as hers. She hated that bug-eyed, skinny nobody.

"Stop at the ice-cream parlor on Madison," she snapped at her driver.

He nodded and negotiated his way across four lanes of noisy New York traffic.

Davina was feeling particularly rattled. She needed a big, sweet ice cream. It had been a bad day at the Broadway theater where she was rehearsing a new *Stars on Mars* song. To begin with, she'd had a sore throat and couldn't hit the high notes. Then had come the horrible incident that had completely unnerved her. Davina angrily scraped her nail down the cream leather upholstery. She didn't often need her parents, but tonight she was glad they would be at home for once.

How dare that weird businessman barge, uninvited, into her dressing room? How he'd got past the security guards she didn't know. And what nerve to suppose that she would want to advertise his ugly line of Fashion House clothes. Didn't he know he should talk to her agent?

The creepy Mr. Cell had given Davina the shivers, and she couldn't erase him from her mind. His eyes seemed to have etched themselves behind Davina's, in the way that staring too long at the sun burns its image into a person's vision. Every time Davina shut her own eyes, she saw his two mad eyeballs staring at her.

The car stopped outside her favorite ice-cream parlor. Davina fastened her black mink coat and put on the matching gloves. She stepped out into the cold night and waved condescendingly at her chauffeur. She would walk home. Enjoying the sound of her high-heeled boots on the pavement, she swept into the parlor.

Inside, she ordered the house specialty. It was called the Mondae-Tuesdae-Wednesdae-Thursdae-Fridae-Saturdae Sundae. Determined to banish all thoughts of the strange businessman from her mind, she pulled out her gold-plated fountain pen and began practicing her autograph on a paper napkin. Should she stick to her curly writing or change her style?

When her enormous sundae arrived, she ate it all.

Twenty minutes later, she was walking home, feeling sick. She realized that a cold March evening wasn't really the best time to eat a large, freezing-cold ice cream.

In the distance, her grand apartment building towered over the street. That was odd, Davina thought—normally the outside of it was lit with green lights. Were they broken? The building really did look drab, all dark. She would complain as soon as she saw the doorman. She could see him now, standing by the front door with his taxi-calling light baton.

She crossed the broad avenue. The building entrance was only a hundred yards away—but now it was a dark hundred yards, lit up at only one point, where a streetlamp cast an oval pool of yellow on the pavement. Davina walked toward it. She liked spotlights.

Something white and rectangular lay on the ground under the light—garbage, Davina suspected—another thing to complain about. However, as Davina approached, she saw that the white rectangle wasn't garbage. It was an envelope. And when she got nearer, she saw something very strange. The envelope had *her* name on it.

A fan letter! Davina thought with pleasure.

She took off her glove, picked up the envelope, and pulled out the letter. It read:

Dear Davina,
Sorry about this, but you know too much.

Suddenly a heavy hand grabbed Davina's arm. She looked up to see a familiar face smiling down at her. Davina felt petrified with fear. Her body went winter cold. Her ears suddenly seemed to stop working. She could no longer hear the sounds of New York. It was as if the cabs and traffic, sirens and horns no longer existed. All Davina could hear was her own voice—her screams as she found herself being dragged toward a parked car. She looked beseechingly up at the uniformed doorman in the distance.

"Help! Help me!"

But the doorman did nothing. He stood motionless, looking the other way. And desperately kicking and struggling, Davina found herself being pushed into a Rolls-Royce as unceremoniously as a stray dog might be forced into a pound van. She was driven away into the night.

TWo

Molly Moon threw a bumper-size packet of Honey Wheat Pufftas up the supermarket aisle. The box flipped through the air, and the fat cartoon bee on it flew, for the first and last real flight of its life, before it landed with a crunch in the shopping cart.

"Bull's-eye! Twenty points to me," Molly said with satisfaction. A shower of Jawdrop bubble gums came raining down into the cart from over the shelves of cereals.

"How can Ruby eat so much gum?" a boy's voice asked from the other shopping aisle. "She's only five."

"She sticks her pictures up with it," said Molly, pushing the metal cart to the canned-fish corner. "How can Roger eat so many sardines? That's what I want to know. Cold, too, straight from the can. Disgusting. You can't stick pictures up with sardines."

"Ten points for those gums and double it, Green Eyes, because I got them in from over the other side." The husky-voiced boy emerged from behind a giant stack of baked beans. His dark-brown face was framed by a white hat with earflaps. He put a large bottle of orange squash concentrate in the cart.

"Thanks, Rocky," Molly said. Orange squash concentrate was Molly Moon's favorite drink. She liked to drink it neat.

She disentangled a pen from behind her ear and messy hair and wrote down their chucking scores in a small worn notebook.

Molly ~~45 100 140 175~~ 210
Rocky ~~40 90 133 183~~ 228

"Okay, wise guy. You win this week. But I'll be the champ before Easter."

Then Molly consulted their list. It said:

Happiness House Shopping . . .
Boring Stuff
~~potatoes~~   ~~onions~~   ~~tomatoes~~
~~parsnips~~   ~~lettuce~~   ~~eggplants~~

7

~~coffee~~   ~~milk~~   ~~cream~~

~~tea bags~~   ~~sugar~~   ~~10 tins sardines~~

~~white flour~~   ~~4 Honey Wheat~~   ~~eggs~~

~~celery~~   ~~Puffitas~~   ~~parakeet food~~

~~chicken~~   ~~oats~~   ~~dog food~~

cashews   ~~frozen peas~~   ~~mouse food~~

~~chops~~   ~~butter~~   ~~baguettes~~

~~sausages~~

Exciting Stuff

~~Qube~~   ~~potato chips~~   ~~cheesy biscuits~~

~~fizzy drinks~~   Moon's   ~~orange squash~~

~~biscuits~~   Marshmallows   ~~concentrate~~

~~ketchup~~   Heaven Bars   magazines

sweets   ~~sherbet~~

Presents

~~Jawdrop gums~~   ~~chocolates~~   ~~teeth whitener~~

~~popcorn~~   ~~lip gloss~~   ~~shaving foam~~
    ~~and razors~~

Happiness House was the orphanage where Molly and Rocky lived. When Molly Moon was a baby, she'd been left on its doorstep in a Moon's Marshmallows box, which is how she'd got her name. Until recently the children's home had been called Hardwick House, and as that name might suggest, it had been an extremely difficult place to live in. But just before Christmas, Molly had been dealt a spectacular, life-changing card.

In the library in the nearby town of Briersville, she'd found a faded old leather-bound book, *The Book of Hypnotism*, by Dr. Logan. It had changed Molly's life. After learning the book's secrets and discovering that she possessed incredibly powerful hypnotic skills, Molly had left the orphanage and gone to New York, accompanied by the orphanage pug, Petula. There she'd used hypnotism to get the starring role in a Broadway musical called *Stars on Mars*. Molly had fooled and controlled *hundreds* of people, and she'd made lots of money. But a crook called Professor Nockman had discovered her secret. He had kidnaped Petula and blackmailed Molly into robbing a bank for him.

It had been dreadful, until Rocky had showed up and helped her sort Nockman out. Molly had left New York behind, bringing with her the money that she'd earned and a large diamond that had come her way the day of the bank robbery *and* Professor Nockman. Back at Hardwick House, things began to get better at last. Molly had removed the witchy orphanage mistress, the building had been renamed, and the kind—although slightly batty—widow called Mrs. Trinklebury, who had worked at the orphanage before had come to help permanently. Molly had told her that the money she'd brought back from America was from a rich person called the Benefactor who wanted to help the children's home. Molly had also hypnotized Nockman and brought him with her to be Mrs. Trinklebury's assistant. She was hoping that by working with someone as kind as Mrs. Trinklebury, Nockman would soon reform and become a genuinely kind person too. So far the experiment was working well.

Molly checked her list. They had about everything now.

All the healthy food—the vegetables and fruit that Mrs. Trinklebury had asked for—lay squashed at the bottom of the cart underneath milk and fizzy drinks. On top were the special items—the presents for the six children from the orphanage who were away.

Gordon Boils and Cynthia Redmon were at an Outward Bound course, where Gordon, wanting to look meaner, had shaved his head. Molly had bought shaving foam and razors for him and chocolates for Cynthia.

Hazel Hackersly and Craig Redmon, Cynthia's twin, were at a ballroom-dancing course, so Molly was sending them lip gloss and teeth whitener.

Jinx and Ruby, the two five-year-olds, were staying at Mrs. Trinklebury's lovely sister's pig farm. Molly was mailing them a package of popcorn and bubble gum.

Molly scratched her head, hoping she hadn't got lice

again. "All that's left now is something for everyone who's still at home. Roger needs his nits . . . I mean his nuts."

"Poor Roger. *He's* nuts," said Rocky, lobbing some cashews into the cart. Indeed, Roger Fibbin was. Since Molly had returned, he had grown more and more muddled by the world. He spent most of his time up the orphanage oak tree.

"Mmm," agreed Molly. "Got my ketchup and Mr. Nockman's parakeet food . . . got Gemma's sherbet and Gerry's cheesy biscuits. Just need our candy and Mrs. Trinklebury's magazines."

Molly pushed the heavily laden cart down the last aisle toward the front of the store and scooped up a carton of toffees, a bag of candy sticks, some Heaven Bars, and a giant package of Moon's Marshmallows.

Rocky plucked *Celebrity Globe* and *Welcome to My World—At Home with the Stars* from the magazine rack.

KID NUTTEL KIDNAP!, the *Briersville Evening Chronicle* declared in black print, but Rocky didn't look at the newspapers. He and Molly piled their purchases onto the checkout conveyor belt. A pretty young woman with thick hair and gentle hands started tapping out prices on her register. Molly looked at her fresh country face and her nylon apron. She could almost belong to a different species from the people on the front of the glossy magazines that lay in front of her.

OSCARS SPECIAL ISSUE, trumpeted the headline on *Celebrity Globe*, beside a close-up photo of a woman with tumbling golden hair and a smile so full of teeth that Molly thought she must have had extra ones put in. Her lips were like shiny pink slugs, and her eyes were like a leopard's. Molly knew her face well. Everyone did.

"Suky Champagne, Academy Award Nominee, Shows Us Her Shoes," it said under the picture.

Mrs. Trinklebury would be pleased. Her favorite time of year was when the Academy Awards came around—the time when Hollywood handed out prizes, the Oscars, to the most talented people in the film business. Mrs. T. usually talked of nothing else for weeks.

Welcome to My World had a picture of a man who looked more like a god than a human. His skin was as dark as coal and he wore a Tarzan-like outfit. His long dreadlocks were blowing perfectly in the wind as he stood in the sun on a cliff top by the sea.

"I'd look just like him if you put me in one of those toga things," said Rocky with a wry smile. "I just need to grow my hair longer."

"And a few muscles," said Molly.

"Hercules Stone Invites Us into His Malibu Villa," ran the words beside the star's glistening stomach.

For a moment, Molly felt a pang of regret. If she'd continued with her starry career in New York, *she* might have been beside the sea in California this week and on the cover of *Welcome to My World*. Her hypnotic talent could have taken her to the very top, but she'd given up her life of fame and wealth to come home and be with her friends and family. Now she was only special in an ordinary way, just like the checkout girl in front of her.

Molly took her change, breathed out happily, and on the way out of the shop tossed all her loose coins into the cardboard cap of the crazy woman who always sat there talking to herself, wrapped in a dirty sleeping bag.

"Thank you, my child," she said with a snaggly-toothed smile.

Molly didn't like people calling her *their* child, because she was nobody's child—she was an orphan. But she felt mean thinking this about the sad woman who slept in the supermarket doorway.

"That's all right," she said. "Happy New Yea . . . erm . . . Happy March."

Three

Mrs. Trinklebury had parked her rusty olive-green car in the parking lot by the River Brier. Molly and Rocky pushed the cart down the main street, past the butcher's, where they often bought Petula tasty scraps to eat, past the camera shop and the baker's. Soon they had loaded the trunk. Rocky set off to return the cart and to pick up some screws from the hardware store.

Molly slid into the passenger seat and pulled her denim jacket around her. She began to pick at some of the foam that was bursting through the white vinyl upholstery and thought about what to do over the rest of the weekend.

She might help Rocky make a go-cart, or go down to the riding stables and ask for a lesson. Perhaps everyone might want to go for a swim at Briersville Pools. None of these ideas really inspired Molly, though, for the truth was that what she really wanted to do, what she'd been dying to do for months, was some hypnotizing. But she couldn't. She'd promised Rocky she wouldn't. She and Rocky had agreed that hypnosis was a dangerous tool that would always land them in trouble. Rocky had also learned from Dr. Logan's book. He could hypnotize people using his voice. Molly hadn't mastered voice hypnosis properly. But her powerful hypnotic eyes were far superior to Rocky's voice.

Hypnotism had changed her life. For the very first time, Molly had known how it felt to be good at something. Molly missed feeling good like this. In fact, she missed it dreadfully. Life just wasn't as exciting without hypnotism. The promise she'd made was driving her crazy.

Another thing had been perplexing Molly since Christmas. Lucy Logan, the person who had made sure that Molly had found and taken *The Book of Hypnotism*, had disappeared. Lucy was the great-granddaughter of the author of the book, and she had worked in the Briersville library. Lucy had hypnotized Molly to find the book in her library and then, after learning its lessons and having some adventures, to return it to her. Molly thought Lucy was a completely brilliant person—

and certainly the most special adult she had ever met. She felt she owed Lucy a big thank-you, and she had been looking forward to making friends with her. But now Lucy Logan had vanished. She'd handed in her notice at the library in January and gone.

The watery March light reflected on the cold surface of the river, where a grubby white duck and drake swam about. Molly watched them, trying to divert her mind from hypnotism and Lucy's disappearance. And then, without meaning to, Molly found herself wondering for the millionth time who her parents were.

This question was like a mosquito that sometimes tried to fly into her life. When the question bit her, Molly couldn't help but itch it.

If she was in a good mood, she would imagine her parents as interesting, fun people who, for some dreadful reason beyond their control, had lost their baby. When she was in a low mood, she saw her parents as two horrible people who had wanted to drown her like an unwanted kitten. But whatever mood she was in, thinking about them was always frustrating. Because however hard she tried to picture them, Molly knew she would never know who they were.

Molly shut her eyes and tried to calm her babbling mind.

She was very good at doing this, as she'd perfected the art of daydreaming when she was very young. Soon she was breathing peacefully and imagining herself drifting upward like a cloud, out of Mrs. Trinklebury's car and along the course of the River Brier, up into the hills and all the way up to its source in the highest peak. Molly imagined that she was hovering. As she felt the weight of the earth and the ancient quality of the mountains beneath her, she was reminded how huge the world was and how unimportant her worries were compared with it.

Feeling refreshed, she opened her eyes. She took one of the baguettes out of a shopping bag and ripped off its end. Opening a new ketchup bottle, she knocked some sauce onto it. For a few minutes, Molly munched her favorite snack and looked out over the river.

On the far bank there were fenced-off gardens with terraced cottages behind them. One garden was larger than the others. It seemed to have two cottages behind it. Some dense green hedges, clipped into the shapes of sitting birds and animals, had recently sprung up in this garden. On the top of one hedge, a huge bird with a long tail was shaped out of branches and leaves, and beside it was a crouching box-hedge hare with two distinct ears. On the top of a yew bush sat a big dog with large hollow eyes, looking as if he was guarding the house.

The spring sunshine danced over the shiny foliage of the bush dog. As the light bounced off a glossy twig where his mouth might have been, the creature seemed to smile at Molly.

Molly remembered how exciting it had been when she'd first hypnotized Petula last November. She sighed and popped the last piece of ketchuppy bread into her mouth. It was so difficult keeping her promise not to hypnotize. It was like resisting the urge to walk on your hands once you'd learned, or like stamping on the impulse to jump high when you actually had the power to leapfrog a tree. Molly longed to experience again the warm "fusion feeling" that washed through her whenever she let her eyes reach their hypnotic peak.

Now, as the dog's leafy eye twinkled at her, Molly was struck by an idea. She had only promised Rocky not to hypnotize any *one*. She had never promised not to hypnotize *things*.

The fusion feeling was lovely. It made Molly feel as if a tropical sun flowed in her veins. The voice in her head urged her on.

Go on, give it a try, Molly. It'll warm you up. Hypnotize the bush dog. What are you afraid of? That it'll jump over the river and bite you? Molly stared at the bush. Hypnotize a bush? A bush couldn't be hypnotized.

Exactly, urged her mind. But it will make you *feel* nice.

So, winding down the window, Molly focused in her special way at the topiary dog. She found the faraway feeling inside herself that made everything apart from the dog-shaped bush look blurred. Then she searched for the feeling of bush in herself, and the more she stared at the bush, the more the leaves of the dog seemed to absorb her and the more the sounds of the town grew muffled.

Molly felt naughty. Rocky wouldn't be pleased if he knew she was doing this. She'd have to do it quickly before he got back. She waited for the fusion sensation to slowly rise through her body. For a moment nothing happened. Then a hint of the feeling began, as if sparks of electricity were traveling up her backbone into her head, to behind her eyes, where they circled and throbbed. Her mind felt slightly fizzy, and tiny zapping noises seemed to pop just inside her ears.

But somehow, something was different. The sensation flaring up in her was not the familiar fusion feeling. As Molly stared at the dog, her eyes pulsing, the sensation seemed to twist and mutate. Instead of being a warm tingling, it turned into an icy-cold prickling under her skin, giving her goose pimples all over. Molly gasped in shock and immediately snapped out of her trance.

A sharp clip, clip, clipping noise from across the river reached her ears, and Molly noticed a pair of steel shears snapping shut under the beak of the big topiary bird. She couldn't see the gardener, but whoever he was, he seemed intent upon keeping his bushes trimmed and tidy, keen to control the wild growth of the privet-hedge creatures.

In the side mirror, Molly saw fat Mrs. Trinklebury wrapped in her crocheted coat, lugging bags of wool back toward the car. Molly's hypnotic experiments would have to wait.

As Mrs. Trinklebury approached, Molly saw that she was looking very flustered.

"Just look at this t-terrible news," she declared, dropping a newspaper on Molly's lap.

The paper shouted out its headline.

Child Star Disappears

Underneath, there was a photograph of Davina Nuttel, dressed in an astronaut costume for her role in *Stars on Mars*.

Davina Nuttel missing from outside her Manhattan home.
Mink glove found at scene.
New York police treating the case as abduction.

Mrs. Trinklebury was beside herself with worry. "The poor girl. Her poor p-parents. Can you imagine it, Molly?"

Molly could easily. She'd had firsthand experience of kidnaping, since her very own Petula had been abducted in New York. But she'd also actually met the famous Davina Nuttel, so the news was extra shocking. Even though Molly hadn't liked Davina much, she felt genuinely concerned for her now.

"That's horrible!" she gulped.

"See, life for the famous isn't all fun," said Mrs. Trinklebury, and tutting like a chaffinch, she plonked a cakey kiss on Molly's forehead.

"I'm p-peckish, aren't you? I hope Mr. N.'s cooking l-lunch. Look, I've got a v-video for us all to watch this afternoon. It's got Gloria Heelheart in it. It's the one she won her Best Actress award for last year. She's marvelous. It'll take our minds off Davina."

As they drove home, Mrs. Trinklebury sang along to the radio, trying to cheer herself up. She was thrilled that the child pop star Billy Bob Bimble was number one with his hit single "Magpie Man."

"Don't let him steal your heart," she trilled along,
"Steal it,
Steel your heart, ooooooooh,
Don't let him have your heart,
Guard it from the start, ooooooooh,
Steel your heart,
Magpie man, oooooh,
Wants the sun and the stars and you, ooooh,
Magpie man."

Twenty minutes later they arrived at Happiness House. The front of the building was crisscrossed with scaffolding poles. Half of the building was a pristine white, while the other half was still its old, gray, flaky self.

Petula shot out the front door like a black furry missile. She jumped onto Molly's lap, wagging her curly, stumpy tail, and dropped a present of a stone. Then she turned around, raced back across the gravel, and came out of the house with a letter between her teeth.

"Thank you, Petula," said Molly, taking the soggy envelope and peering at it.

Molly's name had been printed in neat letters in

green ink, but they had smudged. And the address had been licked off. Obviously Petula had been looking after the envelope for a while.

"Help me with these bags, could you, Molly?" asked Rocky. "They're so heavy, they're cutting into my fingers."

Molly put the envelope into her pocket and took a bag from him. That was why she didn't read the letter until later.

Four

All her life, Molly's home had been a dump. But recently the dump had been given a facelift. Now Happiness House was completely different inside. For instance, the oak-paneled sitting room, which for so long had been a drafty assembly hall, had new rugs on the floor and pictures on the walls. Comfy armchairs and sofas and tables with books on them filled it. A log fire that was always lit in the daytime kept it warm. It smelled of beeswax polish, and today it looked very pretty, with pink apple blossoms in vases, taken from the wild orchard just outside Hardwick village. At one end stood a Ping-Pong table and at the other a trampoline.

After Molly, Rocky, and Mrs. Trinklebury had put away the groceries, it was time for lunch. Mr. Nockman stood in the dining room behind the food counter, with the steam from hot vegetables, sausages, and potatoes wafting up into his face. He looked ten times better than he had when Molly first knew him. His face was much slimmer, with visible cheekbones, and it had a healthy, ruddy complexion. His eyes had whites that were *white*—not yellow and bloodshot—and his bald pate was shiny and clean.

Today he was wearing a pair of baggy gray flannel trousers and a blue zip-up cardigan with a thick red stripe down the back of it. From his shoulder, his favorite parakeet, Chicken Tikka, whistled merrily, occasionally hopping sideways to give him a friendly peck on the ear. All in all, the new, retrained Nockman was happier than he had ever been in his life.

He put three perfectly cooked sausages that he had been saving onto Mrs. Trinklebury's plate.

"Vould you like beans, my dear?" he asked her in his strange German accent—actually an accent that Molly had hypnotized him to have.

"Oh, thank you, Simon," she said as she folded a napkin for him into the shape of a bird.

After lunch, everyone crowded into the small TV room. Mrs. Trinklebury sat in the armchair, and everyone else found a beanbag or a slice of floor to sit on.

Nockman shook the old video machine

25

working, and Mrs. Trinklebury's film, *The Sighing Summer*, began.

Apart from an interval when three of Gerry's mice escaped from his shirt, everyone was glued to the film for two hours. As the final scene played itself out, with Gloria Heelheart throwing herself off a cliff into the sea, Mrs. Trinklebury wept and Molly reached into her pocket to find her some tissues.

Rediscovering the letter Petula had brought her, Molly slipped out of the room to read it. Petula followed her. They climbed to the top of the stairs, where they both sat down.

Molly ripped open the envelope. Inside was a piece of paper, slightly chewed, with the address:

14 Water Meadows Road
Briersville

Underneath, in green ink, was a message that made Molly's heart flutter with excitement and at the same time filled her with relief.

Friday

Dear Molly,

Sorry not to be in touch before now, but I've been in the hospital, as I had an accident. Don't worry, I'm all right, although for a while it was touch and go. I'm back home and would like to see you. I'll tell you all my news, but more importantly, I'm longing to hear about your adventures with hypnotism.

Also, there is something rather important that I would like you to do.

Why don't you come for tea on Sunday at four? I'll see you if I see you. . . . Hope I do. . . . Perfectly punctually?!

Best wishes,

Lucy Logan

"Wow—how about that, Petula?" Molly said, giving her a squeeze. She was really pleased. At last she was in touch with Lucy Logan again. Molly couldn't wait to see her. She wondered what had made her hand in her notice at the library, and she still thought it odd that Lucy hadn't called her, but perhaps she'd been in the hospital all this time.

Molly remembered how she had drifted like a snowflake into the library in the dead of night on Christmas Eve to return the mysterious *Book of Hypnotism* as Lucy had hypnotized her to. Lucy had woken her from her hypnotic instruction with the words *perfectly punctually*. Molly smiled as she read the same words in Lucy's letter.

Molly wondered what Lucy could want her to do. She wanted to thank Lucy, to tell her about New York, and to talk hypnotism with her. There was one other big reason too.

Keeping her promise not to hypnotize anyone really was driving Molly up the wall. It wasn't only frustrating. The thought of never being able to use her powers again was beginning to make Molly feel bereaved, as if something in her had died.

Lucy had told Molly that she used hypnotism to do good things for other people. Molly and Rocky had done their own sort of good hypnotism before they'd left New York. They'd made a hypnotic TV commercial called "Check Out the Kids in Your Neighborhood." They thought it would make people who watched it care more about the children around them. The TV company had promised to show it a lot, and so it had probably done some good. Molly wanted to ask Lucy to tell Rocky that generous, unselfish hypnotism was okay. Then he might agree to break the hypnotizing ban that they'd made. She'd need to explain this all to Lucy without Rocky being there.

For this reason, Molly decided to go to 14 Water Meadows Road alone.

Five

Sunday morning was so bright and shiny that the glossy-leaved trees outside Molly's window looked wet. Molly breathed in the frosty air and felt really thrilled. Today she was going to Lucy Logan's for tea.

As two thrushes landed on a prickly, red-berried shrub and began pecking at its fruit, Molly noticed Roger Fibbin's skinny form scrabbling about in the dead leaves and broken twigs under the oak tree. With his beaky nose and his jerky movements, he looked like a bird pecking around for grubs. He was probably looking for a magical doorway to another world.

Roger had gone a bit mad. He seemed to live in a scary fantasyland where the leaves and stones whispered to him. He roamed the town listening for secret messages, and he made folded-paper darts that had writing inside them. They said things like *Send help quick! Aliens have eaten my brain!* and *Watch out! The brain centipedes are here!* and *Don't judge your body by its skin.*

These he threw around Briersville—through people's mailboxes, over garden walls, into cars and shops. Once, he managed to slip in through the exit door of the cinema and throw fifty of his darts into the audience.

Molly wondered whether the peculiar habit he'd developed—of eating from the Briersville garbage cans—had given him some sort of brain infection, but the doctor said that all he needed was rest, good food, and kindness.

Molly undid the window and called out, "Roger, are you all right?"

Roger looked up nervously and then glanced over his shoulder to check that no one was listening. "Yes, they can't get me today."

"Do you want to go for a bike ride?"

"Can't, Molly. Too much to do. Maybe another day."

"Okay, you just let me know when. It would be good fun."

She shut the window and wondered whether Roger would ever get better.

The morning tipped into the afternoon.

It was a lovely, fresh, downhill bike ride into

Briersville. The roadside was bursting with young green shoots, crocuses and daffodils, and the sky was blue. Blossoming trees nodded in the clear March breeze. Other trees were still cold and bare, but the tips of their branches were tinged with dark pink, where new leaves were nearly ready to break out.

Molly cycled past Hardwick village, down the winding road between fields full of cows, past Briersville Junior School, and into the town. Since it was Sunday, it was very quiet. The Guildhall, with its green pepperpot roof, was closed, and the broad street was deserted.

Water Meadows Road was a narrow, cobbled street, across the bridge and down a turn to the right. Number fourteen was a bay-windowed cottage in a row of very old houses. Molly leaned her bicycle against its front wall and, grasping the lion's-paw knocker on the door, rapped twice. Unzipping her jacket, she looked down at her T-shirt and noticed some gravy that she'd spilled on it at lunchtime. She was trying to suck this off when the door slowly opened. Molly let the shirt drop from her mouth.

In front of her was a shocking sight: a figure from a horror film, yet wearing the neat, pleated skirt, the white collared shirt, and the plain blue cardigan of Lucy Logan. Its entire head was wrapped in white bandages, except for a patch of hair that was arranged in an elegant bun. Molly could see Lucy Logan's familiar blue eyes and her mouth, but the rest of her face was covered with some sort of dressing.

Lucy stood leaning on crutches. Her left foot was in a slipper, but the whole of her right leg was in plaster, and her toes, with pink nail polish on them, popped out of the end of the cast.

Molly's first reaction was to gawp, and for a moment she stood transfixed.

"Oh, Molly, I'm sorry. Of course, this must be an awful shock for you."

Molly barely recognized Lucy's voice, but she nodded and managed to say, "Are you all right? What happened?"

Lucy leaned out into the street and nervously looked left and right. Then she pulled Molly inside.

"I'll tell you all about it, but come in quick—my toes are getting cold."

Molly found herself standing in a small hall. On a semicircular cherry-wood table, a mantel clock ticked quietly. Opposite it, a tiny hanging grandmother clock swung a pendulum. As Lucy took Molly's jacket and put it over the back of a chair, Molly breathed in a smell of toast and wondered why her host had just behaved so warily.

"Come into the warmth," Lucy said, maneuvering

awkwardly on her crutches and leading Molly past a narrow staircase into a meticulously tidy kitchen. It was so immaculate that Molly looked down at her gravy stain and wished she'd changed her top.

"Sit down," Lucy said kindly, inviting Molly to sit on a crescent-shaped bench in the bay window. "Do you drink tea?"

"Er, hot orange squash if you've got it," said Molly, not quite daring to ask for a concentrated orange squash, which she would have preferred. She didn't want Lucy to think she was weird.

"Fine," said Lucy, and she put a kettle on to boil.

Molly sat on the bench with her hands wedged between her knees, trying not to stare at Lucy's bandages. What sort of horrible accident had she had? Molly didn't know what to say, and the palms of her hands began to sweat, as they always did whenever she was nervous. Lucy broke the silence.

"Molly, I'm so sorry I haven't been in touch. You must have thought it was peculiar that I didn't call you. But two things happened. First, something very serious took over my life and I couldn't tell anyone about it. And then I had the accident. My car caught fire. My face is badly burned. I still can't eat much—I have to suck soup from a straw and chew on cookies that dissolve in my mouth. My throat was damaged from all the

33

fumes. My voice has been affected, as you can hear. It's probably always going to be husky. The doctors say my face will be scarred for life and my hair will never grow back in places. But"—she gave a lopsided smile—"I'm lucky to be alive, and now I don't take life for granted."

Molly was shocked into an awkward silence. In the last few months, she had felt annoyed and hurt that Lucy had forgotten her. She had never imagined that something as horrible as this had happened.

"Don't worry about not getting in touch," she said quickly. "I mean, I did wonder where you'd gone, but you know I was busy straightening out the orphanage— the redecorations and things. And it's all thanks to you, Lucy. Everything's much cozier now. Everyone's happier. School's much better too, because Mrs. Toadley left. Well, er, actually she was fired."

"I heard it was because she went around telling everyone what a dreadful teacher she was," said Lucy.

"Which she was," said Molly, hoping that Lucy wouldn't disapprove of the fact that Molly had hypnotized the bullying Mrs. Toadley into behaving like this. "But I haven't done any hypnotizing at all since I got off the plane before Christmas," she added. She hoped Lucy would be impressed by this self-restraint, but the librarian gave her a sharp look.

"You've stopped? Why would you stop? Don't you need anything?"

Molly was taken aback. "I—well—I didn't think about that. I just promised Rocky that I wouldn't use it anymore."

"Oh dear." Lucy fell silent. Then she said, "Bring your drink and these cookies. We'll go into the sitting room." She hobbled through another door. Molly followed, and the glory of the room beyond took her attention away from Lucy's bandages.

The room was a shrine to hypnotism. In the center of it was a table that had a circular swirl inlaid in copper. Molly looked at the pattern. It reminded her of a similar swirl that had been painted on a pendulum she'd once owned. The copper design seemed to draw her eyes toward the dot at the table's center. At once she felt relaxed. Immediately she snapped away. "Is that a hypnotic table?"

"It can be," said Lucy.

"I'll have to watch you this time," said Molly, smiling. "I can't believe you hypnotized me so easily last November in the library."

"Well, as I told you, I wanted you to find the book," said Lucy. "Don't worry—I don't need to hypnotize you ever again."

"I'm too alert to be hypnotized anyway," said Molly, following the copper swirl with her finger.

Indeed Molly was. Everything in this room reminded her of the incredible power of hypnotism. Above the mantelpiece, over a cheerful fire, hung a portrait of a bewhiskered Victorian gentleman in a black tailcoat and top hat. From his waistcoat top pocket came a golden chain that was attached to a shiny pocket watch. Molly instantly recognized the old man from his picture in *The Book of Hypnotism*.

"Yes, there's the great Dr. Logan himself," said Lucy, settling down in a chair. "All over the room are things that belonged to him that have been passed down through the family. The table, and in the cabinet behind you there's the very pocket watch that he's holding in that portrait. He used it as a pendulum. He went all over America, and that's how he made his fortune. I've got lots of pictures of him and his traveling hypnotism show. There's his collection of miniature clocks, too. Have a look."

Molly went to the cabinet. Sepia-colored photographs of Victorian people stood in silver frames. In one, Dr. Logan was on a stage, posing theatrically beside a peculiar figure. Lying flat and balanced between a couple of chairs, her head on one and her feet on another, lay a woman. Nothing supported her body. Her long dress had been bunched up, like a tied-up umbrella, so that it didn't drag on the floor, and she was as stiff as a board. Molly knew it was a hypnotism trick called the human plank.

Molly inspected the golden pocket watch and then looked at the tiny carriage clocks. On the wall beside the cabinet were three more clocks: a round one, a castle-shaped one, a pewter clock. They were all showing the correct time. "I've never seen so many clocks in one home," she said.

"Well you've probably never been in the house of a clock collector," said Lucy. "Clocks remind me that life is short and that I mustn't waste it."

As Molly thought about this, she looked out the sitting-room window. It was then that she noticed that Lucy's garden was the very one where the topiary animals grew. The hare and the dog were very close to the window, making the room darker than it should be.

"Wow! I was looking at your animal bushes yesterday," Molly exclaimed. "Without realizing that they belonged to you. Are they new? I've often looked over the river from the parking lot, and I've never seen them before."

"Yes, they are new. I bought the plants fully grown and clipped them myself."

"I like the dog with the big eyes," said Molly.

Lucy laughed. "It's supposed to be a bush baby. I obviously need to go to topiary classes." She reached for a cookie. "Help yourself, Molly. I shouldn't, really. I've put on so much weight since the accident. I've eaten hundreds of cookies." She shifted uncomfortably in her skirt and undid its zipper a bit. "The bushes are there for a reason," she added. "They're to stop people from looking in."

Lucy suddenly seemed nervous.

"I can't be sure who's watching me at the moment." She paused. "Molly," she said, sounding serious, "I've got an awful lot to tell you today. But first I want to hear all the things that happened to you after you read the book. It's very important that I know."

"Sure," said Molly, curious about Lucy's mysterious business but dying to tell her about her amazing experiences. And so she launched into her story.

"I had an incredible time. In fact the *best* time I've ever had mixed with the *worst* time . . ."

Lucy Logan listened intently, but she wasn't as interested as Molly thought she might be. What Lucy Logan was most intent upon was *whom* Molly had hypnotized and *how*. She questioned Molly about exactly how she had hypnotized an audience at the Briersville talent show so that she'd won, then how she'd hypnotized a flight attendant, and how she'd hypnotized the hotel staff in New York, and how she'd won over the whole audience of New Yorkers in the show *Stars on Mars*. She wanted exact details about the methods Molly and Rocky had used when they had robbed Shorings Bank after Nockman had blackmailed them. Her questions were so thorough, it was almost as if Lucy was testing Molly.

"So," she said eventually, "you gave all the money and jewels back to the bank. That was extremely honest of you. Not many people would have done that."

Molly said nothing. Her fingers automatically reached for the diamond that hung around her neck. She decided not to tell Lucy about that for now. She didn't want Lucy to disapprove of her.

"Lucy," she said instead, wiping her lips on her sleeve, "what about you? Now it's your turn to tell me about your hypnotic adventures."

Lucy's blue eyes looked at Molly from behind their white frame of bandages, and she said in a serious voice, "Molly, we haven't got time for my stories now. The special work that made me hand in my notice to the library is very grave. It's why I didn't get in touch. I didn't want you to get involved, because I didn't want you put in danger. But the time has come for you to know what's been going on." Lucy took a deep breath. "You thought you were coming for an entertaining tea, but I have invited you here to ask you to do something very, very important. I'm extremely sorry, but I have no other choice. Time is running out."

Molly gulped. She didn't like the way the afternoon was turning out.

Lucy stood up. "Please come with me."

Molly followed Lucy through a passageway hung with half a dozen more clocks. A flight of stone stairs led to a basement. Lucy hobbled slowly down them.

At the bottom was a door with four locks on it, two combination padlocks and two locks with keys. Molly wondered what could need such protection.

"There are secrets in here," said Lucy, "that have to be kept hidden. Secrets that will interest you. Come in."

Six

The basement room inside wasn't what Molly expected at all. She associated the librarian with shelves of old books and card-index files, not this high-tech space with its shelves of metal files. On the far wall was a plasma screen. Hidden ceiling lights illuminated the gray carpet and shone on a table in the center of the floor, which bore a white keyboard, a computer mouse, a velvet mouse pad, and two miniature bonsai trees. A glass-sided display case sat under the white screen. It contained six pairs of tiny colored shoes.

"Ah, those are old Chinese lotus shoes," explained Lucy, seeing Molly looking at them. "Some of them date back to the southern Tang Dynasty of A.D. 920. They were worn by girls who'd had their feet bound so they could never grow big. Aren't they lovely?"

"Did you go to China on your . . . adventures?" asked Molly, unsettled by the strange little shoes.

"No." Lucy sat on a chrome swivel chair and gestured to Molly to sit on another. She turned on the computer. Quiet whirring noises came from a wall of steel equipment, and the large screen showed a menu of many labeled files.

"Molly," she said, her tone solemn, "I handed my notice in at the library because I discovered something. And I've spent every moment of the past few months investigating it. It's something very frightening that is going on in the world. Something that will affect you, me, everyone."

Whatever this bad thing was, Molly knew she didn't want to have anything to do with it. She wiped her clammy hands on her jeans as Lucy double-clicked on a computer file called "LA." It summoned up a picture of the front page of the *Los Angeles Times*. The headline read: DAVINA NUTTEL, CHILD STAR, FEARED SNATCHED. There was the familiar face of the young actress grinning as she hugged a puppy.

"I suppose you've heard about this," said Lucy. "The police can't find any leads. The poor girl has completely vanished."

"Poor Davina," said Molly. "I hope she's all right."

"I expect she *isn't*," said Lucy. "I think Davina has been abducted by a person who has a lot of influence over the police force, so there isn't *any* chance that he will *ever* be caught."

"Who?" asked Molly. "How do you know?"

"Before I tell you who I think he is, I want to show you a few things."

A series of pictures filled the screen. Oddly, they were all pictures from advertisements. First there was a red Primospeed sports car, then a green Nicesplice lawn mower, next a Compucell computer, then a Heaven Bar ice cream. Images of different objects that weren't connected passed in front of Molly's eyes. She recognized a lot of them. A blue-and-silver Inspirations fountain pen, a Shlick Shlack knife, a polka-dotted Fashion House dress, a jar of Navy Girl soup, a box of Honey Wheat Pufftas, a roll of Sumpshus toilet paper, a pot of Fresh Space face cream, a Vitawell yogurt, and a squeezy bottle of Bubblealot dishwashing liquid. Molly wondered what these everyday things could possibly have to do with the terrible kidnaping of Davina Nuttel.

Lucy asked suddenly, "How do you choose the things that you buy, Molly?"

"By knowing what I want?" replied Molly, not sure if this was the right answer. A can of Qube jumped about on the screen, as if it was trying to help her.

"But how do you know what you want?" asked Lucy. "There are so many wonderful things. For instance, look at all these candies." Lucy clicked, and dozens of different brands of candies popped up on the screen. Jawdrop gums, Coocoo toffees, Heaven Bar chews. "How do you know which candy to buy?"

"Well, I know the ones I like."

"Yes, but before you *first* tasted those candies that you now know you like, how did you know to try them?"

"Because I'd heard about them?"

"From who?"

"From friends."

"And . . .?"

"From ads?"

"Good," said Lucy.

Molly wondered what Lucy meant. She didn't think ads were very good. Weren't all ads brainwashers?

"It's good that you understand that advertisements have the power to make people buy things," Lucy said. "Now, I want you to look at these faces."

Onto the screen came a selection of famous faces that Molly mostly recognized. There were movie stars and singers and celebrities. Gloria Heelheart, the Queen of Hollywood; Suky Champagne, the young star; Billy

Bob Bimble, the boy singer; Hercules Stone; Cosmo Ace; King Moose, the boxer; and Tony Wam, the karate expert.

"I wonder," said Lucy, stopping on a picture of a red-haired woman with big brown eyes, "whether you know what this woman likes to eat after she's been to the gym."

It was a peculiar question, but then Molly realized that she knew exactly what Stephanie Goulash, the chart-topping singer, liked to eat.

"Mightie Lighties," Molly said, feeling as if she was on a TV quiz show.

"Absolutely correct," said Lucy. "And how about this one, this movie star, Hercules Stone? What deodorant does he use?"

"In the Groove." The words tumbled out of Molly's mouth before she'd even registered that she knew the answer. Craig was always going on about Hercules Stone, about what he ate, what he wore, what he rolled on under his famous armpits.

"Good," said Lucy again. "So you can see how these celebrities, like ads, are also showing people what to buy."

Molly nodded.

"Millions of people know these things, just like you do. And this is what I'm worried about."

Molly couldn't imagine why Lucy should be worried. Perhaps Lucy was old-fashioned and didn't think stars should let people into their private lives. But what on earth did this have to do with Davina's kidnaping?

Lucy clicked up some video clips. There was a Mightie Lightie ad that finished with a tiny Stephanie Goulash sitting on top of a giant version of the famous cereal bar. In another, Hercules Stone brandished a stick of In the Groove as if it was a sword and fought off a pack of little green monsters. Twenty ads, ranging from lipsticks to washing machines, featured showbiz celebrities, sports stars, TV personalities. Molly recognized almost all of them.

"Here's the most important thing," said Lucy. "*All* the products in these ads are made by companies owned by *one man*. Each time any one of these things is sold, he gets richer."

"He must be very rich then," Molly remarked.

"Isn't it an odd coincidence that so many celebrities should choose to advertise *his* products?" said Lucy. "None of them promote *anything else* from *any other* company."

"Well, he probably pays them mountains of money to do it," said Molly.

"I don't think he pays them," said Lucy. With a sudden swivel of her chair, she turned to look Molly full in the face. "I think he hypnotizes them."

"What?!"

"Molly, you must have realized how powerful hypnotism is. You must know that if it gets into the wrong hands, it could be a very dangerous weapon."

Molly nodded slowly. She didn't want to hear what was coming next.

"I've long suspected," Lucy continued, "that one day someone would try to make a lot of money through hypnotism. My great-grandfather always feared this possibility. He was right. Hypnotic power goes to bad as well as to good people. Bad people who can hypnotize are very greedy and destructive. This businessman is very dangerous."

The screen was filled with the giant head and shoulders of a tall, smartly dressed, gray-haired man wearing a baseball cap, who stood arm in arm with two famous baseball players.

"He is a multi-multi-*billionaire*. He is so rich, Molly, that he makes more money in *one day* than all the people in Briersville make *together* in one *year*. His name is Primo Cell."

Molly stared, fascinated, at more pictures of the

suave, tanned tycoon. All his features were unremarkable except for his eyes. One was turquoise, the other brown, and together the duo were stunningly magnetic. Molly just wanted to gaze at them. Here he was on a safari, holding a lion cub, and here a thousand feet up in the basket of a hot-air balloon. There were clips of him coming out of restaurants and at parties with the celebrities who had been on the screen earlier. Suky Champagne, Hercules Stone, Gloria Heelheart, Stephanie Goulash, and Cosmo Ace.

"Primo Cell is a hypnotist, I'm sure of it," said Lucy. "I am also a hypnotist, and a very skillful one. My understanding of the art made me begin to suspect him some time ago. The more I discover, the more I know I'm right. And there's more. Twelve years ago, this man knew no one. Look."

Up came a photograph, recognizable as the same, much younger, man, dressed in a T-shirt and jeans, holding a sign that read MAKE YOUR PETS VEGETARIAN. BUY "NICE PETFOODS."

"His first business was a ridiculous failure."

"It was a nice idea though," said Molly, thinking how Petula liked strawberries.

"That's why they were called Nice Petfoods. Compare that man to today's Primo Cell. Cell is getting richer and more powerful every day. This same man now has *hundreds* of companies and *millions* of people all over the world buying his goods. The stars happily advertise his products—things they normally wouldn't be seen dead with. Look at this picture of Hercules Stone doing the dishes using Bubblealot. This is not doing Stone's career any good. He's supposed to be the sort of glamorous guy who never has to lift a finger. He wouldn't do this ad unless he was forced to—or hypnotized to."

Molly's mind was racing. She was finding Lucy's ideas difficult to take in.

"Can't you go to the police?"

"I have been to the police. It was stupid of me. Of course they thought I was crazy. A week later I had the accident." Lucy shuddered as she remembered. "I was lucky to get out of that burning car. If I hadn't been to the police, it wouldn't have happened, I'm sure of it. Primo Cell watches his back, Molly. Someone with secrets like him has to. He has people under his power high up in the police force here and in America. I'm absolutely certain that if I were to speak out again, I'd have another accident.

"Things are getting worse. Cell's influence is spreading like rot. He is controlling people's minds—close up

49

and from afar—and they don't know it. People's minds are supposed to be free places, Molly. My greatest fear is that Cell has bigger ambitions than making money. Powerful people are already saying that he should run for president."

"What! President of the United States?"

"Exactly. Wouldn't you want to be president if you were a power-crazed egomaniac and could make people do whatever you wanted?"

Molly nodded. This made sense.

"I have no proof yet that he'll run for president this year. But it's very possible. He could make people support him, and he's got all the money to pay for an election campaign."

A puzzling thought struck Molly. "But Lucy, hypnotism wears off. Primo Cell won't be able to keep thousands of people under his control. He'll have to keep hypnotizing all those stars and celebrities and police officers and politicians and whoever else."

Lucy nodded. "You would think that would be the case, but Cell already has so many people under his control, and some of them he's had for years. I think he's somehow found a way to keep his subjects hypnotized *permanently*. I think he's discovered a new hypnosis much more powerful than ours."

Molly screwed up her face as she digested this. It was a frightening idea.

Lucy hadn't finished.

"I'm also sure that Cell is behind Davina Nuttel's disappearance. My research shows that Cell planned to launch a new line of kids' clothes through his Fashion House company this year. I've found several pictures in the papers of him coming out of the Manhattan Theater after seeing the show *Stars on Mars*. He must have wanted Davina to promote Fashion House. My hypnotist instincts tell me that something went wrong. Perhaps Davina didn't go along with his plans. Perhaps she found out his secret. Perhaps somehow, astonishingly, she resisted his hypnotism. Whatever happened, my feeling is he had to get rid of her. The man is out of control."

If you've ever been on a roller-coaster ride, you will know that fearful feeling you get while being cranked up to the top before you swoop terrifyingly downward. Your stomach feels full of waves of apprehension. Molly's instincts told her that a fast, furious ride was seconds away. She found herself gripping the arms of her chair.

Lucy reached for her shoulder as if to prepare her. "We must find out how his *new* kind of hypnotism works. How he keeps his victims under his power permanently."

"We?" asked Molly faintly.

"Molly, you may not realize it, but you have more than a talent for hypnosis. You have a very special gift. Your performance as a hypnotist in New York was absolutely amazing. Only someone as good as you could stand up to Primo Cell. I have never come across anyone with powers like yours. *Because* you can help, you must. If you don't, dreadful things will happen in the world. And think of poor Davina."

Molly blushed from all of Lucy's flattering words, but at the same time she was dreading whatever invitation she felt was coming her way.

"What do you want me to do?"

"I want you to go to Los Angeles, in America, to Primo Cell's headquarters." Up came a photograph of a dark-blue glass office building with palm trees in front of it. "This is where he works. And this is his home." A gray house behind cedar trees, a high wall, and a big metal gate filled the screen.

"First and foremost, you must find out whether Cell is behind Davina's abduction. And then find out where she is. Help her if you can. Investigate Cell. Talk to some of the stars who are under his power.

Report back to me." Lucy paused. "I'll send you money, so you don't have to worry about that. You'll have to use a lot of hypnotism to get information. But I know you can do it. Will you, Molly?"

Molly thought of how miserable her life had been before she had found the hypnotism book. How happy she was now. She owed her happiness to Lucy. How could she refuse to help her? But when she looked up at that impenetrable steel gate, and thought of the gentle librarian fighting to escape from her burning car, she trembled inside. She didn't want to go to America and take on this dangerous man, but she felt herself nodding her head.

"I'll do it," she said. Then she couldn't help blurting out, "But—but what if Primo Cell hypnotizes *me*?"

"This isn't without risk, Molly. I won't pretend it is. But if that should happen, I assure you, I will do everything to get you back."

Molly rubbed her sweaty hands up and down on her jeans.

"You are probably feeling that this is too grown-up for you," Lucy told her. "But it's not. You are a genius hypnotist. And you are a brilliant secret weapon. I'll tell you why.

"You can investigate Cell without casting the slightest

suspicion on yourself, because you, Molly, are a child. Primo Cell will never suspect a child."

Molly felt as if she had just swallowed a pill that was going to change her life.

"So when do I go?" she asked.

Seven

It was lucky that Molly had a light on her bicycle, as she didn't leave Lucy's until after dark. She strapped the briefcase Lucy had given her onto the rear rack and pedaled wearily through Briersville and up the hill out of town.

She felt cheated. She'd arrived at Lucy's cottage wanting to listen to stories about hypnotism. Instead, the afternoon had been hijacked by Primo Cell. Molly disliked him already.

What she had learned felt slightly unreal. Imagine if someone gathered undeniable evidence that proved all birds are really extraterrestrials, here to take over the world. You'd doubt the information was really true, even if the facts were staring you in the face. This was how Molly felt about Primo Cell. Yet Molly knew firsthand just how easy it could be to control people. In her gut she felt that what Lucy had told her was true.

Molly didn't dwell on what might happen should Primo Cell catch her investigating him. If he *had* kidnaped Davina, then he was crazy—a nut case—and really dangerous. She wished she had a fast car with lots of gadgets in it. Instead, she was on an old chopper bike.

But there were two things that excited Molly. Lucy had given her a new license to hypnotize—and Molly was going to Los Angeles.

Back at Happiness House, Gemma and Gerry were cleaning out Gerry's mouse cage. They were about to make a strange discovery.

Gerry's ten mice ran around in a cardboard box, looking confused.

"When did you last do this?" asked Gemma, her face puckering at the smell.

"I've cleaned the worst parts four times since Christmas. I haven't touched the parts over there, as they don't get dirty."

"Why don't they get dirty?"

"Because that's where the mice sleep."

Gemma reached in and pulled out straw and rags. Gerry gave a tug at a pile of paper in the clean corner.

"See," he said, "this paper looks brand-new—just a bit nibbled at the sides." He dropped it on the floor.

"It's got something written on it," said Gemma, picking it up again. She gathered up the torn pages. "It says *The Book of Hy* . . . I can't read that—it's been eaten. This bit says *Ancient Art Revealed*. What do you think that means?"

"Dunno," said Gerry, wringing out a sponge and mopping the cage. "Something about painting pictures in an old-fashioned way?"

"It's a photocopy," said Gemma, gently peeling the pages apart. "About . . . it's about hypnotism. Where did you get this, Gerry? Is there any more of it?" Gemma looked into the back of the cage.

"There might have been—but I probably threw it away. What's hypnotism?"

"You know, where you make someone go all dreamy and then you tell them to do things. Where did this come from?"

"From a garbage can. Ages ago."

"Whose garbage can?"

"I dunno—either Ruby's or Rocky's, they both use the most paper. . . . Rocky always throws away the words of songs he's made up. I thought that was a song. But Gemma, don't read it now, you said you'd help me with my mice."

Gemma was too engrossed to continue her mice work. "This might be *important*," she muttered. "I'm gonna go to the linen cupboard to read this. You can meet me up there."

Twenty minutes later, Gerry and Gemma were crouched cross-legged on piles of towels in the dark linen cupboard, the pencil beam of a small flashlight focused on a scrappy pile of photocopied paper.

"Do you think we could really learn how to do it?" asked Gerry.

"We can try it out on your mice," answered Gemma.

"Now? I've got Victor in my pocket."

"No, we've got to learn it properly first. Pity all the lessons aren't here. Gerry, this is top secret. Understand?"

"Understand," said Gerry, and they knocked their fists together to seal the deal.

Molly arrived back at Happiness House desperate to talk to Rocky. She hoped that he hadn't gone on one of his wanders. He wasn't in the TV room, where Mrs. Trinklebury was watching a program about patchwork. Eventually she found him in the kitchen with Petula on his lap, reading a newspaper. Next to him was Nockman, who was studying a bird-training manual.

"Psssst," Molly whistled from the doorway.

"Uh-oh," Rocky said as he and Petula came out into the corridor and Molly grabbed his sleeve and hurried him upstairs. "What's up? Where'd you get the brief-case?"

Molly ushered him to the window seat at the end of the top-floor hallway and sat him down. There, in a whisper, she told him everything that had happened at Lucy Logan's. Then she opened the case and showed him the photographs and maps of Primo Cell's neighborhoods in Los Angeles.

Rocky shrugged his shoulders. "The whole thing sounds crazy to me. I don't believe it."

"You're just saying you don't believe it because you don't want to come, because it sounds dangerous. But please, Rocky—you've got to help me. I'm not the only one who can hypnotize round here."

"But I'm not a quarter as good as you, Molly."

"So you do believe this is true?"

"I never said that."

"Well, even if you don't believe it, you'd enjoy a vacation in Los Angeles," said Molly confidently.

"But . . ."

"Since when would Rocky Scarlet turn down a trip to sunny L.A.?" urged Molly. "Bet you'd never get asthma there."

"But . . ."

"Rocky, there is no way I'm going by myself," Molly said, louder than she meant to. "Listen, it's much warmer than here, and they have beaches. We'll only be gone a month or so. I can't do it without you, Rocky. Please come with me."

Petula suddenly sat up and wagged her tail hard. Someone was at the end of the corridor.

Gerry and Gemma approached sheepishly. From inside the cupboard, they'd heard the last part of Molly and Rocky's conversation, and now, although embarrassed to have been caught listening, they were burning with curiosity.

"What vacation? What beaches? Where are you goin'? We wanna come too," said Gemma.

"Yes," said Gerry. "You can't leave us behind. Last time you left us behind, it was 'orrid. 'Member?"

"You can't come," Molly began. Then she stopped. Gemma and Gerry had never been on vacation. She thought of them on a beach with buckets and spades, or in the sea, body surfing, or in a tour bus at one of Los Angeles's film studios, and her heart melted. They would love it, and she didn't see how they would get in the way. In fact, it might be an advantage if they came.

"You know, Rocky, if Mrs. Trinklebury came to look after them, we'd look like a normal family on vacation. And Nockman could help too." Molly was thinking that actually Nockman's criminal knowledge might come in useful. He was particularly good at picking locks.

"What about the others?" said Rocky. "They'll all be back from their courses next week."

"Why don't we ask Mrs. Trinklebury's sister to have them stay on her farm?" suggested Molly. Rocky nodded.

"I'll have to have a word with Mr. Struttfield," said Molly, thinking how she would have to hypnotize their headmaster. "Okay, Gemma, when Mrs. T.'s finished watching her program, I'll tell her that we've all been asked to go to L.A. by the Benefactor."

Rocky grinned. "And I'll find a nice hotel there where we can all stay, and Nockman can organize plane tickets—leaving as soon as possible."

"Does that mean we're going?" asked Gerry, not sure what had been agreed.

"Sure does," said Rocky.

"Whoooooooooo!" shouted Gerry. "Whooooooo!" And not knowing what to do with all his excitement, he started jumping up and down like a coffee-drinking kangaroo. "L.A., L.A., L.A., L.A.!" he shouted, running up the hall and back again. For a moment he stopped.

"Where is L.A.?" he asked.

"L.A. stands for Los Angeles," said Rocky. "It's in California, in America."

"Whoa. America? Wow!" After that Gerry was unstoppable. He bounced down the stairs and around the hall and up the stairs again and down again and up again, shouting, "No more school! NO MORE SCHOOOOOOOL!"

Gemma thanked Molly and Rocky ten times and then rushed into her bedroom to pack.

"It's the right decision," said Molly. "Because if we didn't take them and something bad happened to us there, then they'd *never* get a vacation."

"What might happen to us?" asked Rocky, raising an eyebrow.

"The same thing as Davina? I don't know. But this Mr. Cell is a power-crazed maniac. And a brilliant hypnotist. Jeepers, Rocky, what are we letting ourselves in for?"

"Trouble," said Rocky matter-of-factly.

"Yes, ten tons of trouble," agreed Molly.

Eight

Over the next three days, Molly watched Happiness House erupt with anticipation. Mrs. Trinklebury was so delighted about the idea of a vacation that she threw her apron on the fire to celebrate. She was very excited about going to Los Angeles and Hollywood, the movie capital of the world, home of the stars she adored. She harbored hopes that she would meet some of them.

Nockman wasn't entirely pleased to be going back to America. That was where he had, until recently, spent his whole life, and he didn't want to be reminded of his unwholesome past and the crimes he had committed. He worried that he might be tempted to do something bad again, but Mrs. Trinklebury, who was helping him reform, said that it would be good for him. So he carefully constructed a traveling box for his twenty parakeets. Molly had told him that the Benefactor was managing the flight arrangements for all the pets. Nockman automatically believed her. He always respected what Molly said, although he wasn't exactly sure why. He was glad the birds could come, because he wouldn't have gone otherwise.

Two matters had to be dealt with by hypnotism. One by Rocky, the other by Molly.

Rocky's challenge was to find hotel rooms for them. Their trip to Los Angeles coincided with its busiest week of the year. The night of the Academy Awards, when the best actors, actresses, directors, producers, and film people would win the coveted golden Oscar statuettes for their work, was in a week's time. Every single room in every hotel had been booked months in advance.

"I hate to do this," said Rocky as he picked up the phone. "Because of us, some people are going to lose their rooms."

"Aren't you nervous that you've forgotten how to do long-distance hypnosis?" Molly asked. But Rocky shook his head.

"Hypnotizing people is like riding a bicycle, don't you think? Once you've learned, you never forget." Molly was amazed by Rocky's confidence and very impressed when, ten minutes later, he came out of the TV room with the news that they now had two bungalows and a room reserved at a hotel called the Château Marmont.

"All I needed was a bit of time," said Rocky. "As long as they listen to me, they melt like butter in my hands."

Molly, however, was incredibly nervous about her hypnotic challenge. She had to visit their headmaster and hypnotize him into giving his permission—for her, Rocky, Gemma, Roger, and Gerry to go to Los Angeles, and for the rest of the orphanage children to stay on Mrs. Trinklebury's sister's farm. Molly was worried that she might have lost her hypnotic skills, especially since she'd had that ice-cold fusion feeling when she'd tried to hypnotize the bush.

In the headmaster's office, Molly started by explaining that the trip to California was educational. They'd been learning about earthquakes and the desert and the American Congress, she said, so the trip would be very informative.

"The other children have been asked to stay on a pig farm, where they will learn about pigs. . . . You know— pigs and slop and manure and, erm, agriculture. This will also be very educational."

Mr. Struttfield seemed to think the idea splendid, because he said, "I'm very impressed that you have come to ask my permission yourself, Molly. I like children with initiative. A good golf player has initiative. A sense of—if you want that ball to go in a certain direction, learn how to hit it. Don't wait for someone else to hit it for you—eh, don't you agree?"

"Yes, sir."

"If you ask me, farms ought to turn their land over to golf courses. Don't you think?"

Molly said nothing.

"So you're all off to Los Angeles and farms. Well, I hope you have a very educational time and, if you can, play a bit of golf for me, eh?"

"Thank you, sir. Yes, sir."

With that, his phone rang and, picking it up, Mr. Struttfield nodded to Molly that she could go.

Molly couldn't believe it. She'd actually persuaded him to let them all off school without hypnosis! She didn't know exactly how Mr. Struttfield had been so easy to win over, but feeling very pleased with herself, she went back to the classroom.

And so it was that, a few days later, a small minibus was loaded and thirty-eight passengers (five children, two adults, twenty parakeets, ten mice, and one pug), took their places on board. Even Roger was eager to come, happy, he said, to be getting away from the voices he was hearing.

Molly, at last, and for the first time in months, had to test her hypnotic powers. She thought her skills might have grown rusty. But they hadn't. She easily hypnotized the airline attendants. One bolting glare from her green eyes was all it took. The warm fusion feeling blasted through her, and she knew they were under her power. The animals were allowed through, and soon they were all settled on the plane.

The flight wasn't anything like Molly's solitary one to New York before Christmas. This flight was chaotic as well as noisy. When the jumbo took off, Mrs. Trinklebury started a shouting-out-her-prayers thing that lasted off and on for most of the flight.

Halfway across the Atlantic, Gerry lost a mouse. Victor, his prize buck, broke loose and made his way up to the plane toilets, where he got locked in with a hairy backpacker. When she burst out of the cubicle, shouting that she'd seen a squirrel, Victor quietly made his way back to Gerry's seat.

"Madam, it's impossible that a squirrel could get on board," the flight attendant assured the backpacker. "It's a long flight. Perhaps you should drink some water and do some of the calming exercises that we recommend."

Molly would normally have wanted to get off a flight like this, with Mrs. Trinklebury being so embarrassing, but as it was, she wished that it would go on and on—then she wouldn't have to investigate the danger that was Primo Cell.

She told this to Rocky. "If you're scared," he replied, "think how terrified Davina must be, wherever she is. If she *is* alive and if Cell has taken her, she needs *you* to rescue her."

"She's the only reason I'm going," said Molly. "I wouldn't risk my life just to check out those stars. Anyway, I suppose I owe Davina. I did steal her part in *Stars on Mars* before Christmas."

Molly leaned down to put a slice of salami in Petula's basket. Petula was very well-behaved on planes.

After eleven hours, the plane wheeled above the bright lights of Los Angeles. Molly stared out at the enormous city below. It seemed to stretch for hundreds of miles in all directions. She couldn't help wondering where Primo Cell was right now, among those millions of buildings.

Then the tires hit the tarmac and they were safely down. Everyone put their watches back eight hours. It was seven o'clock in the evening.

Soon they were all standing in baggage claim, half asleep, waiting for their suitcases. The only people with any energy left were Gerry and Gemma, who were giving rides on the baggage carousel to Gerry's toy superheroes.

Molly watched a small red case trundling around on the conveyor belt. Exhausted as she was, she let her eyes linger on it, absorbing its rough-textured surface and the color of its tarnished buckles. For a moment the airport seemed very far away, and it was as if she and the suitcase were the only things that existed. A moment later Molly felt as if the suitcase was *inside* her mind. It was a strange feeling, but not a completely new one. It reminded Molly of the sensation she got whenever she was hypnotizing a person. A slipping sensation that happened just before her subject went into a trance, when she could feel their personality weakening and starting to belong to her. Molly thought how odd it was to be feeling this with a suitcase, and then, as she sleepily gazed, the familiar, warm fusion feeling started to spread through her body. But a second later, the feeling turned icy cold. It was exactly the same thing that had happened with the topiary dog. Shocked, Molly snapped her attention away from the case.

It was very peculiar. This obviously had something to do with staring at objects. What would happen, Molly wondered, if she let the freezing feeling continue? Would she find that she'd hypnotized the object she was looking at? That was ridiculous. How could a suitcase be hypnotized? Next time, she decided, she would experiment and see what the cold fusion feeling grew into.

Everyone gathered their bags and cases and hauled them onto luggage carts. Dazed and weary, they made their way to the taxi stand. No one noticed a luggage porter approaching them.

"Hey, 'scuse me," he said, his face beaming with recognition, "but ain't you the girl and the boy on the 'Check Out the Kids in Your Neighborhood' commercial?"

Nine

olly was stunned. It had never crossed her
mind that the hypnotic charity TV ad she
and Rocky had made in New York could
have been watched by people in Los Angeles. How
many more people in the airport had recognized her?

"Um, yeah . . . yeah, that was us," she told him reluctantly.

"Great work," said the smiling porter. "Let me give
you folks some assistance!" He took Molly's cart and
led them straight to the front of the taxi line. Here he
loaded their bags into a waiting minibus and waved
them off.

"So much for Lucy saying that because we're children,
we won't be suspected," whispered Rocky as they sank
into their seats. "Primo Cell probably saw the ad and

has been looking for two kid hypnotists ever since."

Molly was too shaken by the incident to say anything.

Soon the minibus was heading out from underneath concrete columns toward the city of Los Angeles. Molly sat with Petula on her knee, wishing that they hadn't come. She tried to let the new surroundings distract her from thoughts of Primo Cell. But it was an impossible task. Once the bus had left the airport, they headed out on a road dotted with huge billboards. On either side, ads showed Shlick Shlack knives, nutritious Navy Girl soup, and Sumpshus toilet paper, in which the boxer King Moose was pictured having a fight with a giant toilet paper roll. Cell's companies. His influence was everywhere. Another poster that kept being repeated was of a politician in a cowboy hat. Underneath his red, white, and blue jacket, it said in bold letters, GANDOLLI FOR PRESIDENT THIS NOVEMBER. At least, Molly thought, there wasn't one advertising Cell for president.

The minibus turned onto the highway. Brown, scrubby hills stretched into the distance, and on them stood oil-drilling pumps, each the size of a small house. They looked like monster birds with metal legs and beak-shaped ends that seesawed, pecking at the ground.

As Molly looked at the nodding oil pumps, she couldn't help thinking that Primo Cell might already have hit men pecking around the country, trying to find the two children who had made the hypnotic commercial. He probably wanted to do away with them, as he had maybe done away with Davina Nuttel. The great, heartless iron birds made her courage falter.

Soon small houses began to pop up beside the road, and then larger ones. Then they were driving up a long shopping street, full of secondhand-car showrooms and bars, and on to another with clothes boutiques and restaurants. A giant poster had Hercules Stone's smiling face on it. It was advertising the film *Blood of a Stranger*. Big letters proclaimed NOMINATED FOR THREE ACADEMY AWARDS: BEST FILM, BEST ACTRESS—LEADING ROLE, BEST SCREENPLAY. Molly watched a jogger passing a fast-food shop called Emergency Donuts. OPEN 24 HOURS, DON'T PANIC. Petula pricked her ears at a pack of five dogs that were being walked by a woman on roller skates.

"The suburbs are very big here," Molly said to the driver.

"The suburbs?" said the driver. "This ain't the suburbs. This is Los Angeles city itself. This is the City of Angels, angel."

"But where are the skyscrapers?" asked Molly, sure that he must be wrong.

"Oh, there are *some* downtown, but this ain't a sky-scraper city, doll. This is a city of gardens, nice an' green, and *low*-rise buildings, which is best 'cause we gets earthquakes here, bein' on the San Andreas Fault line an' all that. In fact, we're nearly at your hotel, and your hotel is smack in the center of Los Angeles. Mos' places, this is as high as the buildings get."

"But in the center of most cities," Molly said, "the buildings are packed closely together."

"Yeah, that's 'cause mos' cities are old and ain't got space. This is a young city, an' there's always been loadsa space."

At the end of the wide street was a giant bottle-shaped billboard advertising the drink Qube. Behind the billboard were hills with buildings on them receding steeply away.

"Up there," said their driver, "are the San Gabriel Mountains, an' over there"—he pointed behind him—"is Death Valley. But you don't wanna go there—it's so hot, you can fry an egg on the hood of your car."

The minibus found a gap in the oncoming traffic and dived up a steep drive on the other side of the road. Molly saw a small sign half hidden by leaves. The

Château Marmont. Molly looked up at a fairy-tale building with turrets and towers. Windows rose for ten floors, with small balconies in front of them. The entrance was in a cavelike garage under the hotel, where three men who looked more like movie stars than porters were waiting to unpack the minibus.

"Welcome to the Château Marmont."

Everyone was very excited to have arrived, although they were all dazed and dehydrated from the plane, and their eyeballs felt as dry as if they'd been rolled around in tissue and then put back in their sockets. Ascending in the elevator to the hotel's reception area, Molly realized what an odd-looking and scruffy party they made, with boxes of mice and parakeets and Nockman with a nine-o'clock shadow around his chin where he hadn't shaved.

The foyer of the hotel was very smart and dark, with tall ceilings and a stone floor. Next to it was a grand sitting room that was packed with people. A few looked up disapprovingly at the gaggle of children. Nockman walked off to find the men's room.

Molly went to the front desk to check in. A receptionist with a skin like an unpeeled avocado looked worriedly at Roger, who was hugging a small palm tree in a pot.

"Is he with you?" he asked.

"Yes," said Molly. "He'll calm down in a minute—he's just got I've-been-on-a-plane-too-long-itis."

The receptionist looked at the five children in front of him.

"I'm afraid I can't check you in until a responsible adult arrives."

"Uurrgh," growled Molly. "Honestly, we're just as responsible as them." And to avoid wasting any more time, she zapped the avocado man's eyes until he was ready to do exactly what she asked. Then she organized where everyone would sleep.

As the receptionist smiled obediently, Mrs. Trinklebury arrived. She was late because she'd found herself in the elevator with the famous actor Cosmo Ace. She'd followed him up to the seventh floor and into the fitness rooms, where she'd watched him pedal an exercise bike. Molly realized that Mrs. Trinklebury was going to love the Château Marmont.

Nockman took the key to his room and disappeared up the stairs with his birds and his luggage. The rest of the party followed a bellboy outside.

In the gardens, where it was now dark, steel heaters like tall, stubby umbrellas showered down heat on guests at tables beneath them.

As they weaved along a path between urns of pansies, Molly overheard snippets of conversations:

"Steve says he loves your screenplay but he wants Spelkman directing it."

"But Spelkman stinks. His films are slop. He can't get performances out of actors. Oh, no, this is terrible."

"It's the only way, Randy."

"Now listen, Barbara. I don't want anyone who *eats meat* doing my hair or my makeup, or my nails or anything. Is that clear? I don't want any of that bad energy near me."

"Okay, Blake."

"So what are you wearing to the Academy Awards, Jean? Remember, it's watched by people all over the world."

"As little as possible."

They walked along a jungly path overhung with rustling palm trees and lined with staghorn ferns. Mrs. Trinklebury and Roger's bungalow was situated near a sunbathing garden where a waterfall cascaded down from rocks into a swimming pool. Roger patted the trunk of a broad-leafed ficus tree, and the hotel parrot squawked at him from its cage.

The others followed the bellboy again, to the top of a

narrow stone-stepped path, where they came to the best bungalow of all.

It was perfect for Petula, because it had a fenced lawn in front of it with a little wooden gate. It was a modern rectangular building whose whole front was made of glass. Inside, there was a big sitting room with an L-shaped sofa and a TV, and a small kitchen area to one side.

"Someone will come in and clean up whenever you cook," said the bellboy.

On top of a counter was a basket full of potato chips and candy.

"We'll replenish the snack basket every day."

Gemma started to flick through the hotel's leather-bound brochure.

"Look! There's a hotel film library and it's got hundreds of films to borrow. An' music . . ." Gemma spent the next ten minutes on the phone, calling the others in their rooms. She took room service orders, and twenty minutes later the food arrived on trays under silver lids. Steaks, French fries, milk shakes, and, since they didn't have orange squash concentrate, Molly ordered some grenadine instead. The room-service waiter explained that this was made from pomegranates and was a fruity syrup that was supposed to be mixed with lemonade, and when it was mixed with ginger ale, Americans called it a Shirley Temple cocktail.

Molly sipped the concentrated grenadine from a glass full of ice. She knew that Shirley Temple had been a child star in the 1930s, and this made her think of Davina Nuttel. She hoped she was safe, wherever she was.

Molly woke in the middle of the night, her body thinking that it was morning. Back in Briersville, it was already ten A.M. She found it difficult to go back to sleep because Gerry's mice were on their squeaky exercise wheel and, outside, a tree creaked noisily.

She wished that she was in this luxurious hotel to enjoy a vacation, not to embark upon an uncertain mission. Investigating Primo Cell had sounded dangerous back home. Now it felt impossible, too. Molly considered what exactly she and Rocky should do, now they were in Cell territory. Definitely, the most important thing was to find out whether Cell was behind Davina Nuttel's kidnaping and, if he was, to find her.

As Molly tried to get to sleep, two images from the file of photographs that Lucy had given her kept returning to her mind. One was of Cell in hunting clothes with a half-cocked rifle under his arm and two lifeless pheasants over his shoulder. The other was of him on safari, with a larger gun and his foot resting on the flank of a large dead antelope.

Molly reached down the bed to stroke Petula. Primo Cell most certainly liked killing things.

Ten

Early next morning, Gerry tapped on Molly's bedroom door, waking her up. He was wearing swimming trunks, water wings, and a huge hotel bathrobe that trailed on the floor.

"Comin', Molly? Breakfast is by the pool. We're gonna 'ave pancakes."

For a moment, as the sun washed into the room, Molly was still half dreaming that she was back at Happiness House on a boiling hot morning. Then the memory of what she had to do today drowned her carefree thoughts. She groaned.

Half an hour later, Molly and Rocky were sitting in their pajamas on the floor in Molly's room. The contents of Lucy Logan's briefcase were spread out before them.

"Okay," began Molly, "to find anything out, we're going to have to check out Primo Cell's home *and* his headquarters *and* the stars he's hypnotized. If we do all that, we may find something out about Davina."

"I suggest," said Rocky, "that we get Nockman in here, ask him what he needs for lock breaking and computer-code cracking, and then, tonight, when Cell's office building is empty, we should break into it. If Lucy is right, and he is planning to hypnotize and *keep* hypnotized thousands, maybe millions, of people, and if he's already got hundreds under his control, he can't have all the details in his head. He'll have to keep files—either written down or in a computer. And there has to be a secret place where he keeps them—in a locked cabinet or a locked room. I bet there's something there that will tell us whether he's had anything to do with Davina Nuttel."

"But why his headquarters tonight? Why not his home?"

"Because he'll be asleep there, Molly. Wake up."

"Okay, okay." Molly pulled the map of L.A. toward them. "His headquarters are in Westwood, near Beverly Hills. We can catch a sixty-seven bus."

"The bus?"

"That will make us inconspicuous. We'll take Petula

82

and we'll look like a couple of kids walking the dog with our—um—uncle."

Thirty minutes later, Mr. Nockman stood docilely in front of them. He was wearing a short-sleeved shirt decorated with exotic birds and a pair of flower-patterned Bemuda shorts that Mrs. Trinklebury had bought him. His mouth hung open, so Molly could see he had six or seven fillings. Petula sniffed at his hairy flip-flopped feet.

"I hate to hypnotize him again," said Molly. "He was doing so well. And I really hope that doing something criminal doesn't make him miss his old life."

"We're not interfering with his self-improvement," said Rocky. "It's just one night, and it's all for a good cause. He won't remember he's done it."

"Okay," said Molly, concentrating. "You, Nockman, are going to accompany us tonight. You will tell Mrs. Trinklebury that you will be doing some work for the Benefactor—you know, the man who Mrs. T. thinks sends us money at the orphanage. Say you're changing his front door locks for him."

"Yes." Nockman nodded.

"You must bring everything you might need for opening locks, for breaking codes of combination locks, and for cracking codes to access files in computers.

83

Imagine you are going to be robbing a very secure office. Is there anything special you need?" She paused while he thought.

"I—vill need—explosives."

"Well, I'm afraid you can't have them. They're too noisy, and they make too much mess."

"Some locks," said Nockman, shaking his head, "may be impossible—to open." Molly looked at Rocky worriedly. They couldn't use explosives. They didn't want Cell knowing they'd broken in.

"No one is to know about this," said Rocky.

"No—vun."

"Meet us outside the hotel entrance at ten tonight," said Molly. "Now, go and spend the day with your birds and Mrs. Trinklebury. As soon as you leave here, you will come out of your trance."

Nockman nodded like a programmed robot and plodded away.

"Good work," said Rocky, yawning. "We might as well go down to the pool too. We've got the whole day to spare. I want to practice my diving."

"What, and get recognized again?" said Molly sharply. "Who knows who'll be down at the pool? If Cell really is who Lucy says he is, he'll maybe have spies about. We can't risk it."

Rocky breathed out exasperatedly. "I suppose you're

right." He picked up a photograph of Cell and began to draw a beak and wings on him.

In the distance the hotel parrot squawked, "Have a nice day, have a nice day."

Molly closed the curtains against the sun, and picking up the hotel's video-rental menu, she resigned herself to a day of watching movies.

Eleven

At ten that night, Molly left Mrs. Trinklebury sipping a pink drink and eating pretzels in the hotel lobby, where she was blissfully happy to be overhearing Hollywood gossip about the Academy Awards. She was completely ignorant as to where Molly, Rocky, Petula, and Nockman were really going.

Outside, they made their way to the bus stop across the street from the hotel's driveway. Molly and Rocky were wearing canvas hats to help hide their faces. Nockman was dressed in a black turtleneck and black trousers. He was carrying a small canvas bag that Molly supposed had tools in it.

"You look, erm, professional," said Molly.

"Sank you," said Nockman.

"It's his cat-burglar look," Rocky whispered in her ear. "I hope it's not *too* professional looking. We don't want to look suspicious. I'll take the tools."

Petula sniffed the air. For some reason it was full of the scents of lots of dogs very nearby. She looked around and saw behind her a huge cutout of a dog's face. Below it were the words BELLA'S POODLE SALON AND DOG HOTEL. Although the writing didn't make sense to Petula, the smells did. Her nose sensed a Labrador, a Yorkshire terrier, a bulldog, and some sort of oriental-smelling dog. There were other dog breeds she didn't recognize at all. On top of all their scents were shampoo smells, perfumes, and the aromas of essential oils. The place was obviously a dog beauty parlor. Petula hoped that after they'd done whatever was making Molly nervous, she'd get to go there for a wash and blow-dry.

"Arrooof!" she barked at Molly, to show her what she'd found. But Molly hardly heard her. Scary thoughts were rolling around and around her brain like snakes on roller skates.

Perhaps, she thought, Primo Cell had other hypnotists working in the building—big thugs who worked all night as security guards. What would she and Rocky say if they were caught? How would they explain Nockman,

who would be standing there all dopey and hypnotized? To Molly it felt as scary as diving off a boat into
the sea where lots of sharks swam.

"Do you think he works late?" she asked Rocky nervously.

"Nah," Rocky replied. "He likes to go out at night
with all his famous pals. His hypnotized celebrities, I
mean. You can bet he'll be in a fancy restaurant somewhere."

The blue-and-white sixty-seven bus shook them
from their worries by stopping with an air-expelling
sigh. They climbed aboard, and fed the meter with
tokens they'd bought at the hotel. Molly was glad it was
practically empty.

The bus chugged westward. On both sides of the
streets were interesting buildings. The Cowboy's
Retreat was a log cabin fronted with flashing neon
lights. The Emerald Crown was a hotel shaped like a
wedding cake with a carpet that rolled down to the
road like a green beach meeting a tarmac sea. They
passed another GANDOLLI FOR PRESIDENT poster. It
was next to a giant lizard-shaped billboard above a
record store. The purple Groovy Lizzening reptile
was wearing sunglasses and earphones and looked
much more cool than the cheesy cowboy-hatted
politician. Crowds of people swarmed around the

entrance to a music venue called Whiskey-A-Go-Go. A slat board on the side of it showed who was performing tonight.

"Wow, I'd like to go there," said Rocky.

Molly was looking at a person sitting under a lit-up sign that read STAR MAPS FOR SALE HERE.

"What are star maps?" she asked the bus driver.

"They're maps that have all the streets in Beverly Hills and Hollywood on them, and they're marked to show you where all the stars live," he told her, repositioning one of his ornamental cactuses on the dashboard.

"What?" said Molly. "You mean the maps show you *exactly* how you can get to the stars' houses?"

"Yeah, of course. You can see what the outside of their homes look like, but you can't go near 'em. They got security and guards—otherwise fans would be crawlin' over their grounds."

Molly was amazed. "Are we in Beverly Hills now?"

"Yeah. See the way the curb is kept so pretty with all the flowers? And up those streets there, it's even *more* pretty. They got palm-tree avenues an' lawns, an' if you go way up into the hills, you get the real big mansions. But now we're heading toward one of the business districts." The bus shot past a big pink building called the Beverly Hills Hotel.

"It would cost me two weeks' salary just to stay *one* night there in their *cheapest* room," said the driver.

Soon they were in Westwood.

"Nice meetin' ya," the driver said.

With a squirting-air sound, the doors of the bus closed. And as if relieved to have farted, the bus went meandering down the road. Molly, Rocky, Petula, and Nockman stood on a wide sidewalk near the entrance to a smaller street called Orchid Avenue. Halfway down it, big and reflective, its walls made of dark-blue glass, was the Cell Center, Primo Cell's building. Molly recognized it at once. Its flat roof was crowned by a giant golden emblem—a huge disk that looked as if two black claws were turning and swirling around a golden plate. Molly shivered.

A small park with lemon trees lay opposite. Trying to look as unnoticeable as possible, Molly and Rocky led Nockman and Petula over to a bench. Petula began to investigate smells. It was a good spot from which to watch the entrance to Cell's fortress.

"That symbol on top looks like claws grabbing a coin," said Rocky.

"Or black flames devouring a golden world," suggested Molly.

"Or black eyelashes around the golden pupil of an

eye. But if you don't know about Cell, then it just looks like a strange design."

"You don't think Cell is hanging about in there, do you?" asked Molly.

"There's only one way of finding out."

TWelVe

The investigative party made its way up the mosaic path to the night-lit entrance of Cell's building. Under her feet, Molly noticed, was the black-and-white image of a magpie picked out in tiles. Nockman followed, waddling like a penguin.

The black glass door opened as they walked toward it, and a burly security guard with short, spiky hair stared at them ominously, his eyes hooded by forestlike eyebrows.

"Can I help?" he asked, in a voice that suggested he would prefer to strangle them.

"Yes, please," Molly replied politely, but inside she was smoldering. She never liked rude grown-ups. Who did this hyena man think he was? Confidently, she raised her green eyes to his.

Molly's hypnotic power was leagues ahead of any normal hypnotist's. In a few seconds she could absorb the atmosphere that surrounded a person and judge where his weaknesses were. She could feel how much hypnotic pressure he would need before he gave in. As she eyeballed the security guard, the fusion gauge inside her, like a thermometer and an oven timer in one, told her that old Spiky-hair was well and truly cooked. He stood with an expression of awe on his face, as if he'd just seen a goddess.

"Are you alone here?" Molly asked.

"Yes."

Molly glanced around for closed-circuit cameras and spotted two. "Who looks at the film on the cameras?" she asked. "Is someone looking at them now?"

"No." The guard shook his head. "The film—goes into—a memory bank and—is looked at only—if there is a problem. Like a robbery—or a break-in. I have a—panic button—that alerts the—police. They then call the com—pany where the film—can be viewed."

"On no account are you to press that button tonight."

"No, ma'am."

"Okay. You must take us up to Primo Cell's office immediately. Are you expecting anyone in tonight?"

"No, ma'am."

"Do you ever get unannounced visitors? Does Mr. Cell ever—pop in?"

"Sometimes, ma'am."

"Do you know where he is tonight?"

"No, ma'am."

"Well, I think you'd better show us up."

After a ride in a silver-walled elevator, Molly, Petula, Rocky, and Nockman found themselves walking along a blue stone passage into a circular rotunda. There the marble walls bore the same image of the clawlike motif. At a black door, the night watchman punched a code number into an electronic lock. The door opened softly, and they were inside Cell's office.

The room was bathed in a denim-blue light—the street lighting that filtered through the blue glass windows.

"You may return to your desk," said Molly. "When you are out of our sight, you will forget that we are here and that you are hypnotized. You will behave as normally as you can. If Mr. Cell arrives, you must call up to this room—without him hearing—and tell us he's here. We'll let ourselves out. What's the number for the door?"

"Zero—nine—six—zero."

"Good. You can go now." The guard left.

"Okay, let's get down to business," said Molly. "Where does he lock things up?"

She cast her eyes around the modern room. There was a floor-to-ceiling window at one end overlooking the little park. On one wall hung a huge oil painting of a beautiful magpie, sitting in a nest full of shiny things—coins, jewelry, precious golden objects, and a big, icy diamond. The opposite wall was lined with bookshelves. The floor was striped black and white. A black-lacquer art-deco desk stood in front of the window. On it were two white elephant tusks set on silver bases, pointing to the ceiling.

"How disgusting," said Rocky. "I'd rather be shot myself than have an elephant tusk as an ornament." Then he looked at the floor, and his mouth dropped open. He crouched down and stroked it. "The carpet is wall-to-wall zebra skin. A zebra-fur carpet!" Rocky was too appalled to be able to say what he felt about this. Petula sniffed the floor. It smelled like horse.

Feeling like a fish in the blue, waterlike light, Molly threw him a pair of Bubblealot rubber gloves.

"Here," she said. "Put these on. We mustn't leave fingerprints." Wearing her own pair of gloves, she crossed the room to Primo Cell's desk and began opening drawers.

Rocky checked the bookcase for a hidden safe.

Nockman stood silently by, waiting for instructions.

In a bottom drawer Molly came across some documents that showed what businesses Primo had recently bought. More papers listed the money his companies had made. The biggest ones were Primospeed, Compucell, and Cell Oil, but even the smaller ones—In the Groove, Vitawell, Shlick Shlack, Fashion House, and Mightie Lighties—were massively successful. Molly had never seen such big numbers as those that blinked out from Primo Cell's bank statements. But these numbers weren't what they were looking for.

Then, as Molly was about to scoop up what looked like an address book, she felt something soft under her fingers. She pulled it out. In her hand was a small black mink glove. It would have fitted Molly perfectly.

"Rocky, look at this. Is it . . . ?"

She looked in the drawer to find the glove's partner.

"Why would Primo Cell have a child's fur glove in his desk?" she whispered hoarsely.

Rocky was about to open his mouth when they heard voices in the hallway outside.

Thirteen

Molly quickly pulled Nockman behind the desk and pushed him under it. They all sank breathlessly out of sight, like two minnows and a sea slug diving behind a rock.

"You will be as quiet as . . . as a dead person," Molly whispered frantically.

Nockman immediately rolled up his eyes and stuck out his tongue.

"It can't be Primo Cell," hissed Rocky, "or the watchman would have called up."

The electronic lock bleeped four times.

"Petula!" Molly gasped. Petula was examining the mane of the zebra skin in the corner of the room. It smelled of some hot, faraway place. She spat out the stone she was sucking to have a good sniff.

The door to the room opened and a woman's voice, suddenly loud, said, "Sumpshus toilet paper's going well."

Molly prayed desperately that Petula would come over quickly, before the lights were turned on.

"It's been helped by the campaign with that boxer . . ." said the woman.

"King Moose," prompted a man's voice.

"Yeah, by King Moose saying that it's tough enough for him to use."

The lights then blazed. Molly was so scared, she thought she might faint. The vein in her throat was pumping so hard that her neck hurt. If the pair, who-ever they were, came too far toward the window, they would see her, Rocky, and Nockman squashed under the desk. As for Petula, she was an alarm bell just wait-ing to ring.

The people were standing by the magpie picture.

"Have you seen the commercial?" asked the man.

"King Moose having a boxing match with an ani-mated toilet roll, and losing? Yes, it made me laugh."

"And you don't do that too often, Sally."

"No need to be cutting, Sinclair. You're not a bundle of fun yourself."

"The job sobers me up."

"Maybe you should put more comedy on your channels," suggested Sally.

"There's lots of comedy," said Sinclair. "I just don't have time to watch it. Our father works me too hard. Now can we hurry up? Surely you know where the file is; you're in here every day."

All was silent except for the noise of shifting box files as Sally searched. Molly was rigid with nerves. Rocky stared at the floor, trying to be as still as a piece of furniture, hoping that he'd left everything in order.

"This is it," said Sally's voice. "It's a small company that makes watches. It's called Timezze. Dad's letting me handle the project on my own. He thinks we should be able to pump Timezze up until every other person in America wears one of them. I'm going to try my hardest to make it happen. I'll get that Tony Wam to promote them. *'A kung fu kick has to be right ON TIME.'* It'll be that kind of ad campaign. I can't wait to tell Primo."

"You're very eager to please."

"That's all right for you to say, Teacher's Pet."

"Let's not start that argument again. So what do you want me to do?"

"Give the watches some free advertising time on Iceberg TV, of course," said Sally. "Here, you take these copies." Molly froze as the man's steps neared the other side of the desk. Suddenly he said, "I don't believe it. That dog's gotten in here again."

Petula looked up from her corner behind the door. "What dog?"

"This dog, this pug—look. They told me a dog got into the building yesterday, and look, it's back again. How did it get in?"

Molly opened her mouth wide, but no noise came out.

"Poor little thing—I wonder how long it's been here. Here, sweetie." Molly heard Petula shuffling up to the strange woman. She was always a sucker for having her tummy tickled.

"Aw, look at it, the darling. Shall I tickle your tum-tum? I suppose it wants to audition for one of your dog-food ads, Sinclair." Sally laughed. "Aw, she's so sweet. Look at her li'l nose. Oh, you gotta give her a job, Sinclair!"

"I'll call her in for the dog-biscuit commercial next week," said Sinclair, chuckling.

"Shall I take her home?"

Molly bit her lip.

"No, Sally. The dog lives around here. Get a grip. We'll just drop her outside on the way out." With that, the lights in the room went off. "Come on, puggy," said Sinclair with a whistle.

"She doesn't want to come. She wants to sign a contract first," laughed Sally.

Go on. Go ON, thought Molly.

Sally must have picked Petula up then, because the next thing they knew, the door had closed and the conversation between Sinclair and Sally faded.

Molly and Rocky waited for several minutes before daring to crawl out of their hiding place. Molly found her legs were shaking. Until she'd been trapped behind the desk, she hadn't properly realized the seriousness of the situation they were in. They lay on their stomachs and peered out of the window. Soon they saw the heads of Sinclair and Sally emerge from the office. The dark-haired woman put Petula down, then laughed and pointed as Petula walked straight up to the door of the building again. Petula did look like some sort of budding acting dog who couldn't take no for an answer. Sinclair irritatedly beckoned for the woman to get into the sports car parked at the curb. With a noisy rev of its engine, they were gone.

"Brrrrr." Molly shivered. "Let's get on with this. We've gotta get out of here."

She bent down to Nockman. "You can be alive now, but nice and quiet please." Nockman clambered out. "There *must* be somewhere else here where Cell keeps his secret stuff," said Molly.

"Unless he keeps it all at home."

Molly looked up at the picture of the magpie.

Moments later Nockman was balancing on a velvet chair and, wearing Bubblealot gloves, was lifting the picture off the wall. There, like a second sunken picture, was a microwave-oven-sized safe. In the center of it was a copper-colored dial with little numbers etched around it.

"Bing—o," said Nockman, knocking his head against the safe enthusiastically.

"Can you open it?" asked Molly.

"Sure—sing," declared Nockman. "Zis is a Glock and Guttman, 1965. A beauty. I'fe opened sree of zeese before. Zay are—like rich old—ladies—difficult to charm, but worse it."

"Worth it?"

"Yes, worse it."

"I don't think Mrs. Trinklebury would be happy to hear you say that," said Molly, thinking how close to the surface of his skin were his old criminal ways. Nockman looked ashamed.

"But okay, open it," said Molly.

Nockman nodded and thrust his face clumsily toward the safe as if he were about to kiss it. He banged his nose. Then he put his ear up to the copper wheel and with his right hand began to turn the dial.

"I hope he can do it hypnotized," said Rocky.

"Aha!" gloated Nockman, clicking the dial forty-five degrees to the right.

"It better not be alarmed," said Molly.

"Mmmmmnn," mulled Nockman, turning the dial six degrees to the left.

"How does he do it?"

"Beats me. I wish he'd hurry up."

"Haaaaah," grunted Nockman, as if he'd just caught a fox undoing the latch of a chicken run.

While Nockman hummed and tutted and clicked, Molly reached for the micro camera in her bag. What had Cell hidden in the secret safe?

All at once Nockman sighed. He pulled the safe's handle down, and a satisfying clunking noise reverberated inside.

"Hey presto," he said.

The door swung open.

Then his face dropped with disappointment as he saw there were no diamonds or jewels. Instead, four black file folders, one on top of the other, lay inside like sleeping monsters. Nockman passed them to Molly.

"You go first," said Molly.

"No, after you," said Rocky.

Molly opened a file.

"Wow." Molly could hardly believe what she was seeing. Staring up at her from the top sheet of a stack of paper was a photograph of Cosmo Ace. It was stuck above the heading "Heaven Bar Campaign." Dates and addresses were printed below. But this was not the familiar, handsome face from the TV ads. This man looked dazed—or drugged—or . . . hypnotized.

"Lucy was right," said Rocky huskily.

With shaking hands, he and Molly each took a file and rifled through them. They had indeed hit the jackpot. All the sheets inside were laid out in the same way—with the name of a person at the top of the page and a passport-size photograph of them on the right-hand corner, like a stamp on an envelope. Molly and Rocky couldn't contain their amazement.

"So many of them! He's hypnotized practically every star who exists."

Some pages bore a note in red ink. It read simply E DAY.

Molly came to Suky Champagne's sheet. It was strange to see her world-famous face in the small black-and-white photograph. Suky Champagne didn't look her usual lovely, vivacious self at all. This Suky looked dopey. Her sheet also included the words "E Day."

"What do you think E Day is?" asked Molly.

"The day he's got what he wants? I don't know,"

Rocky replied. "Look, Billy Bob Bimble's here too."

"Shall I take a picture of every document?" whispered Molly.

"Yes. I'll hold them up and you photograph them."

So that was what they did. Molly took off her sticky rubber gloves and began snapping away. Photographs of celebrities she recognized and ones that she didn't passed before her camera. There was Hercules Stone looking half asleep, Gloria Heelheart with her mouth open like a goldfish. King Moose, cross-eyed, and Stephanie Goulash smiling like a plastic doll. But there weren't just actors and pop stars in the files. There were American TV announcers, sports stars, newscasters, business leaders, newspaper editors, journalists, artists, writers, restaurant owners, doctors, police chiefs, army commanders, and politicians.

"I wouldn't be surprised if he wants to hypnotize the president of the United States," said Rocky.

The documents were in alphabetical order, and Molly noticed there were lots of empty pages with names on them, but no photograph. Were these the people Primo Cell *planned* to hypnotize? On a few of these the red ink said ACTIVATE BEFORE E DAY.

"What *is* this E Day?" Molly asked again.

"A day he's planning something big. We'll have to find out what it means."

The worst sheet they found was Davina Nuttel's. She stared out of the picture like someone who'd just seen a bomb go off. A bloodred cross traversed her page like a murderer's mark.

"Oh," Molly gasped. "You don't think he's . . ."

Rocky stared in horror. "So Primo Cell really did have something to do with her kidnaping."

"But why?"

"All I know is that we're playing with fire and we should get out of here as fast as we can."

Rocky and Molly worked as quickly as possible. They crouched on the floor, hoping that flashes from the camera wouldn't be seen from the street. Nockman sat on a velvet chair, occasionally muttering "Tick, tick," or "Click, click," or "Hmmmm," and picking at his thumbs.

An hour later, Molly had taken 760 pictures and the magpie picture was back in its place.

"He'll never know we've been here," said Molly.

"Unless he's watching us."

"Don't give me the creeps," said Molly.

The building was quiet as a tomb, the street outside silent as a graveyard except for the distant horns and sirens of the Los Angeles traffic. Molly instructed the security guard to order them a cab and then, after they'd gone, to completely forget that they'd been there at all. Petula was still waiting outside the building. Molly picked her up and gave her a hug.

"You're a naughty monkey, Petula."

Back at the Château Marmont, Nockman was instructed to forget the evening too.

"You can tell Mrs. T. that we spent the evening at the Benefactor's house, which is very fine, er, you know—very posh and full of expensive furniture and thick carpets. You can say you met the Benefactor, but only for a moment, as he was off to a business dinner. Say he looked like . . ."

"Like a kind old man," suggested Rocky.

"Yes, with gray hair, and with a mustache, and wearing . . ."

"A pink suit?"

"Yes, say he looks like Father Christmas in a pink suit. If Mrs. Trinklebury asks you any other details, say you don't remember."

Molly couldn't help adding, "And, er, Mr. Nockman, well done for the way you've improved. You're a much nicer person than you were. Everybody really likes you."

Nockman nodded. Then Molly snapped her fingers and woke him from his trance.

They went back to their bungalow and hid the camera and rolls of film in a drawer in Molly's bedroom. Molly found Lucy's telephone number in the briefcase and dialed her number.

"Lucy will be amazed," she said.

"Hope her phone's not bugged," said Rocky.

At the other end of the line the hollow ring tone continued.

"She must be up—it's ten in the morning in Briersville," said Molly. But there was no answer from the cottage.

"I suppose it takes her ages to do her shopping on crutches," said Rocky, yawning. "Call her tomorrow."

Molly longed to tell Lucy about Davina and the hypnotized stars. She wanted to ask her what they should do next. She put the phone down reluctantly.

"See you in the morning, Marshmallow," Rocky said, trying to make them both feel less scared.

Molly had never felt more like a marshmallow—soft, squashy, and lightheaded as a cloud. She was so exhausted that she hardly had the energy to get undressed. She went to sleep as soon as her head hit the pillow.

Fourteen

The second day at the Château Marmont was hotter than the first. In fact, the temperatures were breaking records. Fans whirred in the lobby, where people sat flapping books under their chins.

The atmosphere of Los Angeles was also heating up, because the Academy Awards were the following night. Already, in the hotels and smart houses, famous directors, producers, actors, actresses, screenwriters, musicians, lawyers, and agents were getting their beauty sleep and preparing themselves for the big event. The clothes designers, hairdressers, beauticians, jewelers, limousine companies, flower shops, image therapists, and speechwriters of the city were working overtime. All over town, parties were being organized, and the names of the Oscar nominees were on everybody's lips. Except Molly's.

She hurried through the lobby. She'd braved the sizzling midday streets to visit a photo lab to have the film developed. Now the precious information was in a large envelope under her arm. She kept her head down, because every time anyone crossed the hotel floor, the whole lobby looked up to see whether they were famous or not. Molly didn't want to be recognized again, and with the knowledge they'd gleaned the night before, she felt very vulnerable. She half expected to find two heavy-duty Cell protectors waiting for her outside their bungalow. But she rejoined Rocky in her cool, air-conditioned bedroom without incident and sat down to look at the photographs.

"That's 217 *not* hypnotized, but 542 already under his power," Rocky said.

"And then, hypnotized or not, alive or dead, there's Davina," Molly solemnly reminded him.

"How do you think Cell does it?" asked Rocky. "Does he use a pendulum, or do you think he does it like me and uses his voice? Or mainly his eyes?"

"We just don't know," said Molly with a shudder. "What's for sure is we're never going to be able to dehypnotize over 700 people."

"All their addresses are here," said Rocky.

"Maybe. But even if we manage to dehypnotize two a day, there's only 365 days in a year. We'd be at it for over two years. And what if Cell goes and hypnotizes them all over again? Anyway, how are we going to dehypnotize them without him realizing we're doing it? He'll be onto us. He'll snap us up like . . . like a crocodile snapping at . . ."

"Wading toddlers?"

"Yes," said Molly, finding the image sickening.

She collected the pictures and locked them in her room's safe. She could hear Mrs. Trinklebury outside telling Roger not to climb quite so high in the tree. Molly wandered onto the lawn to watch the others in the pool below. She looked down at them enviously.

"We'd better call Lucy. She might have a good idea about how to dehypnotize these stars. Oh, wouldn't it be lovely to have nothing to do, no work, no . . . mission."

They could see Mrs. Trinklebury in an old-fashioned bathing suit and a broad-brimmed hat, lounging on her sun chair, with a pile of celebrity magazines on her lap. She was throwing bits of cookie to nearby blackbirds. A white-suited pool waiter was placing a tall green drink on the table beside her. Mr. Nockman was on the diving board about to jump. Roger's feet were dangling from the big-boughed tree near the wall. He was hanging blue paper airplanes on its leaves.

Mr. Nockman bombed into the water, making an almighty splash. This was followed by a yell from Mrs. Trinklebury.

"Simon, how *could* you? You've soaked my *Oscars Special!*"

Molly suddenly brightened. She turned to Rocky. "When are the Oscars, Rocky?"

"Molly, haven't you noticed? The whole place is buzzing with Oscar fever. The Oscars are *tomorrow*. I can't believe you didn't know."

"Well, I kinda did," said Molly thoughtfully. "I just hadn't really realized they were so soon. Who goes to the Oscars, Rocky?"

"Everyone goes. All the important movie people."

"Yes," said Molly. She remembered all the television clips she'd seen of the Academy Awards. There were so many awards. Prizes for the best actors, directors, cameramen, screenwriters, soundtrack composers, special-effects makers, designers, and producers.

"I don't know why I didn't think of it before. It's perfect. Where else could we dehypnotize each and every one of these stupid stars so quickly? We'll go to the Oscars too."

Rocky raised his eyebrows and smiled. "Sounds like fun."

"Fun for some, but the trouble is, Rocky, for us it's

work. If it's *tomorrow*, we've got to get moving. If we're going, we've got to look like movie people's kids. I'll need a dress, we'll both need shoes, and you have got to get a tuxedo."

"A tux what?"

"A special evening suit. We better get to the shops quick. We'll call Lucy later."

With that, Molly ran inside to get her knapsack.

Little did they know that nearby, some new hypnotism students were having their first session.

"I think we need it to be really quiet if we're going to do this," Gemma said, kneeling on the carpet. At that moment there was a scratch at the door. Gerry let Petula in.

"Okay, Petula, you can come in, but no noise."

Petula cocked her head and lay down by the bed to watch what the two young humans were up to. Gemma and Gerry crouched in front of a glass vase. In it sat Victor, the biggest mouse.

Victor was annoyed to have been lifted out of his warm straw bed where he'd been sleeping off his jet lag. He chewed on a piece of seed and shot what he hoped was a filthy look at the two humans outside his container. His favorite human, the boy he called Big One, and the girl who was often with him, were looking at him, their bodies distorted through the glass. The furry beast was there too.

"Okay, so we've done the first bit," said the girl. "You're *sure* that mice squeak like that, Gerry?"

"Yes. It's the kind of squeak they do before they go to sleep." The boy made a whispery, squeaky noise. "*Ssssssss-qqquuuueak.* You do it," he said. The girl copied him.

"That's it. Do that." Gerry studied the photocopied instructions in front of him. "It says," he read, "'*Repeat the ani—mal's voice, in a lullin' way, until the animal be—comes rocked into a tran . . . a tran . . .' I can't read it.*"

"A trance." Gemma took the paper. "It's like a dreamy thing just before you get hypnotized. A bit like being in a sort of daydream."

"We gotta make Victor go into a daydream?"

"A trance. '*Once the animal is in a trance, you will know it from the fusion feeling.*' Okay. Let's do it."

Victor scratched his ear with his back foot and wondered whether there were still any potato chips hidden under his exercise wheel. All of a sudden, the girl outside the vase began to squeak repetitively, like a very large mouse.

After five squeaks, Victor pricked up his ears. The girl seemed to be trying to communicate with him in mouse language. Her tone wasn't exactly "mouse." It had a strong human accent, but was an understandable

115

squeak all the same. It seemed to translate into "Slaap, slaap, slaap." Victor assumed she meant *sleep, sleep, sleep*. He felt slightly peeved. That was *exactly* what he'd been doing before he was so rudely *awakened* and put into this glass vase.

Petula lay with her head between her front paws. She often listened to the mice talking to one another. What was more, Petula understood what Gemma was trying to do as well. Living with Molly in New York, Petula had seen, heard, and, more importantly, *felt* lots of people being hypnotized. Petula could feel Gemma trying to hypnotize Victor. The feeling wasn't right, Petula thought. The girl's voice was calming, but she didn't have that extra something that Molly had.

Petula edged forward until she could see the mouse in the vase. She growled softly.

Victor watched the furry beast approach. He knew it wasn't dangerous, as he'd often run around floors where it had been lying. Once he'd even run over its back by mistake. But one thing he'd never done was look into the furry beast's eyes. Now he did. Petula's eyes looked kindly back at him. Victor found the experience lovely. It was like looking into the eyes of a lovely, big, friendly, relaxing, friendly, relaxing, tasty, friendly, lovely, relaxing cheese. And the more he looked at the cheese—or was it a furry beast?—the more

Victor felt himself tipping sideways.

When he finally slumped onto the bottom of the vase, as comfortable as if he was lying in a predator-free, flower-filled meadow, he felt as if all he *ever* wanted to do was lie in that vase, with the furry cheese sitting there forever.

"Look at Victor," said Gemma. "I think I've done it!"

"You mean Victor's hypnotized? Have you got the fusey feeling?"

"Fusion," Gemma corrected him. "I don't know. But I must have. Now we have to make him do something, Gerry. What shall we make him do?"

"I know," said Gerry, and got up to switch on the tape player.

Victor's meadow was suddenly filled with gentle pan-pipe music. Through the curved bowl, he saw Big One moving about rhythmically to the sound.

Victor was far too relaxed to move. He shut his eyes and imagined that he was sitting in a hammock-shaped petal, under the great big furry beast-cheese.

Gemma and Gerry were disappointed at Victor's failure to dance, but at least they felt they'd hypnotized him—which they hadn't, of course.

Fifteen

At five thirty, Molly and Rocky arrived back in their bungalow. Rocky went to the kitchen to get them both drinks, and Molly checked her alarm clock. She really wanted to call Lucy Logan, who had still not answered the phone. So as soon as Rocky came back with some Qubes, she dialed the number.

The phone was answered by a husky, groggy, half-awake voice.

"Lucy—is that you? It's me."

The librarian coughed and cleared her throat several times. "Yes, yes, it's Lucy here. Molly! Is everything okay? It's the middle of the night."

"Everything's fine," said Molly. "I'm sorry to wake you up. Lucy, we've made some amazing discoveries. You were completely right about Primo Cell." And

Molly launched into a detailed description of the past twenty-four hours.

She told Lucy what they had found in Primo Cell's office. Molly explained that they planned to go to the Academy Awards to dehypnotize as many stars as they could, and to find out, if they could, whether Davina was still alive. Molly hoped Lucy would know what the mysterious red-inked words that spoke of E Day referred to, but she didn't. After ten minutes of talking, the conversation felt like it was coming to an end. Molly asked, "And what about you, Lucy? Have you had any more trouble?"

"I'm fine. It's difficult to get to sleep with my burns, that's all." Lucy sighed. "I'm astounded by how well you're doing, Molly. But please, do be careful. Remember, the man's not normal. He's a monster."

"We'll be careful. And Lucy, is that money arriving soon? Sorry to ask, but we're running up big bills here."

"Of course, Molly. I'll see to it right now." Then she added warmly, "Send my regards to Rocky and take care. Keep in touch. Good-bye."

Molly put down the phone.

"So what did she say?" asked Rocky.

"I'll tell you while we're getting these files mailed to her. But look, we've got the rest of the evening and I think we need to relax. Let's go swimming."

"Are you sure?"

"Why not? If we're going to the Academy Awards, we might as well get used to the idea that people might recognize us. And anyway, even if he did see that ad we made, I'm sure Cell is too busy with Oscars stuff to be worried about a couple of hypnotists."

After a trip to the front desk to organize express post to Briersville, Molly and Rocky moseyed down to the pool. Even though it was almost six, the sun was still oven hot.

There weren't many other guests outside. Mrs. Trinklebury and Gemma waved to them from a shaded table where they were eating ice cream. Molly and Rocky found sun beds near the pool's waterfall. Rocky dived into the turquoise water to join Roger while Molly put on a straw hat. She patted her thin, spammy legs. She wanted them to get nice and warm before she had a swim.

She shut her eyes. The heat of the afternoon, the smell of something being barbecued, and the sweet sound of whistling blackbirds nearby made her feel nicely lethargic. The sun shone on her eyelids, and from behind them everything looked orange. She listened to the waterfall splashing into the pool and she began to unwind.

After a minute or so, Molly looked about.

Two businesswomen were sitting at a table under an umbrella, their backs to her. Both had coiffured hair and wore suits—one light blue, the other fuchsia pink. She looked at the pink-suited woman's hair. It was flecked with white and golden streaks, and a tortoise-shell clip was fixed in the middle of it, catching the sunlight.

The clip twinkled and danced in the sunlight, and the more Molly stared at it, the more the woman's hair looked like the mane of some beautifully groomed horse. It tumbled down the woman's back like spun gold.

Then, as she gazed, with the sun beating down on her, Molly detected a hint of the fusion feeling inside her. And, remembering what had happened when she'd stared at the bush dog—no, bush baby—in Briersville and the suitcase at the airport, she wondered if, by gazing at the tortoiseshell hair clip, she would get the cold fusion feeling again. And she did. Molly felt the strange shift from warm to cold.

As the tingling cold started to creep up her spine, a thought struck Molly. Perhaps if she let the feeling come completely, her hypnotic powers would be made stronger. In a moment of boldness, Molly decided to let the cold fusion feeling blossom inside her. So, staring at the tortoiseshell clip as if she wanted to hypnotize it, Molly invited the feeling in.

At first, the feeling was timid, like a trickle, creeping up her body. Then it began to flow up her legs like a stream. And then, in a sudden arctic wave, it crashed through the rest of her body, making her shake. Molly's veins felt as if they were flowing with ice-cold, sparkling mineral water, and the diamond around her neck felt as cold as a glacier. It was a very weird sensation. Molly didn't feel entirely comfortable with it, but she held the feeling captive. She stared at the hair clip. She felt as if she'd hypnotized it. Had she?

Molly noticed that everything had gone quiet. Very quiet. Even the pool's waterfall was silent. Molly wondered why it had been switched off. Still in her bubble of cool, she turned to look.

What she saw made her jump. For the waterfall had indeed stopped falling. But not in the normal way: It was now a solid sheet of water, as if it had been suddenly frozen. Except it was not iced—it was *shiny*, like wet water. Molly glanced to the left.

Gerry, who had been playing, was still as a statue, and in the most awkward position. He was balanced on one leg while his other foot was in the air, where he had just kicked a ball. His eyes were looking up to where his ball hung, as if from an invisible thread in the sky. To his left, Gemma was giving Mrs. Trinklebury a lick of her ice cream. Mrs. Trinklebury's tongue was poking out of her mouth like a red worm, half buried in the pink icy goo. Gemma was blowing a gum bubble and Mr. Nockman was saying something approving to her, his words silently frozen in the air. The smoke from the businesswomen's cigarettes hung like columns of cloud. The whole world was still as a picture, a three-dimensional picture.

The cold fusion feeling filled Molly completely. All she could hear was the sound of her heart beating and her frightened breath. Molly felt that if she let go, in the same way as she "turned off" her eyes when she hypnotized someone, the cold fusion feeling would go away—at least she hoped it would.

Molly looked for Rocky. He was horizontal in midair, diving into the pool. Petula was lying under a table by the shallow end, playing with a stone. Then Molly saw Roger. He was under the water. Without oxygen, he could be *drowning*. Trying not to panic, Molly focused her mind, and as if she was taking the bottom away from a tank of water, she instantly drained the ice-cold feeling from her body. It flooded out in a nanosecond. And in that time, without so much as a shudder, the world started again. Rocky dived, Petula barked at him, Roger surfaced, Mrs.

Trinklebury licked, and water came crashing into the pool.

The diamond round Molly's neck still felt cold, but Molly felt hot again and very relieved to be back. Shakily, she got up and dived into the pool as well. Water shot up her nose.

"Rocky, something really weird has just happened," she spluttered.

"Yes, you've just dived in with your T-shirt and hat on," said Rocky, before doing a handstand under the water.

Molly pulled her hat off her head and frowned at it.

"No, not that. Rocky. Rocky, listen." She grabbed his arm and pulled. "Something stranger than anything has just happened to me."

"What?" asked Rocky, floating on his back.

"Well," Molly faltered, in a scarcely contained whisper, "I think . . . oh, this is going to sound like I've gone crazy . . ."

"What? Tell me."

"I think I just . . . I think I made . . ." Molly hesitated.

"Made what?"

"I think I just made the world stand still. I think I stopped time!"

Sixteen

"I didn't notice," said Rocky.

"Yes, stupid. *You* were part of the stillness."

"When? I can't remember it happening."

"You're not listening," hissed Molly. "You were *frozen*."

"What—like minus ten degrees?"

"No, not *cold* frozen, frozen *still*. I was cold, though." Molly pointed at the pink-suited woman. "I was concentrating on that woman's hair clip, trying to sort of hypnotize it . . ."

"Why were you doing that?"

"Because . . . well, because I actually first got this feeling in Briersville, but I didn't tell you about it because I thought you'd think I'd broken my promise not to hypnotize anyone. But I wasn't hypnotizing any*body*. I was hypnotizing *things*. . . . That's what makes this cold fusion feeling happen."

Rocky's eyebrows wobbled.

"And anyway," continued Molly, trying to ignore his suspicious look, "I was hypnotizing the hair clip to get the cold fusion feeling, and this time I let the feeling completely come. I went *really* cold, and when I looked up everything had . . ." Molly looked at Rocky's disbelieving face. "Honestly, Rocky, everything had stopped. Time had stopped—except *I* hadn't stopped. You had, Rocky. You were halfway through a dive, stuck in the air. I'm not kidding. Then I let the feeling go and everything started again, and you dived into the water."

Rocky looked worriedly at Molly.

"Did you drink something from the minibar?"

"No!" Molly glared at Rocky. "I'm telling you, this is true."

Rocky put his hand on her shoulder.

"Molly, I think we'd better get out of the water. I know you think what happened was true, but maybe you got too much sun today. I got that thing from the sun once when I went on that long walk, and I had a fever and everything seemed—"

"Cripes, Rocky, sometimes you drive me crazy. If you don't believe me, I'll prove it to you."

Molly swam to the edge of the pool and pulled herself out. Rocky followed her.

"Sit on this sun bed," she told him. "And look at your feet."

Rocky shot her a worried expression but obeyed.

Molly began to stare at the orange life belt that was hooked up on a post. Within a few moments she had summoned up the strange cold feeling again. She drew it up through her body until the life belt pulsed orange in front of her eyes and the rest of the world vanished into a blur. At last, with a cold, sparkling snap, the coldness swamped her. Just as before, everything went quiet. Molly disengaged her eyes from the belt, but a part of her still concentrated on the cold fusion feeling, cupping it in her body and picturing two imaginary stoppers that prevented it from flowing out of her feet. It required tremendous effort.

She looked to her right. Everything was still. Mrs. Trinklebury was holding up her knitting, inspecting it for holes. Gerry was bombing into the pool, splashes frozen like great watery petals. Roger was like a statue. The pool manager was handing drinks to the two suited ladies.

Rocky was staring at his feet. Molly clicked her fingers in front of his eyes, but he didn't blink. She put her ear to his mouth—he wasn't even breathing. She looked about her. It was difficult to believe that no one was watching her—that she was the only person moving. The only person breathing. It was terrifying. What if everything got *stuck* like this? But Molly knew she must do something to prove to Rocky that time had just stopped. Taking a deep breath, she slowly stood up. With enormous concentration, so as not to dispel the fusion feeling, Molly began to walk toward the poolside toy basket. Her body tingled. Each step was scary. Holding the world still was an incredible strain. She picked out an inflatable frog, a duck rubber ring, and a whale-shaped raft. She brought them back to Rocky and put the duck on his head like a crown, the raft under his feet, and the frog on his lap. And to make extra sure he believed her, she picked three yellow flowers from a pot and put one between his toes, one between his fingers, and the last in his mouth.

For a moment she sat still trying to understand what was happening to her. She looked beyond the pool. Was the whole of Los Angeles still? Was the *whole world* still? The idea was too crazy to contemplate. Yet Molly felt it was so. And then, like an animal sensing approaching rain, she sensed something else. For a moment, Molly was sure she felt movement some-where—somewhere out there. Then she couldn't tell what she was feeling. Her heart was beating too fast and she was too scared. She desperately wanted everything to move again, *now*.

She switched off her concentration and unplugged the fusion feeling. Simultaneously, Rocky jumped in surprise and threw the pool toys off him. He spat out the flower.

"Aaaarrrgggh!" he shouted. He turned to Molly in amazement.

"How? How did you do that? How long was I still for? How did you do it, Molly? Did you find another book?"

Molly went to bed that night feeling exhausted and nervous. The prospect of gate-crashing the Oscars the next day was frightening, and she was very concerned that she and Rocky would be caught. But even more disturbing was the new hypnotic skill she'd discovered. Nowhere in Dr. Logan's hypnotism book had stopping the world been mentioned. Having no wise words on the subject, Molly felt she was sailing in completely uncharted waters. She didn't know whether stopping the world was a good thing or a bad thing. She didn't know whether it was dangerous. It was certainly spooky. She heard a tap at her door and Rocky came in.

"I'm tired but I don't feel sleepy," he said, sitting on the end of her bed.

"Same here," said Molly.

"I checked the TV to see whether the time is right everywhere in America and in the rest of the world. It is. You've bitten off a lot to chew with this stopping-time stuff," he went on worriedly. "I'm glad it's you who can do it and not anyone else. I mean, imagine what you could do. You could get away with murder."

"Oh, don't," said Molly, shivering and pulling Petula up onto the bed.

"I don't mean real murder, I just mean you could play all sorts of tricks on people. If you were a criminal, you could easily do burglaries or kidnap someone. Stop the world. Do the kidnap. As far as everyone was concerned, the person would just suddenly disappear. Or if you wanted your football team to win, you could freeze the world during a penalty and you could re-position the ball so that it went into the goal."

Molly buried her nose in Petula's fur. The idea that she, one small person on the planet, had made the whole world stop made her feel dizzy and terrified. She felt it was a power too big for her.

"I'm going to call Lucy in the morning and ask her if she knows about this," she said. "I'll try not to think

any more about it now. We must get some sleep, Rocky.
We're going to need loads of energy tomorrow."

Rocky nodded and switched off the light.

"Sweet dreams, Marshmallow," he said as he shut the
door.

"You mean, 'Good luck with your nightmares,'" said
Molly, and she pulled her blanket up over her head.

Seventeen

The day of the Academy Awards rose sunny with cloudless skies. Petula woke before everyone else. She checked the small stash of stones that she'd hidden behind the TV set, chose an egg-shaped one to suck, and slipped out of the bungalow grounds via a hedge tunnel. From the steps above the swimming pool, she could see the giant painted poodle jumping over the sign for Bella's Poodle Salon and Dog Hotel. She could smell some sort of tasty meat breakfast that the guests there were being fed. Petula looked down at her paws. Her claws most definitely needed a clip. And her skin had felt itchy ever since the plane journey. The doggy-shampoo-smelling place reminded Petula of a comfortable washing house she'd visited in another big city. Knowing that a good grooming would really revive her, she turned toward the hotel's driveway.

Crossing the four lanes of road to Bella's was quite difficult, and Petula found herself standing on the central partition for five minutes as she waited for a lull in the traffic. But soon she was walking up to the blue metal gate of the dog salon, which she pushed open with her paw. Down some steps was a door. This swung open as an athletic man came out of the shop with a Pekingese under his arm. The Pekingese smelled of lilies and had four pink ribbons in his hair. Petula trotted smartly past them. She was looking forward to this.

Inside the shop, everything was for dogs. There were racks of collars and leashes, hanging like tempting jewelery. There were beautiful fur cushions for dogs to relax on, fine feeding bowls, displays of specialty dog foods, snacks, chew bones, and edible dog cigars. There were piles of luxury dog toys and bottles of dog fragrances, dog coats in every size, and even dog shoes for those days when dirty paws weren't wanted. A woman with frizzy blond hair and huge hooped earrings was sitting behind a counter, adding up a bill. Behind her was the salon, where a big furry chow chow was standing in a special glass box that was blow-drying his coat. As Petula crossed the shop floor, her long nails made a distinct clicking sound.

Bella, the salon owner, looked up, expecting to see that one of her dog clients had escaped from the spa room next door. Instead, she saw Petula approaching her, wagging her tail. Petula put her front paws on the woman's lap.

"Why, aren't you the most adorable li'l thingummy-bobbit! Where's your owner, cutie pie? Oh, my, aren't your claws long!"

Of course, Petula said nothing. She gave Bella one of her most winning looks, her head tilted charmingly to one side. Bella looked at the door and then down at the velvety black pug.

"Why aren't you wearing a collar, honey?" Bella got up and peered outside. The pug dog seemed to be ownerless. Petula barked. Bella smiled and patted her. She could always tell when dogs wanted a grooming. She looked at the chow chow enjoying his blow-dry and consulted her watch.

"Okay, my darlin'. You're a precious li'l thing, you are! Come with me. Let's give you the treatment!"

This was how Petula found herself getting the full pampering that she felt she deserved. First Bella took her to the wet room and washed her in rosemary shampoo. Then Petula was massaged, rinsed, dried, clipped, polished, and groomed until she felt like a dog from the Land of Perfection. Lastly she was taken to the salon's spa room to relax.

Here she socialized with the dogs who had been booked into the dog hotel. There was a giant, silky Afghan hound who was very interested in what Petula had had for yesterday's supper, a French bulldog with bat ears and no manners, who sniffed at her bottom with no invitation at all, a silvery-coated Samoyed, the chow chow, a sausage dachshund, and a Chinese crested dog.

The small, hairless, gray-and-pink Chinese crested dog interested Petula the most. She'd never met one before. He really had no hair, except for a tufty bit on the top of his head, and his ears were enormous and pointed. Petula liked his looks, and he certainly smelled nice—of parsley and clever thoughts. Petula lay down on a pink divan with him and made friends. For an hour, the two dogs communicated as dogs do, sending thoughts and memories to each other telepathically. The Chinese crested dog was staying at the dog hotel, as his owners were having an Oscars party with fireworks and lots of people in the house.

Bella returned and took Petula back to the shop, where she picked out a collar encrusted with fake diamonds, which she fastened around her neck.

The bell above the door rang, announcing another

customer, and sensing that Molly needed her, Petula took this opportunity to slip out of the salon.

Back at the Château Marmont, Petula found Molly still asleep. She was tangled tightly in the sheets, whimpering unhappily. Petula jumped onto the bed and snuggled close to comfort her.

Molly was having a horrible nightmare in which she was at the Academy Awards in a cage on the stage. Primo Cell stood beside it, laughing as the audience threw dead magpies at her. Then the scene froze and she was the only being alive in a still world where nothing would ever move again.

Molly awoke to find she'd drooled all over the pillow. Her forehead was hot and clammy. Petula licked her face as Molly struggled to sit up. Then Molly grabbed the phone from the bedside table and dialed Lucy Logan's number.

She could hear the phone ringing thousands of miles away in Lucy's little cottage. It rang on and on. She thought of Lucy's clocks ticking in accompaniment. The clocks. For the first time Molly wondered about them. Surely Lucy knew something about time stopping. Why else would she collect clocks? Molly needed desperately to speak to her, but no one answered. She finally put the receiver down. Where was Lucy? Had something happened to her? Molly chewed her hand. Petula barked.

"Petula . . . ." She hugged her. "You smell fantastic . . . and who gave you this lovely collar? Where *have* you been?"

Petula wagged her tail, but Molly still felt as if she was in a nightmare. She didn't want to think of the terrifying prospect of the Academy Awards. But she knew that as surely as land approaches a falling parachutist, the afternoon would come. And so it did.

By two o'clock, Molly and Rocky were dressed. Rocky wore his smart black tuxedo and new black sneakers. Molly put on the outfit that she'd bought. It was an emerald-green dress with green shoes that matched.

"Molly, you ought to do something about your hair. It looks like your hairdresser was a tornado," said Rocky.

Molly wrestled her hair down.

"It's gone loony-bin curly. You should look a bit more, well, Oscar-y," said Rocky. "Do you think we'll get in? I mean, do we look like stars' kids?" He tugged at his bow tie. "I'm taking this off. It looks stupid, and anyhow I don't know how to tie it."

"We have to get in—otherwise dehypnotizing all these

stars is going to take years." Molly picked up a piece of white card that she had been writing on and reread the instructions on it.

"I won't be much help getting in," said Rocky. "Your eyes will have to get us past the door people."

"This card will get us in, or at least I hope it will. You can help dehypnotize stars inside, Rocky. We'll find a quiet place where you can work on them with your voice."

Molly pulled out a list of Hollywood names from her dress pocket.

"How long do the Oscars last?"

"Six hours, Mrs. Trinklebury said," replied Rocky. "That's plenty of time to get lots of hits."

"We might be the ones that get hit."

Petula trotted in. She was ready for an evening out and barked at Molly to show her that she was coming. Molly picked her up.

"You look much more starry than we do," she told Petula. "Your coat is as shiny as your diamonds!"

The phone rang and Rocky answered it.

"Ready or not," he said, "the car's here. Oscars, here we come."

Eighteen

In front of the hotel steps, a black limousine waited like a shiny wheeled beast. A smart, gray-suited driver with dark glasses opened the car door, and Molly, Petula, and Rocky climbed in.

No one noticed them going. Mrs. Trinklebury was glued to her TV set, watching a pre-Academy Awards commentary program, Nockman was practicing opening his room's safe without knowing its combination, and Gemma and Gerry were training Gerry's mice to race along a cardboard track they'd made. Roger was busy up his tree, getting ready to spend the night there.

The limousine coasted away from the hotel and drove toward Hollywood Boulevard. This had once been the most important movie and theater street in the world. Now it was more a souvenir of the past, but it was still exciting, with the famous Grauman's Chinese Theatre with its copper-green, pagoda-style roof. Here the biggest stars in movie history had their footprints and handprints set forever in concrete.

As they continued toward the Kodak Theatre, venue of the Oscars, the traffic thickened.

"Whoa, look at the people," their driver said as they slowed to a crawling pace. Molly could see, through the darkened windows, policemen waving flags, urging on cars with gawping passengers and telling other cars to drop their loads quickly. Halfway up the street there was a stationary glut of vehicles, and the sidewalks thronged with crowds who had come to catch a glimpse of their favorite celebrities. The limousine crept closer.

"I bet you guys are excited about walking up that red carpet."

Molly nodded vaguely. She was hoping that her legs would remember how to walk without tripping over each other. She felt sick. She thought of all the TV cameras and newspaper photographers waiting along-side the famous red carpet.

"You don't think anyone will recognize me from *Stars on Mars*, do you?" she whispered to Rocky nervously. "It could really mess things up. I don't want anyone taking a picture of me while I'm hypnotizing the guards on the gates."

"New York's the other side of America—and you weren't on Broadway for that long," said Rocky uncertainly, picking nervously at his trousers. "If people recognize you from the TV, they'll just think you're the nice girl from the charity commercial. That's all."

Molly fell silent as they pulled up behind a shiny Lincoln. Their driver got out, eager to see for himself what was going on, and opened Molly's door.

The challenge ahead made her stomach churn and her head dizzy. As she swallowed the lump of nerves that had lodged in her throat, she managed a "Thank you" and stepped out of the car. Petula bounced after her. The noise of cheering and whistling filled the air. Molly was so shaky that the ground felt as if it was moving.

Under her green shoes, bronze stars embedded in the sidewalk showed the names of bygone movie icons. After fifteen paces, and after pushing through a throng of people, Molly, Petula, and Rocky stepped into the cordoned-off area and onto the shore of a bloodred carpet that rolled like a river through the security gates. This carpet would take them through the fenced-off part of Hollywood Boulevard and into the Kodak Theatre itself. There was no turning back now.

Only people who had Oscars invitations stepped onto the red carpet. Immediately people were interested in who she and Rocky were. A thousand cameras seemed to flash. The carpet turned into a blur as Molly walked along it.

"Are they actors?" she heard someone ask.

Ahead were the gates—low arches covered with flowers. As Molly saw guests pass through them, giving their bags to be put through the X-ray machines, she realized that the arches were camouflaged metal detectors, to check for hidden weapons or explosives.

"High security," said Rocky.

"Hope it's not so high that I can't hypnotize them," muttered Molly, clutching her white card. For luck, she touched her diamond, hidden under the top of her dress.

Behind them, someone extremely famous arrived. The crowds began yelling and screaming. This was good. It gave Molly a chance to work without people watching her.

Molly gritted her teeth, turned her eyes up to full glare, and prepared to floor one of the gatekeepers. Her hypnotism would have to work swiftly, without anyone else being aware of it.

The man on this particular gate was tough and professional. Molly didn't look him in the eye until she was right in front of him. When she did, her hypnotism was like a wallop in the face.

"Look at my invitation," Molly said quietly, and of course the man did.

It read:

THIS IS A GENUINE
ACADEMY AWARDS INVITATION.
LET ME, MY FRIEND, AND MY DOG
THROUGH WITHOUT ANY TROUBLE.
BEHAVE NORMALLY.
FORGET US ONCE WE ARE IN.

The man nodded, and he saw exactly what he expected to see—a fancy invitation with curly, gold-embossed letters on it, and with the picture of the gold Oscar statuette at the top.

He ushered Molly, Petula, and Rocky through the metal detector. Then Molly gave the "invitation" to Rocky, who folded it and put it in his pocket. They were in.

Hollywood Boulevard lay ahead of them, flanked by tall palm trees and completely covered with red carpet. The road looked like a calm, flat, red lake. And on it stood hundreds of people, mostly stars Molly recognized, who looked like gods walking on water. They were all dressed impeccably in the most spectacular, most expensive evening clothes that money can buy. The men wore mostly black silk or velvet or fine-weave suits; the women were in gorgeous gowns from the world's most exclusive designers. Some were in flimsy, short dresses, but a lot were in long ones. And because Molly couldn't see their feet, they looked as if they were gliding, like multicolored swans, on the red lake. Behind brass barriers were tiered platforms or bleachers on which stood hundreds of lucky people who had won standing-room tickets to watch the glitterati of the film world arrive.

"Oh no," said Molly. "Look at the cameras."

Arching over the boulevard was a bridge. On this stood banks of photographers. Stars waved up at them and smiled professionally. Alongside the carpet stood TV cameras and interviewers holding microphones. The stars posed and smiled, knowing that the whole world was watching. Enormous lenses pointed left and right, and even though it was still broad daylight, the air prickled nonstop with electronic flashes.

"Hey," said Rocky happily. "So this is what it feels like to be a star."

Molly had experienced the world of stardom for a few brief weeks in New York, but she felt very out of practice and much more unsure of herself than Rocky.

The feeling that gnawed at her most was the fear that someone would put a hand on her shoulder and shout, "Hey, you aren't supposed to be here. You can stop right now, turn around, and get out!"

"Rocky, do you think anyone will realize we're not supposed to be here?"

"Only if you talk like that," said Rocky, smiling at a camera. "There'll be lip-readers watching this on TV."

Miles away in Oklahoma, a deaf boy called Ben was watching the Oscars on TV. He always enjoyed reading the lips of people on television. Being able to lip-read was one of the good parts about being deaf. Television was much more interesting. For instance, he knew the president and his wife very well because he lip-read what they said to each other when they were away from the microphones. Tonight, as he watched a film director being interviewed, he noticed a couple of kids standing close behind. He saw them speak.

"Just enjoy this, Molly. No one knows you weren't invited. I've already persuaded myself that I was," said the good-looking black boy who, Ben thought, did look like a young star.

Beside him, the girl in the green dress with the messy hair said, "You're right. This is too good to worry about. But let's get into the theater as soon as we can."

"Go for it," thought Ben, wishing he could be with the kids on TV too.

Cameras flashed constantly. White, bright light bounced off pearly sets of teeth that smiled super-perfect Hollywood smiles. It sparkled on diamond necklaces, platinum bracelets, and gold cufflinks.

Petula's new collar shone, and so did Petula. She loved all the energy and excitement in the air.

Molly glanced around at the famous faces. Right away she saw five or six of the celebrities whose names were on her list—Primo Cell's victims.

There was Stephanie Goulash, in a dark-blue see-through dress, her piled-up hair red as flames. A few steps away, Cosmo Ace, in a silver suit, was talking to a TV journalist. Molly could see Hercules Stone, dressed in a white tuxedo, stepping though the throng with a beautiful Chinese woman on his arm.

Then she saw something that made her insides jump. A few feet away from her, a short woman in a dark suit was studying Molly. Her microphone had a large shield on it that read THE NEW YORK REPORTER. Molly recognized her as the arts correspondent of New York's biggest newspaper. She had interviewed Molly when she performed in *Stars on Mars*. Molly pulled Rocky away, but it was too late.

"Hey, excuse me, Molly! Molly Moon!" the journalist cried excitedly. The heads of nearby cameramen swiveled in Molly's direction.

"Molly, what a lovely surprise to see you here! And Petula, too! People have been wondering when you'd be back."

Nineteen

olly's past had caught up with her, and there was no escape.

"So have you and Petula recovered from her kidnaping?" the woman questioned.

"Er, yes, thank you," said Molly, trying to avoid a large lens that had zoomed in on her. Petula looked up at it and barked happily.

"And is your appearance here a sign that you'll be coming back to the stage, or maybe to the screen instead?"

Molly tried not to look flustered. "Er, no," she said. "I'm just here to spend some time with a friend. Thank you—I have to go."

"This is the friend who made the commercial with

you? The one about checking out the kids in your neighborhood?" pushed the journalist.

"Yes, I am," said Rocky. "Nice to meet you." Rocky smiled at the camera and would have happily given an interview, but Molly stepped on his toe and gave him a "don't you *dare*" look.

As Molly tugged Rocky away, she heard the journalist say, "As usual, Molly Moon is as mysterious as ever. But it's great to see her back. Perhaps a film career is in the cards."

Molly led Rocky deep into the crowd.

"Uuurgh," she said, "that was scary. These newspaper people have really good memories." Then she noticed that Petula hadn't kept up with them.

"Oh, no, Petula's got stuck back there," Molly said, looking worriedly over her shoulder. "I hope she's all right."

Molly needn't have worried. Petula was having the time of her life. She'd loved the limelight when she was in New York. It felt good to be bathing in it again. She turned her face this way and that for the cameras. She stood on her hind legs and begged. She hopped around in circles. The photographers loved her. Then she gave a foxy bark and trotted off to find Molly. On the way, she passed a tall, velvet-clad man with a deep tan and black hair pulled back in a ponytail. Petula paused—he smelled like someone she'd met before, who'd been behind the camera at some TV studios in New York.

Although Petula didn't know it, the man who smiled down at her was in fact a top Hollywood director. He was an Italian called Gino Pucci. His latest movie, *Blood of a Stranger*, was nominated for Best Picture tonight. Petula liked his smell. She stood up and put her paws on his leg, and as he bent down to talk to her, she shot him one of her most charming expressions. It was a devastating look. Gino was too stunned to say anything. Petula barked seductively and then trotted off.

Molly and Rocky were now standing near a heavy stone arch—the entrance to the Kodak building. A giant golden Oscar statue, almost as high as the arch itself, stood like an ancient idol, as if the Kodak Theatre was a temple to worship stars in.

"Wow," said Rocky, laughing quietly. "There are so many actors here that I feel like I'm *in* a film!"

Molly was struck by how many of the actors were smaller than she'd imagined. Watching them on big movie screens had made her think they were super-human size. In fact, a lot of them were short. Up close, the stars were all so human. There was one scratching his nose, another one itching her ear. Molly was surprised by the ordinariness of them all.

"It's funny, isn't it?" said Molly. "We know all their faces so well, but they don't know ours at all. At least I hope they don't."

For a few minutes, Molly and Rocky absorbed the scene, knowing that it was something they'd remember all their lives.

"Okay," said Molly, "enough of this starstruck stuff. Let's get inside."

Petula had caught up, and the three of them hurried ahead.

Inside the covered forecourt of the Kodak, it was cooler and quieter. Cameras weren't allowed in here, and it was less crowded. The wide passage before them, which was normally a shopping promenade, was decorated with flowers, and its walls were hung with piped red curtains. A grand, red-carpeted staircase, like an enormous red tongue, led to the theater entrance.

Groups of celebrities were standing about greeting each other and star-spotting other celebrities.

A sudden hush fell as none other than Gloria Heelheart came through the door. She was accompanied by a distinguished-looking old man. The waiting crowd tensed with admiration. Gloria Heelheart was such a huge star that everyone watching felt they were tiny sparks compared to her.

Tonight she was dressed in what looked like a golden coil. It was shiny silk sewn into long spaghetti-thin tubes that had been coiled and stitched together into a shimmering dress that clung to every inch of her famous body. Her swanlike neck was strangled in a real golden coil, so it looked like an expensive spring joined her head to her shoulders. The same coils were on her upper arms. Her oriental eyes were as beautiful and mysterious as ever. A few people greeted her with polite good-evenings while others looked on in silent respect, wishing that they knew her too. Gloria Heelheart smiled her glorious smile and stepped past, raising her bejeweled fingers in a gracious wave.

Molly, staring at the spectacular golden curves stalking majestically across the foyer, thought how incredible it was that the Queen of Hollywood could ever have been caught in Primo Cell's net. She seemed so dignified, but really she was as helpless as a slave.

"This is the perfect place," said Molly.

"But how are we going to nail them?" whispered Rocky. "We can't just walk up and hypnotize them in front of everyone. Besides, Cell is bound to be here somewhere."

Molly looked around nervously. This was an extremely disturbing thought—one that she had not dwelled on before. The idea that Primo Cell was there felt as scary as seeing a tiger on the loose.

"We have to find somewhere quiet." Then her eyes brightened.

"I know where."

Twenty

"**B**ut Molly, I can't just loiter in the gents'," Rocky complained. "There aren't many cubicles, you know. Everything happens right there in front of you, if you see what I mean. Can't I come with you and Petula?"

"Shh, Rocky, of course you can't. Look, this idea is good. The toilets are probably nice and quiet. You can at least have a go at dehypnotizing some male stars. I'll cover the ladies' room."

"But I'm not as good as you. I need to talk for quite a while for my voice to have an effect."

"Rocky, have a go. Please. You're really charming. You can ask them lots of long questions about themselves."

Reluctantly, Rocky set off for the men's room on the

other side of the foyer. Molly and Petula went into the ladies' powder room.

It was very brightly lit. A white-tiled, circular chamber with basins and mirrors led to a long, thin corridor lined with silver cubicles that housed the toilets. A few women were touching up their makeup. They didn't notice Molly, who sat herself on a stool by the door, or Petula, who perched politely under the dressing-table ledge.

Molly knew that sooner or later, some of the stars on her list would come into the room. And when they did, she would be ready for them.

The bathroom attendant came out of a cubicle where she had been arranging the roll of toilet paper so that its loose end was folded into a neat triangle. She was dressed in a starched stripy uniform with a small white apron, and her fair hair was carefully coiffured in tight curls. She was a big woman who could eat two tubs of ice cream in one sitting, but tonight she was too tense and excited to eat anything. This was the greatest night of her forty-year career as a Los Angeles bathroom attendant. She was enormously proud to be wiping toilet seats after famous bottoms had sat on them. Whenever a guest came out of a cubicle, she shot in after them to clean and polish.

She was so obviously enjoying her work that Molly

felt it was a shame to stop her. But the hypnotizing had to be done, and Molly got to work.

She was soon in command of the attendant.

"You won't notice me hypnotizing people," Molly whispered. "You will simply ignore me and get on with your work. After I've gone, you'll forget I was here."

The cleaner nodded.

"What's your name?"

"Brenda—Cartwright," said the woman slowly.

"Well, Brenda, after tonight you will feel that you did the best job you possibly could and everyone loved you. Don't be nervous. Enjoy it."

Brenda nodded, smiled dreamily, and floated off, humming a song from the musical *Hello, Dolly!*

To Molly's surprise and delight, the next person to come into the powder room was Suky Champagne. Now she could get down to business.

Miss Champagne was dressed in an extraordinary mermaid outfit. It was green and silver with velvety sea flowers dangling from it. It had small teardrop shapes of net all over it, a halter neck, a very low front, and a circular gap at stomach level revealing Suky's emerald-studded belly button. The skirt of the dress narrowed so tightly at the knees that her legs could take only tiny steps, then it flowed into a train, making it look as if she was dragging a swathe of seaweed behind her.

She leaned toward a mirror and took a lipstick from her evening bag. She gave herself her special look—as if the breeze from a breaking wave had just caught her by surprise and made her take a sharp intake of breath. Satisfied with her beauty, she touched her curtain of hair. That was when she saw Molly's reflected green eyes looking at her.

In a few seconds, Suky Champagne's mouth was hanging open and her lipstick had dropped into the basin.

"Now," said Molly, talking as quickly as possible. "You are under my power. Completely, utterly, all of that."

The powder-room door swung open again. Molly sucked in a breath and sank back as Gloria Heelheart swayed past her, moving rather like an eel in her golden coils. Seeing Suky Champagne, but not pausing to look at her, Gloria Heelheart headed for her own mirror.

"Suky, darling, congratulations," she drawled. "Congratulations on being a nominee! What a very special night for you."

Molly watched as Gloria opened her golden evening bag and pulled out a picture of some Pekingese dogs, which she kissed.

Suky Champagne, still in her trance, stared at herself in the mirror as if she'd had her brain removed.

"Are you all right?" asked the Queen of Hollywood, frowning—although she couldn't really, because she'd had so many antifrown Botox injections in her forehead. She dabbed at her wide mouth with a scarlet lipstick. "You don't seem all here, darrrling."

Suky's tongue popped out of the corner of her mouth.

"Dddth, dde dotha," she said.

Quickly, Molly tapped Gloria Heelheart on the shoulder.

"She told me she's feeling wonderful. Are *you* getting an award tonight?" she asked. Gloria turned imperiously to see who dared to speak to her—and as Molly's eyes met the famous actress's, Molly zapped, her too. Gloria Heelheart stood like a drugged animal. Her pogo-stick neck drooped and she dropped her clutch bag.

"Right," said Molly, eyeing the door and hoping that no more Hollywood creatures would enter. "You are both entirely under my power, and I want you to do something for me."

The two nodded.

"Think about Primo Cell," she said. "He hypnotized you, didn't he?"

Both women nodded. Molly's heart jolted with excitement.

"I want you to remember what Primo Cell ordered you to do."

Again there were nods.

"Okay. I have power over and above Primo Cell's. And I now order you to forget all Primo Cell's orders. You must erase his instructions from your minds. From this day on you are free to do as you please. You will never again obey Primo Cell. In fact, you won't go near him."

She paused. Gloria Heelheart and Suky Champagne were shaking their magnificent heads of hair.

"Can—not," said Gloria in a monotone.

"I—can—not—o—bey," echoed Suky.

"You *will,*" said Molly sternly, feeling like a schoolmistress dealing with disobedient pupils. "I won't have any of this nonsense." She had to sort these actresses out before anyone else came in.

She turned up the force of her eye glare until Gloria Heelheart's head began to twitch and Suky Champagne's body began to sink to the ground, her stiletto shoes twisting beneath her. Petula whined. Molly didn't really like to see them like this, but it couldn't be helped.

"Tell me what Primo has ordered you do," she ordered Gloria.

"Top—secret," stated the Queen of Hollywood.

"Listen, Gloria," said Molly, astonished and worried that none of her instructions were working. "If you know what's good for you, you *will tell me now*."

"I can—not tell you—anything," croaked Gloria, starting to quake. "It—is—im—possible."

Both stars were resisting Molly's pressure. Normally people submitted completely to this sort of hypnotic power. Cell had hypnotized them so completely that even Molly's strongest efforts couldn't free them. How had he done it?

"All right," she said, giving up and wanting to put the pair into a more dignified state. "In a minute, when I click my fingers, you will forget that you have been in a trance and you will continue as usual."

At that moment, Molly saw an irresistible opportunity staring her in the face. Even though she couldn't break Primo Cell's hold on them, Molly could still change these people's lives—or ask them to do anything for her. Why, she could make them invite her and Rocky to their houses for lunch. She could ask them to insist that she, Molly, star with them in their next movies. She could tell Suky Champagne to campaign to help save the rain forests.

Instead, hearing Brenda Cartwright humming happily, and in a sudden gesture of generosity, Molly said, "Suky and Gloria, you will both notice tonight how brilliant the bathroom attendant, Brenda Cartwright, is. In fact, you'll write to her afterward and tell her your evening wouldn't have been the same without her amazing work. You will even invite her over for tea. You will both feel that she is the most memorable thing about the Oscars. Now, whenever I say, er, 'Powder Puff,' you will both be under my powder, I mean my power, again." Molly clicked her fingers once more, and both women came around.

"I said, are you all right?" repeated Gloria Heelheart, picking up where she had left off.

"Of course. You know I'm a nominee tonight for my role in *Blood of a Stranger*?"

"Yes, darling, I just congratulated you."

"Did you?" Suky Champagne couldn't understand how she hadn't heard Gloria's greeting. Then she let out a strange low cry—the sort of noise a moose burping might make.

"Oh, nooo! I dropped my lipstick and it's snapped off. That's a bad omen! Willomena Dreiksland created that lipstick color for me. See, it matches the water flowers on my dress perfectly. Oh, heavens above, I don't think I'll win that Oscar now."

Gloria Heelheart wasn't listening. As she'd bent to pick up her bag, she'd caught sight of Petula.

"Oh, what a cuuuuuute dawg," she drawled. "Is she

yours?" she asked Molly. "I'm not usually partial to pugs. I'm a Pekingese person, but what a wonderful dawg." She bent down, cupped Petula's head in her hands, and kissed her nose. Petula was quite overwhelmed by her perfume and very glad when Brenda Cartwright came out of a cubicle and Gloria's attention was diverted.

"Brenda, darrrling," Gloria enthused. "You've done the most marrrrrrrrrvellous job tonight. *You* should be getting an award."

Brenda was too overwhelmed to speak.

After a few more pats of Petula, more thank-yous to Brenda for her fine work, and several squirts of perfume, the two actresses were gone.

Molly sank onto her stool. She couldn't understand why she hadn't been able to dehypnotize the two stars.

In *The Book of Hypnotism*, there had been nothing about hypnosis that couldn't be undone. Molly thought everyone who was ever hypnotized could always be released. Somehow Cell had locked his hypnosis in permanently, just as Lucy Logan had guessed. Molly didn't know how he'd done it. She felt as if she was facing a solid steel door fastened with an iron padlock, and she didn't have the key. She began to see the true extent of Cell's power.

If he could keep them under his control for as long

as he wanted, he was invincible. This thought was very frightening. He'd get more and more powerful and richer and richer. And he'd control more and more people all over America—all over the world, probably. Primo Cell knew mountains more about hypnotism than Molly did. And he was probably in the building right now. Molly felt scared.

Outside, Molly heard a loudspeaker call people to their seats in the auditorium. A few more people hurried into the powder room to use it before the ceremony began. Molly decided not to give up hope. Maybe other Cell victims would walk into her web—others who perhaps weren't so severely hypnotized. She must try to learn more about what had happened to them.

But as the evening wore on, her hopes were dashed.

Molly met major and minor film stars, as well as three directors, four producers, five screenwriters, a camerawoman, and a costume designer. She found that the more famous the women were, the more likely they were to have been hypnotized by Cell. He had hypnotized two of the directors and a producer. Again all his instructions to them were firm and unmovable.

The evening purred by for the Academy Awards audience. They watched clips of the year's best films. Oscar after Oscar was awarded. Thrilled and emotional people stepped up to collect them. Petula whined, wishing that she could go and watch.

Eventually there was a tap on the powder-room door. It was Rocky. He was very disgruntled. Everyone who'd come into the men's room had been in too much of a rush to talk to him.

"It's been really embarrassing," he said crossly.

Molly told him what she'd discovered.

"But how's it done?" Rocky asked.

"I don't know. It's like he's sealed it inside them. Screwed the lid on it. It's weird."

"It's dangerous."

"I've had enough," said Molly. "Let's go home."

Twenty-one

To Petula's delight, they ventured out into the empty foyer. There they could hear the muffled hum of the people inside the theater. Molly and Rocky decided that they had to take a quick look before they left. Silently, they slipped inside and hid behind a curtain at the dark edge of the auditorium.

The place was enormous—like a cavernous red mouth lined with toothlike seats. On these teeth sat hundreds of people in their tuxedos and gowns and jewels, watching, listening, applauding, and enjoying themselves.

From the sides of the auditorium, swooping cameras on metal arms scanned the audience. They were filming the celebrities for their reactions as each winner was announced. Every star was aware of the millions of people watching all over the world.

The ceremony had reached the award for Best Actress in a Leading Role. The giant screen showed a clip of Tanya Tolayly starring in *Into the Wilderness*, and then it split into five. The live cameras zoomed in on the five actresses nominated for this Oscar, and their expectant faces, six feet high, loomed above the stage. Suky Champagne was, of course, one of them.

The presenter of the award, a Spanish actress in a winged dress that looked as if it was about to take off, held the sealed Oscar envelope. She tore it open, pulled out the card inside . . . the audience held its breath . . . and she announced, "And the veener ees . . . Suky Champagne for *Blood of a Stranger!*"

There was a shriek from the auditorium as Suky realized she had won. On the screen the four other actresses tried to hide their disappointment. The audience clapped wildly.

Trembling, Suky stood up. She kissed the people beside her—her sister and the director of the film, Gino Pucci—gathered up her mermaid gown, and tried to glide gracefully down the aisle. When she reached the stage, she put her hand over her mouth in astonishment. All her life, she'd fantasized about this moment, and now she could hardly think straight.

"Vell done, vell done," congratulated the Spanish actress, thrusting the golden Oscar into her hands and pushing her toward the microphone.

Suky Champagne felt the cameras on her face. She smiled, aware her parted lips were on millions of TV screens around the world.

Back at the Château Marmont, Mrs. Trinklebury was weeping with joy at Suky Champagne's victory.

"She deserves every inch of that little statue," said Mrs. Trinklebury. "Oooh, what a wonderful day for her. I expect her mother's so proud."

"Maybe she's an orphan," said Gemma.

"I wonder what she'll say," said Mrs. Trinklebury. "She looks awfully nervous."

On the television, Suky's small face looked as if she was waiting for the applause to subside. In fact, she was desperately trying to remember the speech she had prepared. The shock of winning had emptied everything from her head.

Mrs. Trinklebury dabbed at her eyes.

"Thank you," began Suky Champagne, combing her brain to find her lost speech. At last she found it.

"Yes," she sighed, "I want to thank everyone who made this film possible for me. It was a fabulous experience, and without you all I wouldn't be up here today. So thank you. But most of all, my thanks are due to the marvelous Brenda Cartwright, who is here tonight. She keeps the Kodak Theatre powder room so perfectly that I could have spent the whole evening in it. I've never seen such beautifully polished toilet seats. Yes, Brenda, thank you—you've made my evening a complete pleasure."

"What a lovely girl," said Mrs. Trinklebury.

The audience wondered whether or not to laugh, and some of them did. Others sympathized with Suky Champagne. They knew that she must be deeply moved by her victory, so they began to clap. A few directors marked Miss Champagne down as a much more eccentric and interesting actress than they had thought.

Suky Champagne smiled bewilderedly and left the stage.

Rocky looked sideways at Molly.

"Strange behavior. Don't suppose it had anything to do with you?"

"I didn't mean her to say *that*," said Molly guiltily.

From behind their curtain, Molly, Petula, and Rocky watched the ceremony roll by. At last it was all over, and excited, babbling crowds poured out to fill the foyer and the corridors. Jostled this way and that, Molly caught the edge of a conversation about the Davina Nuttel abduction.

"Do you think it's a kidnaping? I mean, why hasn't

the Nuttel family received a ransom demand?" one man asked.

"All I know," his companion replied, "is that I've hired a bodyguard to accompany my children to school. I'm not letting them go out by themselves anymore."

Molly and Rocky suddenly felt they should have left earlier. To avoid the cameras, they decided to leave through the caterers' entrance. It was then that a hand tapped Molly on the shoulder.

She swung around. The tall, commanding figure of a gray-haired man towered over her. Molly lurched sideways and she just managed to stifle a scream.

Primo Cell smiled. "I'm so sorry to make you jump," he said. Molly tried to wipe the horror off her face. Cell was looking straight at her. Molly recognized his eyes, with their different colors. One was turquoise, the other a strange shade of brown.

"Glad to catch you," he said in a warm, friendly voice. "You're Molly Moon, aren't you? My name's Primo Cell. My son Sinclair here has been telling me all about your shooting-star time in New York. Apparently you're the star of the twenty-first century." Behind Cell, Molly could see Sinclair. He was fair haired, blue eyed, fit, and tanned. Molly knew instantly that Sinclair was the same man who'd walked into Cell's office that night they'd hidden under the

169

desk. She stepped in front of Petula to hide her.

"It's a *treat* to meet you," Primo Cell contrived. "I'm always interested in young stars." His voice was fluid and smooth, as if his voice box, tongue, and teeth were all lubricated with liquid silicon. Primo offered his well-manicured hand for her to shake. She didn't take it.

Molly's hesitation looked to Primo Cell like reserve. He said, "Oh, of course. You have no idea who I am, do you?"

Pretending, Molly shook her head. His voice was horribly alluring—she must stop listening to it as soon as she could. "Nice to meet you," Molly mumbled, and began to turn away.

Primo wasn't deterred. This budding starlet had probably been warned that Hollywood was a shark tank and that everyone would want a bite of her.

"I'd really like to know you better," he purred. "Molly, I'm hosting the hottest party in Hollywood tonight. Everyone will be there. It's *the* place to be. I'd love it if you and your friend would be my guests." Cell handed Molly two black invitations with gold magpies on them.

"Hope to see you there." Primo Cell smiled once more, and he and Sinclair disappeared into the noisy crowd.

Molly and Rocky looked at their invitations. Neither of them spoke.

Molly eventually broke the silence. "We only have to go for a while."

"We don't have to go at all," said Rocky. "Did you see the way he looked at you?"

"We should go," insisted Molly, her mind already made up. "Think about it—it'll give us the perfect chance to find out more about him. We've got to find out how he does his unstoppable hypnosis. Maybe something at the house will show us how. He's probably got a special hypnotizing room that will give us some clues. And if Cell did take Davina, maybe she's locked in an attic or something. Rocky, I know it feels like walking into the lion's den, but we've got to go."

"Molly, thinking we can safely snoop about Cell's house is like thinking it's safe to play in a power station without getting electrocuted."

"No," said Molly, picking Petula up, "because we're not going to play. We're going there to turn the power off."

Twenty-two

Molly and Rocky were a bit stumped as to how they would get to Primo Cell's. Their driver had gone, and they realized that getting a cab outside the Kodak building would be tricky, as there were throngs of people there. So when they spotted a long-legged actor in a denim suit with a magpie invitation in his suntanned hand, they politely asked if they could hitch a lift. Molly recognized him from old cowboy films in the video cupboard at Happiness House. His name was Dusty Goldman.

"As long as you don't mind travelin' rough, I'd love to take ya. My car's parked out back," he said, a grin wrinkling his weathered face.

Pleased to meet someone who seemed real, and not

caring how rough his car was, Molly and Rocky followed Dusty Goldman toward the rear exit of the Kodak Theatre.

"I'm surprised you recognized me," he said modestly. "I haven't made a big film for years."

"Why were you at the Awards?" asked Rocky.

"An old friend of mine directed a movie that got nominated for best soundtrack and her husband couldn't go—caught some sort of bug—so she offered me his ticket and the party invitation. Thought I'd go for old time's sake."

Outside the theater's service entrance, the sun had gone down and it was getting cold. Dusty led Molly, Petula, and Rocky to a beat-up convertible. It was rusty, dented, and muddy.

"Why don't more people leave by the back entrance?" asked Molly. "There aren't any crowds here."

"Well, precisely. People like to be seen, especially by the cameras," said Dusty. "The more times their picture gets published, the more famous they get. The more famous they get, the more cameras wanna take their picture. It's a spiral that goes around and around, and most of them want to ride it. They want to get higher on that spiral than anyone else has ever got before. Higher than Marilyn Monroe or Elvis. They want to become gods for the people. That's why not many leave out back." He climbed into the front seat of his unlocked car. "I'm not saying that lots of the people here aren't real talented. There are real good actors, and world-class directors, but a lot of them get sucked into this ugly spiral thing."

Molly and Rocky liked Dusty. He had his feet on the ground and his head screwed on. They hopped into his Thunderbird, slipping into its worn-out leather seats. Dusty took the battered wheel in his left hand and twisted the ignition with his right, and with a few shifts of the gear stick and a growl from the engine, they were off.

It was refreshing but cold to be driving in an open-topped car. Dusty gave Molly a jacket to wrap around herself. Petula sat on her lap, licking at the breeze. They drove back along Hollywood Boulevard and picked up speed as they coasted through West Hollywood, the bright lights of restaurants, hotels, and bars flashing past them. Petula's ears flapped in the wind.

"You like music?"

"Love it," said Rocky. Dusty switched on a country-and-western radio station.

"Do you play anything?"

"Guitar," said Rocky.

"Have you ever been in there?" Molly asked as they

passed the Beverly Hills Hotel.

"Yeah. It's very expensive—all gold an' pink an' fulla cushions. It's like the inside of a tissue box in there." He concentrated on the road. "Ah, see up there? That's Primo Cell's mansion all lit up."

Molly recognized Cell's home from Lucy's photographs. It was high up on the hill, huge and set in a cedar-filled park. Its gray stone walls and gardens were illuminated with silvery spotlights. As they drove upward, less and less of the grounds was visible, until eventually all they could see was the high wall that surrounded the mansion.

Dusty drove up to the imposing gate, turned off his music, and flashed their invitations at the security guards.

"Never been here before," he commented.

"Neither have we."

Molly hoped her rash decision to come had not been unwise.

Dusty followed a line of other cars up the long, winding drive, past the cedar trees and small lakes with colored lights under the water. The undulating lawns were dotted with monster-sized sculptures of jagged-steel beasts that looked as if they were grazing under the full moon. Here and there, small lights moved about on the grass.

"An art lover. I s'pose there'll be quite a collection inside. So," said Dusty dryly, "even if the people aren't interesting, maybe the stuff covering the walls will be. And by looking at our host's art, we'll be able to see what he's like."

The drive rolled into a graveled area above and behind the main building, where a parking attendant directed Dusty to a space by a wall. In the middle of the parking lot, a large stone magpie, poised for flight, was set in the center of a fountain. Water sprayed out of its wing tips.

Molly got out of the car and drank in the view. Below them were the roofs, chimneys, and top-floor windows of Primo Cell's house. Beyond, the vast expanse of Los Angeles spread out like an eiderdown of millions of Christmas lights, some in neat rows, others a hodge-podge of color and winking neon.

"I've heard about this view. The city looks like a computer circuit board from here, don't it?" said Dusty as they made their way down the stone steps that led to the back of the house.

Ornamental rose gardens were laid out to the left and right, each the home of more steel sculptures. A peacock ruffled up its feathers as Petula walked past. At the bottom of the steps there was a Japanese water garden with blossoming trees. Fragrant purple wisteria hung in clumps from a curving wooden footbridge. In the pond below, huge orange-and-white-mottled fish swam beneath the lily pads.

"Chinese carp," Dusty pointed out as they crossed the bridge. Molly realized that this was the first time she'd ever been to a *really* rich person's house. Molly thought how extraordinary it must be to come home to a place like this every day. They passed under an arch and came to a circular cobbled courtyard, where a sculpture of an egg surprised them by suddenly shooting a shaft of orange flame out of its top. Ahead was an ornately carved door. Here, another security guard checked their invitations. Then Molly, Petula, and Rocky followed Dusty into a tall lobby.

They found themselves looking over a balustrade into a large hall. A huge flight of oak stairs led down to a patterned marble floor that looked as if someone had spilled jugs of coffee on it. Jazzy music floated out from a room beyond. Everywhere was busy with waiters and waitresses hurrying in and out of rooms with trays of glasses and food.

"Let's go out front," said Dusty, and he led them into Primo Cell's drawing room.

The huge space, now filled up with guests, had been emptied of furniture for the party. A colossal chandelier with crystal pieces dripping from it like a thousand dewdrops hung from the center of the ceiling. A four-piece band was playing "I've Got You Under My Skin." Dusty did a funny wiggly dance as they walked past the musicians.

As they emerged onto a terrace the size of a tennis court, a voice shrilled, "Hey, Dusty, you made it!"

A tall, beautiful Arab woman in a red gauze dress threw her arms around the old film star's neck.

"Have a great evening—nice meetin' ya," Dusty said, winking at Molly and Rocky as he turned to join his director friend.

Molly and Rocky were offered fruit punch by a waiter. Petula ate an olive that she found on the floor. Then she began sucking on its pit. Molly stared up at Primo Cell's house.

It had four floors. Looking in through the windows of the ground-floor rooms, she could see people celebrating—holding flutes of champagne and triangular cocktail glasses. Gloria Heelheart was hugging Gino Pucci; Hercules Stone was admiring Suky Champagne's Oscar; Stephanie Goulash was greeting King Moose with a kiss. Even the politician Gandolli, whom Molly recognized from election-campaign posters around town, was there. Gossip, laughter, and excitement filled the night air. People basked in the satisfaction of knowing this was the best party in

Hollywood tonight. Many of them were "working" the rooms, making sure that they talked to the most important people. Actors were trying to charm directors, directors were flattering producers, producers were seeking out stars who they thought could make their next film a box-office hit.

But Molly was thinking how lucky it was that they had found their way here on a night like this. Downstairs, the mansion might be buzzing with noise and movement, but behind the windows of the upstairs rooms were no signs of activity. Nice and quiet, she thought, for a little exploring.

Twenty-three

Molly and Rocky finished their fruit punches and returned to the coffee-spattered marble hall. The oak staircase they had come down was flooded with noisy people, and two security guards were standing on the landing at the top. Molly and Rocky decided to look downstairs first. Squeezing between a woman in a gold kaftan who was as wide as a cow and a fat man with a white mustache, they entered an emptier room. It was full of modern art and lit by a large steel-and-glass chandelier.

"Remember what Dusty said," Rocky reminded Molly. "By looking at Cell's art, we'll be able to see what he's like."

To the left was a very weird green-and-gray picture of lots of tiny people the size of mice wearing nothing except leashes, being pulled along by an organ-grinder's monkey that was also on a leash. Opposite was a portrait of Cell himself, so huge that its canvas completely hid the wall. His eyes, one brown, one turquoise, showed the reflection of a flying magpie in their pupils.

"I wonder where he is right now," whispered Molly as a waiter approached them with a tray. On it was an artistic arrangement of what looked like fried crabs and a bowl of black sauce.

"What is it?" Molly asked.

"Soft-shell crab," replied the waiter. When he saw Molly's puzzled look, he added, "You can eat them whole—they're a special kind of crab."

"Er, no thanks," Molly said. Rocky took one.

"Mmmmnn, crunchy," he pronounced.

Rocky was now too excited by the party to find the thought of Cell scary.

"I shouldn't think he's *that* interested in us. He's got much bigger fish to fry."

"I don't want to be fried at all," said Molly, looking at the soft-shell crabs as they went by again.

Molly, Petula, and Rocky began to weave, unnoticed, through the increasingly animated guests, in search of Cell's private rooms. They followed the marble hall to its end and opened a door that led to a conservatory. Thick jungle foliage climbed pillars that sheltered hundreds of blooming orchids, and the air smelled moist and sweet. At one end was an indoor fountain where three people were playing guitars and singing.

There was a tall, thin teenage boy with a large nose and shaggy hair, and a girl of about sixteen, with an urchin haircut and one eyebrow with a section cut out of it. The other one, to Molly and Rocky's amazement, was Billy Bob Bimble. They stopped to listen. Molly could see Rocky was desperate to pick up a guitar and join in, but she glared at him to remind him of their more important mission.

Rocky began to hum along.

"Cool, man," the shaggy one said, nodding his head and shutting his eyes as he played.

Then Rocky began to talk in time to the music. Molly was impressed. He was making up words as he went along and sounded really good. But when he gave her a signal, she walked away with Petula, right to the other end of the conservatory. Molly didn't want to be hypnotized by Rocky. She waited for a few minutes. When she came back, she found the three guitar players staring fixedly at him.

"Coooool," said the shaggy one. They were all in trances.

Molly gave each of them an extra eye glare. Then she asked them whether they'd been hypnotized by Cell.

They had. On her instruction to forget all his instructions, the girl with the eyebrow said, "No way, man. What—Primo says—sticks."

"Yeah," said Billy Bob Bimble. "Primo's—cool. Gotta write—a song—about him."

"You already have, haven't you? Your magpie song is about him," said Molly, thinking of the tune that had been played on radios all over the world.

"No, man, that—track is—about a woman who's gonna have her heart broken. It's a love song."

Molly realized that, on the surface, Bimble was oblivious to Primo Cell's true self. But deep down inside he must, she thought, understand the kind of man Cell was. His song showed that.

"Sing the magpie song," she said.

Billy Bob's caramel-coated voice rang out.

"Don't let him steal your heart,
Steal it,
Steel your heart, oooooooooh,
Don't let him have your heart,
Guard it from the start, oooooooh,
Steel your heart,
Magpie man, oooooh,
Wants the sun and the stars and you, ooooh,
Magpie man."

"Where did Cell hypnotize you?"

"In—the movie—room," said Billy Bob Bimble.

"Where's that?"

"Downstairs." He pointed to some stairs at the far end of the conservatory.

"Outside in the croquet garden," said Shaggy Hair. The girl nodded.

Molly instructed them not to remember meeting Rocky or her and released the musicians from their trance. Then they left them to their strumming and went to find the movie room.

It was a fabulous private cinema-cum-theater with armchair-sized reclining seats. Plush silk curtains were drawn back from a huge screen on which two very fast Ferraris were chasing each other along a cliff-top road. A young man with a serious face was showing a film he had made to an old producer.

Reluctantly Molly and Rocky returned the way they had come.

"We won't be able to find any clues in there," said Molly.

"Wish we could just party and watch movies all night," said Rocky as they made their way outside again. Beside a small croquet lawn surrounded by out-door heaters, they found Tony Wam, the karate star, and two other famous actors from big TV soap operas. They were talking about fan mail. Petula sniffed at their trousers. Molly went to eavesdrop on two women who were sitting talking under a lemon tree. An old actress was giving a pretty young girl some advice.

"To be frank, dear, you should have your cheekbones enhanced—they'd just put a bit of extra bone under the skin—it would make all the difference to your face. And a few nice Botox injections in your forehead would be good, because then you could say good-bye to those nasty frown lines that you're getting. I've had Botox. Look at this—I'm frowning now but you can't see I am, can you?"

"No, there aren't any lines."

"Exactly."

"But don't we need lines? How does the audience know you're frowning, or angry or sad?" asked the young actress.

"I don't know, darling, but I'm not going to grimace just because some *part* demands it. I'm not ruining my face for that."

Molly checked these two out and found that they too were loyal to Primo Cell. She also made the first significant discovery of the evening.

"Where did Primo Cell hypnotize you?" she asked the Botoxed woman.

"Up—stairs—in his—private rooms," she replied.

"How do you get to them?"

"You go up the front stairs and follow the landing to the right, past all the pretty bedrooms."

"They're so beautiful—I stayed there once." The young actress sighed.

"You walk along to the end until you come to a special door . . . ."

"A dreamy door . . ."

"It leads up some more stairs. . . ."

"Exquisite stairs . . ."

"If you are lucky, you may go up there with Primo and have tea."

"Oh, it's paradise up there. . . ."

"You will see Primo's *wonderful* private rooms—his workrooms and his library and his study. He's a very interesting, intelligent . . ."

"He's a brilliant man. He ought to be president."

"The man is a genius. . . ."

"That was where he spoke to me."

"And me."

Molly looked at Rocky, who had joined her. They had to go upstairs.

Twenty-four

olly, Rocky, and Petula waited in the main hall for an opportunity to get to the upstairs corridors without being seen. Partygoers were still arriving, and the stairs were busy with people coming and going. The security guards kept a watchful eye on the scene. Eventually they were distracted by a journalist who was trying to gate-crash. As quick as a couple of chipmunks scrambling up a nut-laden tree, Molly, carrying Petula, and Rocky shot up the stairs and turned right. In a moment they were panting behind a pillar, halfway down the corridor. For a minute they watched the landing to make sure they hadn't been spotted. Then, with their hearts knocking in their chests, they sneaked down the hall and round a corner. Seconds later, they came face to face with a security guard, but Molly soon zapped him, and they walked on.

They found endless bedrooms—all of which seemed to be occupied, as the different clothes laid out on the beds testified.

"He obviously likes having guests," whispered Molly, touching an embroidered silk bedspread. "This place is like a castle, isn't it?"

"Not as cold, though," said Rocky. "And I hope it doesn't have a dungeon."

"It's like an art gallery, too," observed Molly as they walked quietly along. A series of airbrushed pictures of rabbits in the headlights of cars lined the wall. These were followed by portraits of people whose heads were spinning off their bodies.

"It's what he dreams of," whispered Molly, "that everyone he hypnotizes will lose their heads to him."

"Do you think he painted these?" asked Rocky.

"No. He's a collector. But these suit him, don't they? They show what he's like underneath."

They had reached the farthest end of this wing of the house. Beside a closed door, a blue neon sign flashed the words A STITCH IN TIME SAVES NINE. They guessed they were about to enter Primo Cell's quarters.

Rocky tried the door. It wasn't locked. Behind it, green marble stairs led upward.

Molly felt that this was like some sort of witch's

tower, where a sinister spinning wheel stood waiting for them. Shutting the door behind her, she followed Rocky up the stairs. They entered a small sitting room with yellow leather walls and a lit fireplace. The burning wood smelled of limes, and the flames made shadows and light dance across the ceiling. It felt as if the room was watching its guests.

Molly went over to the desk, which was covered with paperweights—each one a dandelion flower in a hard ball of clear resin.

"Don't touch it—it's probably alarmed."

"Rocky, we're not going to find out anything if I don't." Molly rattled the drawers of the desk. They were locked.

"This must be where those two Cell worshipers said they had tea with him," she said.

There were two other rooms. One had file cabinets and wall cabinets in it, but these were also locked.

"Should have learned how to pick locks from Nockman," whispered Molly. But Rocky didn't hear her. He was already in the room opposite, eager to get out as soon as he could.

This next room was a small library, lined with wooden shelves from floor to ceiling. There were all sorts of books—novels, encyclopedias, reference books, biographies, art books, plays, and books of photographs. Two cream armchairs sat on either side of another lit fire. On a low table was a sculpture of a hand trying to grasp a heart that was flying away. Two more strange pictures hung on the walls. One was of a magpie wearing a crown and a blindfold. The other was of a magpie in flight, suspended by strings attached to its wings and tail.

Molly read the words that were woven around the rim of the brown carpet under her feet.

"Knowledge is power Knowledge is power Knowledge is power Knowledge is power."

She followed the words along the floor. At one point the carpet had an odd bump in it, as if something was underneath. Molly bent down and felt the lump. Smiling, she lifted the carpet to reveal a brass key. Molly looked at the desk. The key was too big for the locks in its drawers—it looked like a door key. Perhaps it was for the door they'd just come through. Then Rocky saw where the key belonged. Silently, he pointed to a spot in the middle of the wall, where some hairline cracks gave away the position of a concealed door. Near the floor was a small keyhole. As quietly as she could, Molly tried the key in the lock and turned it. It clicked smoothly and the secret door swung inward. Whatever they found behind it was something that Primo Cell didn't want anyone to see.

The hidden room was another library. This one was

a lot smaller than the first. In the middle was a maroon leather-topped desk with a high-backed chair. Molly, Petula, and Rocky crept in.

The walls were completely lined with books. But unlike those in the previous room, they were all the same size and the same thickness. And their bindings were all the same color—maroon. Some were bright, some were faded, but Molly got the impression that all the books had originally been exactly the same color. Molly recognized the color, but she couldn't quite place it. But when she read the gold writing on the spine of one of the books, she knew, in a horrible flash, exactly why it felt so familiar.

"I don't believe it!" she gasped.

For there, on *every* single shelf of the room, were copies of the same book—a book that Molly and Rocky knew very well.

H

Y

P

N

O

T

I

S

M

"I thought the Briersville book was the only copy left in the world," gulped Molly.

"So did I," whispered Rocky. "But lots must originally have been printed."

"How do you think he got all of these?" asked Molly. "They must all have belonged to different people."

"Different hypnotists," said Rocky.

Something that Molly had thought only happened in cartoons now happened to her. Her legs began to shake so much that her knees actually knocked together.

"I wonder where they are now."

Rocky said nothing.

"Dead?" Molly blurted out in a hoarse whisper like a donkey's cough. Petula whined in sympathy.

"M-maybe he just made them forget everything they knew about hypnotism and sent them back to where they came from," said Rocky, not wanting to acknowledge how evil Primo Cell might really be.

"They're like trophies," hissed Molly. "They're like shrunken heads of all the hypnotists he's overpowered." Her hands were sweating as if she was in a sauna. "I don't like this. We've got to get out of here." Cell's overwhelming collection of the book that had changed her life had completely unnerved her. Her own skills felt like plastic toys compared to Cell's high-tech machines. She pushed away all ideas of searching for Davina. All she wanted to do was get out of the building safely.

They locked the room, rehid the key, and cautiously made their way out of the terrible house.

Downstairs, Primo Cell was pacing. For him, this was just another power-building opportunity. He liked being the center of attention and being on intimate terms with so many of Hollywood's biggest stars. They were all people he considered "his," but their devotion to him made them less interesting. The guests who interested him were those he hadn't met before, and right now, the person who intrigued him most was that plain-looking child Molly Moon.

In New York she'd been headline news with her part in *Stars on Mars*. Her support could be very useful to him on his children's channel. He already used the pop star Billy Bob Bimble, but a famous girl would really help Cell win the hearts of American children. It had crossed his mind that the child was a hypnotist. Her sudden rise to fame, her mystery, her ordinariness and yet her stardom—all had the stamp of a hypnotist. It was always a thrill to meet his own kind, although, of course, *adult* hypnotists eventually had to be disposed of.

Cell sighed as he thought of Davina Nuttel. He had planned to have her spearhead a big promotion campaign for Fashion House girls' wear. He didn't understand why she'd been impossible to hypnotize. Worse, it was as if something within Davina had weakened him. Molly Moon would probably be easier to hypnotize—though he'd have to be careful. *She* could be the new face of Fashion House.

Where was Molly Moon? Primo scoured the balcony and the garden below. An owly old screenwriter was standing by the door smoking a cigarette.

"You know that kid star Molly Moon? Have you seen her?" Primo Cell asked.

"Yeahhsssss," the man replied. "It goes like this. Pan across hall to oaken front door to see girl and friend squeezing through crowd to leave. Close-up on girl's face. She smiles uncomfortably. Someone has recognized her. Focus on girl's pug dog. It follows kids through door. Fade."

"How long ago was that?" asked Primo.

"Fifteen minutes."

"They'll be in a cab by now," Primo said to himself, pressing the pad of his thumb up against his sharp incisor.

"Next time," suggested the screenwriter, exhaling a column of smoke, "maybe you ought to hire a children's entertainer."

Molly and Rocky walked down the drive and out of

Cell's front gates. They decided that it was simpler to walk all the way back to the Château Marmont.

Primo Cell's secret library had scared them both badly.

"I mean, why should we have to sort the Primo Cell problem out?" said Rocky. "We're never going to stop him. He's too powerful."

Molly agreed.

"It's really a job for some sort of trained agent," she said, looking across the road at a poster for an action movie. "The idea that *I* should be able to do it is ridiculous."

"And not fair."

"Not at all fair. Why doesn't *Lucy* wait until she's better and then come and do it herself?" said Molly.

"Here we are in one of the most amazing places on earth," complained Rocky, "and we go to a party that most people would cut their right foot off to go to, but we have to miss the fun and instead snoop about and risk getting caught by Mr. Weirdo. It's not fair."

"Or reasonable."

Grumbling like this, the two friends walked through the chilly night.

Back in their bungalow, Rocky made drinks—proper Shirley Temples. Molly reached into a cupboard for a packet of marshmallows.

"When are you going to call Lucy Logan and tell her you can't do the job?" asked Rocky.

"It'll be seven in the morning there now. I don't think I should wake her up like I did last time. I'll call her tomorrow." Rocky knew that Molly was putting the moment off, but he didn't comment.

Molly put a marshmallow in her mouth and let it dissolve. She wanted to forget Cell and think about something nice, but she couldn't. It was impossible to get him out of her mind.

"If you were him," she said, giving up, "what would you be planning?"

"I wouldn't stop," said Rocky, drawing squirly, hypnotized eyes on the faces of people in the newspaper in front of him. "I'd want to control the whole of America, so that everyone did as I said. I'd want to become president."

"Why stop there? What about world domination?" said Molly. "Lucy thinks he's planning that. What's for sure, he certainly isn't going to just skip off into the sunset. I bet he wants it all."

Molly looked at the familiar Moon's Marshmallows bag in her hand. The moon on it was a round white marshmallow. The earth below it was drawn like a blue marble. When Molly was little, she'd thought the moon was made of marshmallow and that all the marshmallows in a bag of Moon's Marshmallows came from the moon. She'd also thought that babies turned up all over the world in cardboard boxes or baby carriages, like she and Rocky had. She'd thought they zoomed in from outer space in flying cardboard boxes and baby carriages.

"Do you think we're the only people in the world who know what Cell's up to?" she asked.

"I don't know and I don't care," said Rocky. He stopped drawing and began to tune his guitar.

Molly cupped the package of marshmallows so that the little planet earth was nestled in her hands.

"Imagine if we don't do anything about him, Rocky. Imagine if he starts to do really, really bad things."

"We could always see what happens. We can sort things out later if we need to."

"Later will be too late," said Molly.

Molly felt most peculiar. The more she looked at the small globe on the bag, the more she felt herself part of the problem of Primo Cell. If she was the only person who could do something about him, but she did nothing, then she would, in effect, be helping him. She would be behaving as if she *wanted* him to succeed. And she didn't want this. She thought of all the billions of people living in the world, all the free-thinking people Primo would like to control. The small blue planet in her hands seemed to tug at Molly's heart. She couldn't let Primo win. It was totally out of the question.

"It's now or never," she said to Rocky. "We *have* to try to help Davina. We *have* to find the secret of how Cell makes his hypnotism permanent. If we knew that, we could release his victims. Then his power would start to crumble. That's what we must do. We'll never forgive ourselves if we don't at least *try* to stop him."

Rocky looked longingly at his guitar and groaned.

"I suppose we'll have to go back to the house. When?"

"Tomorrow," said Molly. "Before we completely lose our nerve. You know what they say about falling off a horse? You're supposed to get right back on before you lose your nerve."

"My nerve is already the size of a pea," said Rocky.

"Mine's the size of a lentil."

Twenty-five

The next morning, Molly and Rocky woke to banging on their doors. For a moment both panicked, thinking that Primo Cell had come to get them. Then they heard Gerry's voice begging to let him in.

"Come on, you two. Wake up," he shouted. "We're goin' to Knott's Berry Farm."

Blearily, Molly opened her door. Warm morning sunshine poured in, along with a bouncing Gerry.

"It's an amusement park. They've got the Perilous Plunge. Gemma says it's the wettest roller coaster in the world. *And* there's the Boomerang ride and another one called the Jaguar. Mr. Nockman's takin' us all an' even Roger's comin', but we gotta go soon or there'll be big lines."

"What time is it?"

"Ten or somethin', I think, so get your clothes, 'cause we gotta go now."

Molly shook her head.

"We can't, Gerry. We've got to do something for the Benefactor."

"Again? Oh, that's so stupid, Molly. This is going to be brilliant fun."

Molly sighed. "I know, don't rub it in. Believe me, we'd love to come with you, but we can't. But look, we will another time."

"Okay," said Gerry disappointedly.

"Have a great time. Don't eat too much cotton candy or you'll go all buzzy like a fly—remember last time? And don't take your mice. They'll fall out of your pockets in the rides and get hurt."

"Okay," sang Gerry over his shoulder, already halfway down the path.

Molly and Rocky tried to cheer themselves up by having a nice breakfast outside on their patio, but it was difficult when the Knott's Berry Farm roller coasters beckoned them and the Primo Cell business squatted, unmovable, in front of them like an ugly fat monster.

Molly finished her omelette and poured herself a concentrated grenadine syrup. Rocky opened the papers and began to study the sports pages. All at once, Molly felt slightly peculiar. She looked at her plate and hoped that she hadn't just eaten a bad egg, but in that very second, an icy chill swept through her. It wasn't nausea, it was—something else. Instinctively, Molly resisted it, and in amazement she watched as around her the world stopped still. Rocky froze as he scratched his head.

For a moment, Molly thought she must be dreaming. But she wasn't. This was real. Molly looked fearfully toward the hills. Whoever had caused this time stop was somewhere over there. Quite far away, but not far away enough.

Molly scooped a still wasp from the air and sat forward and listened.

The world was so quiet. Apart from her anxious breathing, there was no noise. No traffic, no music, no vacuum cleaners, no lawnmowers. Just silence. For this moment, the whole world was silent. No one was laughing or crying or shouting or singing. The winds and the seas were quiet.

Then, suddenly, as if the pause button on the world's video player had been released, everything started again. The wasp in Molly's hand began buzzing. Molly let it go.

"What are you doing, you idiot?" said Rocky. "Want to get stung?"

Then, because Molly had her green-frog-sitting-under-a-rock look, he asked, "Are you okay?"

Molly leaned toward him, anxious in case the world stopped again. She told Rocky what had happened.

It was hard for Rocky to believe her.

"Perhaps time stopping happens naturally, like an earthquake," he suggested. "This is the place for earthquakes—maybe it's like a *time*quake. Maybe the earth did it by itself."

Both considered this geological possibility. Molly didn't know what to think.

"And another thing," Molly added, very perplexed. "Feel my diamond."

Rocky touched it. "It's freezing."

"It's not normal for diamonds to go all cold like that, is it?" she asked. "I mean, everything around the diamond is warm. My skin's warm. Shouldn't the diamond be the same temperature?"

"Maybe the diamond gets charged up with cold when you get the cold fusion feeling. Maybe it holds the cold like, you know, metal holds heat when it comes out of the oven."

After breakfast Molly and Rocky dressed themselves in jeans and T-shirts. Molly couldn't stop thinking about the strange time stop. She decided that this time it would be best if Petula stayed behind.

Reluctantly they set off. Their plan was a daring one. They intended to hide in Cell's private rooms. It was the only way they could discover how his hypnotism worked and, they hoped, what had happened to Davina.

They took a cab and were soon cruising down Sunset Strip. Molly looked out of the window at people in their cars doing safe things like going to work or to the shops. She thought how lucky they all were. Once or twice, Gandolli, the smiling politician, grinned down at them from red-white-and-blue election posters. Molly thought that he wouldn't stand a chance of winning if Primo Cell was after the presidency.

The previous night, on their way out of Primo's mansion, Molly had hypnotized the gatekeeper to let her and Rocky pass whenever they wanted. Now they slipped into the grounds with ease.

However, making their way to the front door was extremely difficult. It was as if the night before had not ended. Constant traffic motored up the gravel drive. Chauffeur-driven stretch limousines with darkened windows drove by. Molly and Rocky had to dart behind bushes and hide every half minute. What should have taken ten minutes took forty.

"Looks like he's having another party," said Molly, peering at the front door over the shell of a giant tortoise that was munching at the rosebush they were hiding behind. They watched as lots of important-looking men and women in suits arrived, accompanied by bodyguards.

Molly scrutinized the arriving guests. "Those people look like politicians, don't they?"

"Yup," whispered Rocky. "In fact, that's the governor of California. I've seen his picture in the paper. What *is* Cell up to?"

Getting into the house through the front door was impossible. So Molly and Rocky commando-crawled along the top rose garden—Molly unfortunately through a pile of peacock droppings. They sneaked past the sculptures and the Chinese carp pond until they were at the far end of the gray mansion. Here they found a small, low window that was ajar. Going first, Molly squeezed through. She felt one foot land somewhere wet. As she wiggled the rest of her body inside, she found that she'd trodden in a large sink of water. She was in a flower-arranging room. Vases, baskets, and pruning shears stood on the counters, and buckets of exotic flowers lined the floor. With one foot dripping, she quietly jumped down to the linoleum floor and warned Rocky to watch his step. She wiped the peacock muck off her jeans with a cloth.

"Birds' turds are s'posed to be lucky," whispered Rocky.

"Only if they land on you from above. Anyhow, I'm not superstitious," said Molly.

They could hear what sounded like household staff talking outside the room. There was nowhere to hide among the flowers, so Molly crept to the door, ready for instant hypnosis if it should be needed. But the voices passed by, and after a moment, she peeped out into a short hallway. At the end of it was what looked like a service staircase. As quiet as cats, and glad that the walls were blue and that their denim clothes helped to camouflage them, they made a break for it and slipped upstairs.

They were at the opposite end of the house from where they had been the night before, and they could just hear the rumbling hum of talk and laughter from the main reception rooms. Furtively, they slipped up the next flight of stairs and came to a landing with a purple carpet. They followed it to the left.

There were doors on either side of this corridor. When Molly and Rocky heard footsteps coming, they dived through the nearest one and hid behind a four-poster bed.

They found themselves in a luxurious suite, with a sitting room and bathroom attached to the bedroom. It was decorated in pinks and whites, and fluffy cushions were scattered all over the chairs and bed. Small tables with lace cloths on them displayed vases of pink lilies and tiny porcelain ornaments of dogs. The guest staying in it seemed to have really made herself at home. On the dressing table was a little silver tree hung with diamond rings. In an open box beside it were three diamond necklaces. When they saw Gloria Heelheart's face smiling out of a framed photograph, with several white dogs cuddling up to her, they realized that they must be in the star's bedroom. A second later they heard a growl.

Molly looked again at the bed. Its cover, which she had mistaken for a fur counterpane, was in fact a mass of live fur, still attached to its living owners. Gloria Heelheart's ten white Pekingeses were snuggled up to one another, enjoying a midday snooze. The one in the middle had woken up.

Molly and Rocky felt as if they were the matches that were about to set off a box of very noisy fireworks. As silently as snakes, they slipped out.

They discovered that all the suites along the passage had stars staying in them. Every room was lived in, and even had its own style, as if it had been customized for its owner.

On one desktop in a man's room, Molly found a bank statement with Hercules Stone's name at the top of it. Underneath was printed an address: Magpie Manor, North Crescent Drive, West Hollywood.

"He's well and truly settled if this is where his bank stuff is sent," said Rocky. "I wonder how long he's staying here for." Then, as he read the statement, he added, "Wow, he doesn't have to worry about money. Thirty-four million dollars! He's rolling in it."

Molly found an aerosol can of something called Bye-Bye-Bald. She sprayed some onto her hand, and immediately her palm looked as if a patch of black hair had grown out of it.

"His hair's obviously falling out," she said. She looked at two ruby cufflinks on the bedside table and a photograph of Hercules Stone hugging Primo Cell.

"Cell keeps them here like prize possessions. Like caged birds. I suppose they entertain him. He must have them to stay for weeks at a time."

"Amazing entertainment," said Rocky. "Imagine having any star you wanted staying with you."

"We still haven't found any clues to Davina," said Molly. "But if today is business as usual for Cell, it probably means hypnotizing people, which means, if we want to know how he works, we've got to get to his rooms quickly, Rocky. Let's not hang about here."

They left Hercules Stone's bedroom and went toward the landing above the huge oak staircase. Voices greeting each other echoed up from the marble hall. From where they were, they had a bird's-eye view of heads: bald ones, half-bald ones, and others that looked like well-groomed hairy animals.

"Politicians, army swells, *and* celebrities," said Molly. "I see his game. He gets government and army people here by promising that they'll meet the stars. He knows that even politicians get starstruck. I wouldn't be surprised if Cell plans to get a few politicians under his thumb before the end of today."

Molly and Rocky darted along the hall to Cell's wing of the house. They passed the pictures of rabbits beings stunned in the glare of lights. They came to the blue neon sign that flashed A STITCH IN TIME SAVES NINE, and then, tremulously, they stepped up the green marble stairs that led to Primo Cell's nerve center. They were gambling that Cell would be entertaining his guests downstairs, but the thought that they might come face-to-face with him was like a menacing black cloud in their minds. Molly's ears thumped as her heart pumped hard and sent blood throbbing through her head.

But when they got to the top of the stairs, the coast was clear. They slipped quickly into Cell's lime-smelling study.

Just as they did so, they heard two deep voices echoing in the hallway. The voices were coming their way.

Twenty-Six

olly's wits went on strike, and she didn't know what to do. She found herself looking in the fire's log basket to see whether she could hide there. Luckily, Rocky kept his head and tugged her toward the open curtains. They each took a side of material and pulled the dark-green velvet about them, letting it settle so that the drop of the curtains looked natural. Molly concentrated on quieting her breathing. As she looked up inside the green tube of material around her, she felt like a caterpillar in a cocoon.

The door clicked open and then shut as the two people entered. Molly immediately recognized Primo Cell's liquid-velvet voice.

"So here's where I make it all happen," he was saying.

"My home study. This is where I think and relax. Oh—and where I write checks."

Molly heard Primo, agonizingly near to her hiding place, turning a key and opening a drawer in his desk. She swallowed—inside her head it sounded like water sluicing down a drain.

"Ah yes, my charity checkbook. Here it is."

"This really is very kind of you, Mr. Cell," said another man's voice.

"Not at all, General. It really is my pleasure. Please, call me Primo."

Molly's chest tightened. As far as she could remember, general was the highest rank in the army.

"Thank you, and you must call me Donald."

"Donald, it's nothing. My own mother was a widow, so I myself never grew up with a father. I know firsthand how much it will help these families if they get help from your charity. Please sit down."

Molly heard a leather chair give way under the general's bottom, and then a creak as Primo Cell sat too.

"Who should I make the check out to?" asked Cell.

"The U.S. Army Widows' Fund," came the reply.

"Will ten million dollars be sufficient for now?"

The general gave an audible gulp.

"Er, absolutely. More than enough. I'm stunned by your generosity."

For a moment Molly wondered whether she, Rocky, and Lucy Logan had Primo figured all wrong. Perhaps he was using his hypnotism to do good.

There was silence, and Molly pricked up her ears. The sound of a nib on paper scratched the air. There was a long pause, and then she heard a noise that sounded something like this:

"Bdeughhhh."

It came from the general.

Molly knew at once what was happening. *Now* they were going to find out how Primo Cell locked his hypnotism in.

"Good," said Cell as if he was talking to a child. "Now you, Donald, are totally under my power. You will forget that I promised your charity a gift. You won't remember our meeting here. Instead, you will remember a wonderful lunch party at my house. In a minute, you will return to the other guests, thinking that you have merely been to the bathroom. From this moment on, you will do my bidding. And your obedience will be firm and unmovable. You will stay under my power, always . . . always . . . always."

Behind the curtain, Molly shivered. A chill as cold as a breeze from the heart of a glacier rose through her, and her diamond suddenly froze.

She let the icy feeling wash through her but not seize her. And as time stopped, she realized two things. The first was the startling fact that Primo Cell could stop time, and the second was that *this* was how he locked in his hypnosis. He stopped the world *while his victims were hypnotized*, and somehow that sealed his power.

In his chair opposite the general, Primo Cell sat up as if someone had given him an electric shock. The hairs on the back of his neck bristled as he sensed resistance. Someone alert and breathing was here in this very room. He rose and with three powerful steps crossed to the window. He snatched the velvet aside. Molly would have screamed, but terror had seized her throat.

For a second, Primo Cell looked shocked. Amazed even. He rarely came across people who could keep moving in a time stop.

"You?" he barked. "Molly Moon. I should have guessed."

Recovering, Molly focused her eyes on him.

He began to laugh.

"Oh, you disappoint me," he said. "I had thought you might be pupil material, but I can see from your face that this is not the case. And no doubt your accomplice is here too." Cell whisked Rocky's curtain roughly aside. "Ha. But still as a statue. Not as accomplished as you, I see." Cell grabbed Molly's arm. "You two are going to wish you'd stayed at home today," he hissed.

He hauled Molly toward the frozen general. Then, putting his hand on the man's shoulder, he did an astounding thing. Molly felt Primo Cell send a wave of cold fusion feeling out of himself into the general, so that the man stirred, and suddenly the general could move again.

"Pick up the boy," Primo Cell ordered him. "But at no point let my hand lose touch with you." This, Molly realized, was so the man didn't freeze again. The general obediently rose and picked up Rocky, who bent like a rag doll under his left arm.

"Now, hold the girl. Don't let her go." The general's massive right hand clenched Molly's puny biceps. "Good. Now we must hurry."

With his free hand Primo Cell reached for a button inside the top drawer of his desk. A bookshelf in the room sprang open to reveal a door.

"We may look ridiculous like this," said Cell as he maneuvered himself behind Molly and the general, "but looks can be deceiving, especially in Hollywood. Take me, for instance." He pushed them toward the secret door. "People think I'm a marvelous person. A benefactor. Someone they can look up to. But I'm not any of those things. I'm selfish and greedy."

Molly suddenly found her wits as she saw a stairwell below her. Was this where Cell had brought Davina? She pulled away from the general's hand and began to shout.

"Help! Somebody HELP ME!"

But of course no one could hear her. In the grand sitting room, politicians stood like sculptures, champagne glasses in their hands and rigid expressions of enthrallment on their faces as they spoke to celebrities. If the world *had* been moving, the hubbub of conversations would have drowned Molly's cries. As it was, the air was still as a picture, with sound suspended, so Molly's distant screams, as Primo propelled her down the stairs, were audible in the hall.

One person did hear the shouting. One person had casually walked away from the frozen lunch party and was cleaning his nails with a toothpick. As he placed the used toothpick into the outstretched hand of Stephanie Goulash, Sinclair Cell's phone went off. He pressed its answer button.

"I'm on my way," he said lazily.

"Sinclair, get here right now," came his father's impatient reply. Sinclair looked into his phone's screen at Cell's stern face.

"As you can hear, I'm having a bit of trouble." Cell turned his phone to transmit a picture of Molly yelling and the general with a frozen Rocky under his arm. "Come here and help me."

"Okay. Coming up. Trouble is, I was talking to Mrs. Grozztucke when you stopped the clock. She'll wonder how I suddenly disappeared when things start moving again."

"Forget her. The woman drinks too much anyway. She'll just think she's having a hallucination."

"Okay."

Molly was pushed roughly down the stone staircase. It went farther and farther down, as if it was spiraling to hell itself. Her arm felt sore in the general's iron grip.

She was starting to feel exhausted. It was very tiring resisting the freeze while shouting at the same time.

"Get off me," she yelled again and again. But her efforts were useless. Twisting, Molly turned her eyes on Cell.

Her smoldering look rolled off him like water off wax.

"You've got a nerve! Little girls shouldn't play with fire, you know. Or ice, for that matter." Primo Cell suddenly brought his strange party to a halt. "Take off the crystal."

Molly wondered how on earth Cell knew she was wearing a diamond.

"No. I won't," she said. "It's mine."

"Take it off or I'll take it off for you," Primo said grimly.

Molly was amazed. Primo Cell had to be one of the richest people in the world, and at a moment like this he had his mind on diamonds. He was completely materialistic. Molly supposed it was her payment, her punishment.

"You're a mean, greedy, ugly man," she shot back. "You're worse—you're *scum*. You don't need this. But I do." Molly thought of the orphanage children, of the unpaid bill back at the hotel, of the dwindling money at Happiness House, of nothing much to eat, of difficult times ahead. "You *can't* have it."

"You won't be needing it where you're going," Cell stated coldly. "Give it to me right now."

Molly heard the threatening tone of his voice and quailed. She was so tired. She had no more strength to resist. She reached for the catch on her necklace's chain. The diamond had absorbed the cold from her body and felt like ice against her skin. She undid the catch but still clutched the diamond.

"I suppose you'll let Gloria Heelheart borrow it, and won't she be thrilled?" she whispered. "But you know what? If she knew what you were really like, she'd *hate* you. All your hypnotized people would."

"Oh, my, so you have no idea of your crystal's true power," said Cell dryly. "Hmmmm." He reached out and took the jewel from Molly's hand.

And although Molly didn't know it, she froze.

Twenty-Seven

The general now carried two still children down the stone stairwell. They had descended below ground level, and as they wound farther down, light came up from below. The stone wall was replaced by thick glass. And the staircase descended like a tube of ice into a vast, white, cathedral-sized space. They reached the bottom and stopped.

This room was massive and modern, like a very big art gallery, although there was no art on its walls. Instead, in its center was what looked like a strange sculpture. It was a large steel tower. From its top a long pole stretched parallel to the ceiling and, in the distance, something large and heavy was fixed to the end of it. At the foot of the tower was a steel bench.

Sinclair Cell sat on it, looking at his reflection in a pocket mirror.

"Sinclair, you could have come and helped me, you lazy toad," said Primo. "Help me now. Tie their arms behind their backs."

Cell instructed the general to put Molly and Rocky on the ground. The immobile pair lay there like dead fish, and Sinclair came over and tied them up.

Then Cell let the world come out of its freeze. Immediately Molly and Rocky's time started again. Both were shocked to find how they'd been moved. As far as Rocky was concerned, he had just been behind the curtain, while Molly's time had stopped when Primo had snatched the diamond from her. A few seconds later she gasped as she realized what had happened.

"So the *diamond* is connected to time stopping!"

Primo paid no attention to her. He was standing by a small metal box and turning dials inside it.

Molly and Rocky struggled to sit up. Both their eyes were drawn like magnets to the pole at the top of the tower and the heavy object on the end of it. Something solid and menacing—all black and white. At the same time, Primo Cell pulled a handle. The black-and-white thing began to tumble. Then it was swooping downward, and in the next second, a huge metal magpie, with wings outstretched in full flight, was plummeting toward them.

It flew past, a heavy, deadly bird of prey, its thick, swordlike beak and weighty body hurtling low over the steel bench. If Sinclair had still been sitting there, the bird would have slammed right into him. Molly followed its flight. On its long pole it was guided up to the other side of the gallery ceiling, where it hovered as its weight shifted. Then, as gravity pulled it down again, it began its backward descent, targeting the seat. Its guillotine-sharp tail cut through the air with a *whoooomph* noise, sending a breeze through Molly's hair.

"I'm glad you're not superstitious," Rocky said to Molly, "because one magpie's supposed to mean bad luck."

"Beautiful, isn't it?" said Cell as if showing them a priceless treasure. "It's my magpie pendulum. It can even keep time. It can swing backward and forward all day long, and there's a clock on the wall up there. Do you see?" Looking proudly up at his monster, Cell pushed a button and, with a mechanical, birdlike screech, the magpie stopped high in the air. Cell walked over toward the bench and lightly patted its metal seat.

"Here, Molly, you sit here." Molly shook her head in horror. Sitting in the line of the killer magpie was the last place in the world that she wanted to be.

"Bring her over," Cell ordered the general, who, like a hypnotized retrieving dog, lifted Molly over to the bench. Sinclair kept a firm hand on Rocky. As soon as Molly's feet were under the seat, two metal clamps seized her ankles.

"NO," Molly angrily. "YOU CAN'T MAKE ME SIT HERE. YOU'RE COMPLETELY INSANE!" She struggled wildly with the metal bonds, but Cell was as unperturbed as if he was waiting for the kettle to boil. He watched Sinclair shove Rocky, kicking and shouting, onto the bench beside Molly. Sinclair checked that both sets of ankle locks were tightly fastened.

Activated by a remote-control device in Cell's hand, metal belts slid like evil snakes from behind the prisoners and snapped shut about their waists.

"Now, time for a bit of fun," said Cell with a laugh. Molly raised her eyes to the horrible death bird above her. She and Rocky were directly in its path.

"You wouldn't dare," she shouted, looking from Primo to the control box to the remote in his murderous hand.

Cell pulled back the sleeve of his cashmere suit and checked his gold watch. Then he took Molly's diamond from his top pocket and handed it to Sinclair. As if with telepathic understanding, Sinclair put it back around Molly's neck. Cell tapped a few buttons in the remote control.

"Miss Magpie is programmed," he announced. "In roughly two and a half minutes, she will fall again. When she does—well, you've seen my princess in action. I'm sure you can imagine the weight of her. Her beak is as sharp as a . . . what do we call those kitchen knives we sell, Sinclair?"

"Shlick Shlacks."

"As sharp as a Shlick Shlack, and her tail is deadly. Both are exquisitely sharp and heavy, so you needn't worry—whichever end you choose, it'll be quick."

"YOU'RE CRAZY!" screamed Molly. She was confused as to why Sinclair had hung her diamond around her neck, but unable to take her eyes off the killer bird. "You can't chop us up with your magpie! What kind of lunatic are you?"

But then she noticed the drain grilles on the floor and a silver reel of hose attached to the wall. She turned desperately to Rocky. The look that he returned was as wild and frightened as her own.

Molly's lower lip trembled.

"Please, Mr. Cell," she said in a small, surrendering voice. "Please don't do this to us. Just let us go and we won't bother you anymore. Please. Please don't make us sit here when the bird falls."

Primo Cell ignored her.

"I correct myself; in *two* minutes, the magpie will move again. You, of course, Molly Moon, can freeze the world. Sinclair has given you back the crystal. So you actually have longer than the two minutes I'm allowing you, to decide on your exact fate. How long can you stop the world for? Personally, I find ten minutes is about my limit. It's so exhausting, isn't it? Thanks to you, I'm now tired before my lunch party, which is irritating. I prefer to be well rested whenever I work." Cell loosened his silk tie.

"You know, Molly, it's odd how you never realized that crystals are essential to stopping time. Didn't you notice how cold it became when you used it? Didn't you realize that crystal is not a conductor of heat? Don't they teach you anything at school these days?" Cell unbuttoned his collar and pulled out a thin silver chain from under his shirt. On it was a huge, clear crystal that reflected and refracted the white light of the torture chamber, sparkling as if in sinister greeting.

"Show them yours," he ordered Sinclair. Sinclair wore a strip of leather round his neck, on which was yet another large, shiny gem.

"Now," said Cell, examining his cufflink, "I'd love to talk about all this, but I really must be getting back to my guests. Maybe another time . . . Ah, I forgot."

Primo eyed the drains. "What a waste. Anyway, Molly, and, er—I never did catch your friend's name—have a good eleven minutes. Bon voyage."

As Cell lifted a hand in farewell, Molly summoned all her strength to turn her eyes up to full hypnotic power, and she raised them to Primo Cell's. Her gaze flew through the air and hit him full in the face. The impact almost knocked him backward.

"My, my, Molly! I wasn't expecting *that*." Then he turned away, repeating, "What a waste." He beckoned for his son and the general to follow him, and they started up the glass stairs. Molly heard him say, "Sinclair, this staircase is beautiful, but it's a bore to climb. Remind me to install an elevator."

Twenty-eight

Molly and Rocky sat rigidly on the death bench, with the iron vises around their ankles and their bodies held firmly by the cruel steel straps. Rocky could feel his chest tightening. Molly reached forward to see if she could lean below the point where the magpie's beak would sweep by.

"It's useless. I can't get out of the firing line." She stared at the hideous instrument of death with terror in her eyes. "Rocky, I don't want my backbone sliced off. B-but, but if we sit up, we'll be mashed head on by the bird."

"The beak will hit me," said Rocky, his voice wheezing asthmatically. "I saw where it comes. It'll skewer me . . . then the side of its wings will rip us. And when it returns, its tail will slice our heads clean off."

Desperately he began to claw at the metal belt.

"Oh, Rocky! Oh, please, someone . . . help!" Molly yelled at the top of her voice, struggling uselessly. "This can't be happening. He's just trying to scare us. He'll be back. I'm sure he will. He couldn't want to . . . to . . ."

"Murder us?"

"Oh, I don't believe it, Rocky!" gasped Molly. "He's going to murder us." Molly screamed louder than she had ever screamed in her life. "HELP! HELP! SOMEBODY! HELP US!"

Rocky took Molly's hand.

"The two minutes are almost up."

Molly stopped. Despite her panic, she noticed how still and calm he was. "No one can hear us, can they?"

Rocky shook his head. He had tears in his eyes. "Sorry, Molly."

"But there must be something we can do," pleaded Molly. "We must be able to break these things . . ." All her hypnotic powers felt useless. "This can't be it."

All of a sudden the magpie gave a deafening screech. Molly almost fainted with fear.

"You can stop the world now," said Rocky. "And give us just a bit more time."

"Yes," Molly panted. "Of course, of course . . . yes." Molly stared at the drain beside them and pulled her mind into sharp focus. She had only a few seconds. From a part of her mind a small voice cried, *What's the point, Molly? It'll hit you eventually*. Molly ignored it. At lightning speed, she achieved the cold fusion feeling. And as it flooded her body, she heard the bird's charging swoop. She saw it coming. With a massive effort, she sucked the cold sensation to its summit. In a split second, the bird was upon them, and yet it wasn't quite there. Just in time, the world had stopped. Tremulously, Molly looked up. The magpie's beak was only a few inches from Rocky's neck. His eyes were tight shut. The spread of one wing was a few feet away from Molly's chest. Molly put her hand on Rocky's shoulder and, just as she had seen Primo Cell resuscitate the general, she sent the fusion feeling down her arm and into him. Rocky opened his eyes, instinctively straining away from the pickax beak.

"It's frozen," said Molly.

"How long for?" he wheezed. "It's going to rip me open. And how come I'm moving?"

Molly held the frozen feeling inside her more determinedly than she had ever held on to anything in her life before. "As long as you're touching me, you're not frozen," she told him. "And the magpie is still for as long as I hold it there."

Molly could feel, somewhere in the house above them,

Sinclair and Primo Cell's resistance to her freeze. She thought of Cell's irritation at not being able to continue showing off to a guest at his lunch party. He'd have to leave a sentence unfinished, and remember exactly what he was saying when time started again.

When the world moved once again . . . *if* it did, Molly and Rocky would be dead. Molly stared at the black-and-white killing machine in front of her. Did the world have to start again? Of course it did.

Rocky touched the tip of the magpie's beak.

"How many people has this magpie tortured before us?" The bird's metal eyes stared blankly at them.

"What shall we do?" said Molly. "I mean, if these are . . . you know . . . our last moments alive." She felt like crying.

"I suppose we should be enjoying it," said Rocky. "If we're going to die, we might as well. I mean, when it happens, Molly, it'll happen so fast I don't think we'll feel it. We'll die instantly. So we might as well try and be happy now."

"What, you mean tell each other jokes?" Molly said, a hard lump in her throat sending a pain up the back of her neck. "Or should we be remembering, you know, good times?" She took several deep breaths. It was taking huge concentration to both talk and hold the world still.

"There's no shoulds about it," said Rocky. Then he said, "Cell didn't even give us a last request—like in the movies. *And* this *is* Hollywood. Talk about mean."

Molly looked at her friend. Rocky looked genuinely annoyed. He'd almost made her smile.

"What would you have asked for?"

"My guitar. Then I might have been able to use my voice and hypnotize him with a song. What about you?"

"A gun."

Molly felt the stopped world, like a powerful jack-in-the-box ready to spring, trying to force her to let it move again. She pushed it into submission. It made her feel cold—so cold. Molly groaned.

"All right?" asked Rocky.

"I'm getting a bit tired."

"I'm glad you were delivered to the orphanage all those years ago," Rocky suddenly said.

"Same here with you." Molly knew this conversation was going to hurt worse than anything she'd ever felt before. "Rocky, all my life I've wanted to know who my parents are. Now I'm glad I don't. I'm glad I'm an orphan, because if I wasn't, I wouldn't know you, Rocky. You've been the best friend anyone could ever have. And you're the best singer—your songs are brilliant. The world would have loved them if . . . Rocky, what do you think death is like?"

"I think it feels like sleep, but without the dreams. A deep sleep where you don't think or feel anything."

"Do you think we'll ever wake up again?"

"I don't think we will, no. I think we—our spirits called Molly and Rocky—will be in a big sleep forever and we won't even know it. But maybe the energy that comes out of us when we die, the energy that has no feelings or thoughts—that will go into something else. Like a battery. The energy that was the power behind our lives will wait until something else plugs into it. What would you like your energy battery to be used for next, Molly?"

Molly thought for a second. "Petula's puppies, if she ever has them."

Rocky stroked Molly's hand.

"You mustn't be scared of dying, Molly."

"But how do you know all this?"

"It's just what I believe," said Rocky. "It's common sense. I never was a big one for religion. Religions have great music, that's for sure, and cool buildings, but religions seem to make people fight each other too much. If you treat people and animals around you as well as you can, that's enough religion. Don't you think?"

"Do you think we've treated people and animals well enough?" asked Molly.

"We're not perfect, but you're lovely, Molly."

"So are you. . . . But if everything dies and goes to a place like sleep, what is the point of life?"

"That's like asking what's the point of a beautiful sunrise, or a fantastic piece of music."

"Okay, so what's the point in those things?"

"Why does there have to be a point?" asked Rocky.

"Maybe there *is* a point behind it all," said Molly. "Maybe we're going to find out what that point is."

Molly was shivering uncontrollably. She felt her strength slip as the world pushed her to let it move again. The pressure of all the trillions of people and animals and insects and plants and machines in the world that were trying to burst out, to continue, to move on. Molly imagined the stillness all over the world. People in the middle of a joke—laughing but with no noise coming out of their mouths. People fighting, their punching fists frozen in the air. There were always wars in the world. There must be bullets that had been arrested in midair, bombs that had just been detonated. The violent things were too horrible to think about. Molly thought of good things. A child taking her first steps. A person in a hospital emerging from a coma. Perhaps somewhere a person was about to write the number that would win the lottery. Babies were being born, people were winning races, inventors and artists were, right now, having ideas. Scientists could, at this moment, be discovering something really important. And all these people wanted to continue moving. Molly gritted her teeth. With every passing minute, the pressure was becoming more difficult to bear. She knew she couldn't talk anymore. Eight minutes had passed.

She stared with hatred at the metal bird in front of her, despising it, wishing it would just disappear. She felt sick and more and more lightheaded. Molly held the world still for another four minutes. Then another four.

She held on so tight that she thought she might shatter.

She was holding on to a cliff edge, dangling over a precipice, looking down into a chasm that was death. Rocky seemed to be clinging to her legs, and now only the tips of her fingers held on. Her nails grated over the surface of the rock, trying to find a grip but slipping, slipping.

"I can't hold on," she murmured. "I feel so, so, *so* cold."

Then she shut her eyes and felt gravity pull her down into the chasm, as time swallowed her.

TWenty-nine

That evening, Cell had dinner with all his resident stars.

He always found their company amusing, and it did him good to remind himself how powerful he was.

They sat around his grand dining-room table, behind elaborate place settings of cut glass and solid-gold cutlery, and he listened to how their day had gone.

Gloria Heelheart was thrilled, because Gino Pucci, the director of the film she'd been shooting all year, had just found a replacement for the dog role in it.

"You know, Primo, I told you how the *first* dawg had a heart attack? We didn't know *how* we were going to find another one that would be as charrrrming. I couldn't let one of my little Peekies take the role, as the other nine would get jealous. And now, Gino has found a simply fabulous dawg to play the role. A pug! We're going to reshoot all the dog scenes next week. So the movie should be ready by early November."

Primo stuck his teaspoon into the raw sea urchin in front of him. He scooped up its salty center and put it into his mouth.

"That's good." He nodded.

Hercules Stone looked at his plate and frowned. "I can't eat this," he snarled. His personal butler appeared magically at his side. "I thought we told the chef how I like my burgers. The cheese goes on top of the meat, and the pickles go between the tomato and the lettuce, not on top of the lettuce. The mustard goes under the meat, not on top, and the mayo should be between the pickle and the tomato."

"I'm sorry, sir," said the butler, "it's just very difficult for the chef to remember, as the order of the pile-up changes all the time."

"I can't eat this," insisted Hercules Stone, and like a spoiled child, he turned his plate upside down.

"Oh, gross!" said Suky Champagne from the other side of the table. "I can't digest my salad now."

Cosmo Ace was more sympathetic. "Don't worry, Herc."

But King Moose, who was sitting next to Suky,

moved the eight-pronged candelabrum aside so that he could look Hercules Stone in the eye.

"I'm tellin' ya, Stone," he growled, "any more behavior like that and I'll give ya a knuckle sandwich for your dinner. And it won't have no mayo or pickles or mustard on it. It'll come as it comes—and it'll knock all those nice teeth of yours out, so from now on you'll be eating soup."

"Just you try, Moose—I'll sue," said Hercules, flexing his biceps.

"If we're talking food, Moose," said Tony Wam, the karate star, "how would ya like to taste one of my Koofoo chops?"

"Primo, please stop them. I hate it when they argue," whined Suky.

"Enough!" said Primo Cell. And at once all the stars in the room hung their heads obediently. Sinclair Cell arrived and apologized for being late.

"Another fight?" he asked.

"It wasn't too bad tonight," said Cell.

After dinner, everyone retired downstairs to the movie theater. The big cinema screen had been dismantled, and in the space behind it was a curtained stage. On it, a man in white tie and tails sat at a grand piano.

They all sat down, knowing exactly what entertainment to expect. It was one show about which they never spoke.

Cell settled in his armchair. This was his favorite part of the day. He clapped his hands and the lights dimmed to two white spotlights that shone on the pianist, who launched into the tune of Cell's favorite song. And then the star came on.

Davina Nuttel stepped out of the wings. She looked thinner and more tired than the Davina of the magazine photo shoots. A guard stood beside her, still as a tin soldier.

She glared out into the dark auditorium.

"I won't sing," she said defiantly.

Cell looked at her and exhaled thoughtfully. He wondered for the hundredth time what it was about Davina that challenged his hypnotic power. When he had tried to hypnotize her, she had twisted away from his magnetism like a lizard avoiding a net. But although this perplexed Cell, he didn't let it worry him, because there was a part of Davina that filled him with awe. He'd found that her singing made him feel better than anything else could. Why, he didn't know. Her voice had become a calming drug to him, and now he couldn't do without it.

"Oh, dear, Davina," Cell's silky voice replied. "Do

you think you can really put up with another day of raw sea urchins for breakfast, lunch, and dinner? You know how much you hate them. Think of what else could be on the menu. We've got a wonderful new chef who makes the most delicious chocolate cake and homemade butterscotch doughnuts."

For a moment Davina's lower lip quivered. Then she stamped her foot.

"I'm not a caged nightingale, Cell. I won't just sing when you feel like it. People *pay* me to sing. I don't do it for free. And I *especially* won't do it for you. I HATE YOU."

"Now, now, Davina. One song is all I ask. Then you can live like a princess again. You can have a lovely bath in all those exotic oils. You can wash your hair." Davina stared out into the dark auditorium, her eyes gray and ringed. She shook her head angrily. But she knew she was beaten.

"All right, all right, I'll sing."

With that, the piano replayed the refrain.

Cell leaned back. The song that Davina was about to sing was the only thing that ever made him feel any emotion. Perhaps, he thought, his mother had sung it to him as a baby. He wasn't sure why it produced tender feelings in him, but it did. Feelings of regret and long- ing. And when it was sung by this child, for some reason it became ten times more powerful. Davina wasn't a pleasant girl, but that didn't matter. She reminded Cell of something he had lost. His childhood, perhaps.

Davina's pure voice cut through the air like a fresh spring breeze.

> *"Sitting on an island in the ocean*
> *May seem kinda free.*
> *Lying on a beach of golden sand*
> *May sound as life should be.*
> *Sounds like heaven,*
> *But it ain't heaven,*
> *No siree.*
> *A billion waves of sea, you see,*
> *Divide you from me.*
> *Only you can make my world*
> *Heavenly."*

Cell sighed. And Davina sang on in the heavenly white light.

Thirty

The light was white as the light of heaven. Molly opened her eyes, and as she looked around, she shook with shock. She was in a completely different place from where she'd been seconds before. And, she instantly knew, she *felt* thoroughly different.

Molly didn't feel exhausted, frozen, desperate, and terrified to die. She felt rested, warm, and calm, as if she'd left the stresses and strains of life far behind. She felt as if she was in paradise.

She was no longer trapped on the steel bench with the killer magpie a foot away from her. Instead, she sat on an old chair in a dry wooden hut through which blew a soft breeze, warmed by the sun. She could see a peeling, white-painted bench outside. Beyond that, a jetty and the blue of an ocean.

Rocky sat on a chair beside her looking out to sea too. For a moment, they both sat motionless, listening to the distant slap of small waves and the cries of gulls.

"Rocky," Molly said. "We're dead. We're in heaven."

She looked at the white room. There were two beds, each with sheets, a blanket, and a pillow. To her right was a small kitchen, and to the left a doorway to a tiny bathroom. A guitar hung on the wall.

"I don't remember the bird hitting us," said Rocky. "Wouldn't we remember that split second as it hit us? A second of pain?"

"Maybe we died before the message of pain got to our brains."

Molly stared at two chairs by the opposite wall. Some clothes lay on them. Faded, ragged clothes. Underneath one chair sat her sneakers. They were different—they were worn out. And her T-shirt had a rip in it. Molly stood up and, feeling very unreal, as if she was walking on air, went and picked up her jeans. They had been cut short to knee length and were frayed. Was heaven a place where you kept the clothes that you died in?

"Crikey, Molly, you're so brown," said Rocky. "Look at the color of your legs."

Molly looked. Instead of being spammy, her legs were golden.

Rocky contemplated his, too. "I've never been this dark before."

"We must have been de—" Molly found it difficult to say the word. " . . . for quite a while." She picked up Rocky's shirt. There were no signs of death, of blood, on it. It was now a pale shade of orange, and its sleeves had been cut off.

Rocky walked to the open door of the hut. Outside was a creaky wooden balcony with a fence around it. Steps led down to a sun-bleached jetty. Fifteen feet away, it stopped. Then there was nothing but sea, its waves like egg cartons, and a far horizon with the sun shining above it. Molly joined Rocky and picked up a large mother-of-pearl shell from the balcony.

"It all looks so familiar," she said. She licked her lips and tasted the salty air.

"Like we've been here before," agreed Rocky. At that moment, Petula came around the corner of the hut.

"Oh, Petula!" Molly knelt down and hugged Petula to her, burying her face in her fur. Moments ago, she'd thought she'd never see Petula again. Petula wagged her tail and gave Molly's face a friendly lick.

"Petula must have died too." Molly paused. "But hang on a minute. I don't *feel* dead at all. I just feel as if we've been here for . . ."

"For ages and ages," Rocky finished.

"Because I *know* that jetty. I know exactly where to dive off it," said Molly, frowning.

"And that shell you're holding," said Rocky. "I think I found it, but I can't remember how." Rocky and Molly looked at each other.

Their hut seemed to be set at the bottom of a sheer cliff. There was a cave, but there was no visible access by land. The cliff face continued for miles. They could be anywhere in the world, Molly thought. There were absolutely no clues to tell them where, except that the temperature was balmy.

"We've been here for ages without realizing it," said Molly. "It feels like some sort of time hurricane has swirled us up and carried us here."

"I think," said Rocky, "we've been hypnotized."

A gull let out a harsh cry above them. At the same time a noise came from the side of the hut. Turning, Molly and Rocky saw a blond man in a blue tracksuit walking toward them. He held two full glasses in his hands. It was Sinclair Cell.

"A Qube for you," he said to Rocky. "And for you, Molly, a grenadine concentrate on the rocks."

Molly felt as if her feelings were in a washing machine. First she'd thought she was dead, then she'd felt relief that she wasn't, then amazement had taken over, and now she was very scared. This man wanted her dead. He must have come to kill her. She backed away, wondering if they could escape by jumping into the sea. She looked at the drinks in his hands. Did he want to poison her and Rocky this time?

Then her shocked brain seemed to shift as she realized that he *hadn't* killed her before—the magpie *hadn't* speared them. And a fierce anger rose in Molly as she concluded that Sinclair had been their hypnotist. Outrage gripped her. Like a chameleon changing color, Molly's mood was transformed from fear to fury.

"So you've been nosing about in our brains, have you?" she spat at him. "Kept us like rabbits in a hutch and made us tell you everything you wanted to know about our lives. How long have we been your little hypnotized guinea pigs? Two weeks? Three?"

Sinclair put the drinks down on a driftwood table.

"Oh, dear, I thought you might react like this," he said kindly. "Molly, I saved your lives."

But Molly was raging.

"Even if you save someone's life, it doesn't give you the right to go rummaging round in their minds."

Sinclair shook his head. "I didn't."

"Do you think we believe that?" Molly looked scornfully at him. "Well, I know what you *did* do. You switched our lives off, didn't you?"

Sinclair looked at his feet.

"How many weeks?" Molly demanded.

Sinclair nudged a shell with the toe of his shoe. He'd been dreading this moment.

"Seven and a half months," he said quietly.

Molly was dumbstruck. She counted the months in her head. That meant that she and Rocky had been living without their identities for half of March, April, May, June, July, August, September, and October.

"What date is it?" she whispered.

Sinclair told her. "It's the third of November."

"Wow!" exclaimed Rocky.

"But what about the others?" cried Molly. "Mrs. Trinklebury, Gemma, Gerry, and everybody else, too— back at the orphanage? Where are they?"

"They're fine. They're all living in Malibu. The others have flown over from Briersville. I rented a big house for them on the coast. They're fine, I promise."

This was when Molly blew up.

"You promise? Who are you to promise anything to us? Do you think we'd trust you after you blanked out seven and a half months of our lives? Do you think you're God or something? You're crazy. Come on, Rocky. Let's go. There must be some way out of here." She strode round the corner of the hut in the direction Sinclair had appeared from. Rocky shook his head in disgust and followed.

A burly, seven-foot bouncer stepped out from the side veranda and blocked their way.

"I'm sorry, Molly and Rocky," Sinclair apologized, "but you have to listen to me. First of all, though, I'll give you your memories back." Sinclair clapped his hands and said firmly, "Remember."

It was as if flood barriers in Molly's and Rocky's minds were swept away. Months and months full of summer memories poured through their brains, tickling their synapses with sights and sounds and smells and feelings of days spent living by the sea.

Memories of catching fish and cooking them over an open fire, of Rocky playing the guitar, of reading scores of books, collecting shells, swimming, snorkeling, surfing. Of Rocky losing a toenail, of kite flying, painting, writing, throwing sticks for Petula, sitting around the campfire at night, singing songs, of learning to speak a new language.

"*Hemos aprendido a hablar Espãnol?* Have we learned to speak Spanish?" asked Rocky.

"*Sí,*" said the big guy, whose name was Earl.

"I thought you might as well learn a language," explained Sinclair.

Molly discovered many lovely memories of Sinclair throughout the summer—not the lazy, vain, murderous son of Primo Cell, but Sinclair as a friend. She looked

246

at his familiar face, his shoulder-length hair, and his sympathetic blue eyes, and felt confused.

"But why?" she asked. "Why did you keep us hypnotized?"

"Because you wouldn't have stayed," said Sinclair.

"So maybe we wouldn't have stayed," began Molly. "But it's up to *us* what we do with our lives. Not you. So even if we did have an amazing summer, it wasn't our choice. That's the point, Sinclair. You should have let us choose for ourselves."

"I couldn't risk it."

"Why?"

"Two reasons. One, I worried that you wouldn't give up on beating Primo. The next time he caught you, he'd make sure you died. Two, there was the problem of my own safety. Primo would kill me if he knew that I'd betrayed him by saving you."

"So how *did* you save us?" Molly asked quietly, taking a sip of her grenadine. She was beginning to feel she could trust Sinclair.

"From the top of the stairs, I watched you holding the world still," he said. "I couldn't deprogram the bird, because only Primo has the combination code. I waited as you got more and more tired—until you had almost given up, and just before you did, I took over and stopped the world too."

"So there were two of us, you *and* me, freezing the world?"

"Yes. Anyway, you fainted, and froze, and of course Rocky froze with you," Sinclair explained. "When you blacked out, time didn't start again because *I* was holding it still. The magpie never hit you because *I* was holding it back. Then I immediately released you, and Earl and I"—he pointed to his bodyguard—"we carried you away. We came straight here, to the hut."

"Weren't you scared Cell would catch you?"

"A little. But he thought I was clearing up all the mess. Hosing all the blood down the drains and getting rid of the bodies."

"Does he kill everyone who's a threat to him?" asked Rocky.

"No," answered Sinclair. "Everyone just disappears. Primo wipes away their identities, making sure they don't know who they are ever again. He turns them into lost souls who hear voices in their heads. Then he dumps them in faraway places."

"Like garbage."

"Yes. Nobody will ever know who they are, least of all themselves." Sinclair shifted uncomfortably, obviously not enjoying the conversation. But Molly was too full of questions to let him be.

"Didn't you ever try to save them?"

"Yes, but Primo never involved me in the identity wiping, and so it was difficult to help. If I'm honest, there were some who I might have been able to help, but I was scared. I hate myself for that. But you see, I'm not a hero. I'm weak."

"You saved us," said Molly. "That was brave. But why didn't you go to the police?"

"Molly, Primo controls the L.A. police. He controls practically the whole of the American police force. You have no idea how powerful he is. The same goes for the newspapers. Most of the editors are under his thumb. If I went to reporters and told them everything, Primo would know about it immediately. Then he'd get me."

"Couldn't you *de*hypnotize some of his victims?" suggested Rocky. "You can stop the world, too. We know Cell makes his hypnosis permanent by stopping time. You could stop it again and *de*hypnotize them."

"Sounds easy," said Sinclair. "What you don't know is that Primo uses special secret passwords. It's what completely locks in his hypnosis."

"Passwords?" said Molly.

"Yes. They are the real keys. Without his passwords, his victims can't be released. I don't know what Primo's passwords are."

"So why did you finally wake us up?" asked Molly.

"Because I need your help. Since your ordeal in the

magpie chamber, something else has happened. Primo has become much more dangerous. Time is running out."

"It's about E Day, isn't it?" said Rocky. "It must be getting closer."

"Yes."

"What does it mean?" asked Molly.

"You don't know?"

"No," they said in unison.

"E Day," said Sinclair, "is Election Day." Sinclair looked at Molly and Rocky's quizzical expressions. "Primo intends to become the next president of the United States."

"But he can't," said Molly incredulously. "To become president, you have to have hundreds of supporters, you have to be in charge of a whole political party, you have to have been a politician for *years*."

"That's not true. Anyone can become president," said Sinclair, "as long as they were born in America and are thirty-five years or older. It's November the third now and Primo began his campaign in June—really late, but he's done it brilliantly."

Sinclair proceeded to tell them about the summer's "Cell for President" campaign. Cell had pumped millions and millions of dollars into it, running as an independent, meaning that he didn't belong to any political party. The campaign had stretched the length and breadth of America and been so intense and lavish that every citizen of the country couldn't fail to know about him. "Cell for President" posters had adorned thousands of walls. "Cell for President" hot-air balloons had floated over cities and towns. He'd been to every state and rented stadiums where the public had been treated to the spectacle of their favorite celebrities making speeches. Cell's hypnotized stars had talked about how much better life would be with him as president, and why they'd be voting for Cell. At each venue, Cell had given a speech, his face projected so that it was a hundred feet high on screens. Everyone who looked at the screen was, of course, hypnotized by him.

The splendor and power of his campaign had completely overshadowed Gandolli's and the other candidates'.

The desire for Cell as president had spread like a wildly contagious disease. "American Souls and American Cells—Need America's Cell." That was his slogan.

"You're talking as if Election Day already happened," Rocky observed. Sinclair shuffled and looked at his feet.

"It already has."

"It already has?" cried Molly, so loudly that Petula

barked. "And what happened? Did he win?" Sinclair avoided her eyes. He dropped a newspaper at her feet.

PRIMO CELL WINS PRESIDENTIAL RACE ran the headline.

"It was a landslide victory," Sinclair mumbled. "Election Day always happens on the first Tuesday in November. That was yesterday. November the second. This is this morning's paper."

For a moment there was silence. Then Molly's tongue and brain connected.

"Are you crazy, Sinclair? Why did you wait this long to wake us up? We could have sabotaged his campaign, we could have tried to work out his passwords, we could have done something, but instead, you left us *here*. Are you stupid or something?" Molly paused. "I'm sorry, Sinclair. It's just it seems to me you've left it much, *much* too late to wake us up."

"I couldn't risk it. Dad thought you were dead, and that's what has kept you safe," said Sinclair. "But today . . . after his victory . . ." Sinclair's voice shook. "I had a crazy hope that he wouldn't win. But of course he did. Now he's the most dangerous man on the planet."

Molly thought of Cell as a huge slimy creature, with slithery tentacles reaching into every country of the world.

"Why does he want to be so powerful?" she said.

"Because he's crazy," said Sinclair. "I don't know."

Molly suddenly felt sorry for Sinclair. It had to be very difficult for him to betray his own father. She also thought he must be a very good person. After all, as Primo Cell rose to the top, he took Sinclair with him, but Sinclair didn't want that ride. He cared more about other people than himself.

"Oh, I wish this hadn't happened," moaned Molly.

"He's not actually president yet," said Sinclair more brightly. Molly and Rocky looked perplexed.

Sinclair explained.

"There is a bit of hope. At the moment, Primo is president elect. He has a few months to prepare his advisors and organize his government before he's handed the reins of power by the current president. This is how it always works. He's not THE president until he's sworn in on January twentieth. We still have time to blow him off his tracks."

"The security around Cell is going to be double—triple, now," Rocky said.

"But I'm his son, and he trusts me," said Sinclair. "At least, he does at the moment. And he doesn't know you're alive, Molly, so we've got an ace up our sleeve."

Molly was beginning to think that Sinclair was as crazy as Primo Cell. The reality of the sinister hypnotist's becoming president of the United States was more than her mind could cope with. What could she, a child, possibly do about it?

"I can't help you, Sinclair. Look what happened when I tried before. I am not the magic solution to all of this."

"You're wrong," said Sinclair. "There is a tiny window of hope. But I don't want to talk about it now." He jumped up, eager to change the subject. "I'll tell you about it at my house." Earl handed him a baseball cap, some sunglasses, and keys. "And no doubt you'll want to know about your gang in Malibu."

"Where are we going?" asked Molly.

"Back to Hollywood. There's someone special I want you to meet."

Thirty-one

The cave in the cliffs behind the hut was amazing. Sinclair and Earl led Molly, Petula, and Rocky over a narrow walkway into the spacious, greenly lit cavern. The water inside was ten feet deep and so clear that they could see the sandy bottom.

Stalactites clung to the damp, algaed ceiling. At the far end was a concrete wall, and set in this was the steel door of an elevator. Minutes later, they were all shooting smoothly upward inside the cliff. At the top, a cream, suede-covered wall and a highly polished glass door greeted them. Sinclair pressed a button on the wall. The door slid open, and they found themselves standing outside the concrete bunker that housed the elevator. It was disguised to look like a large rock.

The view was spectacular.

"Hawaii's over there," Sinclair pointed out. "Perhaps when all this is over, we can make sure Primo lends you his private jet."

"Have we learned how to fly planes?" asked Molly, wrinkling her nose as she tried to remember the lessons.

"No," laughed Sinclair. "It comes with a pilot."

Sinclair's Aston Martin was parked beside the concrete bunker. Petula barked at him to open the door. It was windy on the cliff top, and the breeze was getting under her fur. They all climbed in. Sinclair revved the engine until it sounded like a lion purring. Soon they were driving up a winding, walled track to the cliff's summit. Before them was a highway.

"This is the Pacific Coast Highway," said Sinclair. "It goes all the way up the west coast of America. That way"—he pointed to his left—"is north—San Francisco, then Portland, Seattle, until you get to Canada. And this way"—he gestured to his right—"is south—Malibu, then Los Angeles, and eventually Mexico."

"Wow," said Rocky. "Where are we now?"

"This is a place called Dune Beach. It's a two-hour drive to get back to Hollywood, so let's hit the road."

The Aston Martin swooped out onto the highway.

"If we're passing Malibu, can we drop in and see

everyone?" asked Molly. Sinclair shook his head and put the gear shift into Power Drive.

"Sorry. Not just yet, Molly. At the moment they think you're working for the Benefactor. I had to hypnotize them all not to worry about you being gone. I hope you don't mind. But they're all really fine—and if you reunite today, there's a danger that Primo would find out that you're still alive, and we don't want that."

Molly held Petula on her lap and settled back into the blue leather upholstery. She shut her eyes. She felt quite strange. As if she'd traveled up a time shaft, up a cylinder of time in which she'd viewed the summer and autumn months but hadn't properly experienced them. So this was what it felt like to be hypnotized over a long period. Molly felt guilty about people whose minds she'd meddled with—although she didn't feel bad about hypnotizing Nockman to be better. He was enjoying life more, wasn't he? And soon her hypnotism of him would wear off completely, and he would have metamorphized into a good person.

"What have Nockman and Mrs. Trinklebury been doing? Anything exciting?" she asked.

"Yes, they have," Sinclair replied, smiling as he pressed the stereo controls. "If you want some in-car entertainment, look at the screen." A small screen on the ceiling in front of them flickered, and to Rocky and

Molly's amazement, a home video began.

It showed all the children from the orphanage having some sort of party with Mr. Nockman and Mrs. Trinklebury. The microphone picked up the end of a speech that Nockman was making.

"Now at last," he said, "I know how vunderful ze verld is."

Everyone clapped.

"Whose birthday?" asked Molly. "Nockman's?"

"No, it's a party to celebrate Mr. Nockman and Mrs. Trinklebury's engagement. It was in July."

"Their what?" Molly and Rocky stared in shock.

"Are you sure?" said Molly. "Are they, you know, in love?"

"Yup, like two turtledoves."

"Yuck," said Rocky.

"Well, they're very happy," said Sinclair. Molly looked at Rocky. "As long as he doesn't lead her into a life of crime."

"No way," said Sinclair. "From what I see, the guy's nuts about her and will do whatever needs to be done to please her."

"Well, I'm happy if Mrs. T. is," said Molly. "What about the others?"

Sinclair fast-forwarded the tape. In a sitting room, Gemma and Gerry put on a show for the other orphanage children. Gemma invited Hazel to come forward and said that she was going to hypnotize her. Molly and Rocky couldn't believe it. Gemma and Gerry then hypnotized Hazel and convinced her that she was on the top of a very high wall, and that every time Gemma blew, the wall swayed. Hazel lay flat in the middle of the stage, trying not to be blown off.

"But who taught them?" asked Rocky.

"*You* did," said Sinclair. "Well, indirectly."

"Me?"

"Yes," said Sinclair. "It seems you photocopied the original hypnotism book and they found a part of the copy. They're quite good at *looking like* they're real hypnotists."

"But they are real, aren't they? Their show looks brilliant!"

"Well, don't be too deceived. Hazel's acting. Gemma and Gerry have no hypnotic skills at all. I've checked. Mind you, they are very good animal trainers. Look at this."

A table stood at the front of the same room with a miniature gymnasium on it. It had little slides and swings, seesaws, and merry-go-rounds. Molly and Rocky watched in wonder as Gerry got his mice to go down a slide, to ride on the swings, to seesaw, and to whizz around and around. They even stood on top of each other in little mouse triangles.

"Gerry sure can handle those mice," said Sinclair, as the tape came to an end. Petula glanced at the screen and blinked.

For a while they drove in silence. Sinclair concentrated on the road, but he seemed agitated, speeding up and then slowing down again and tapping the steering wheel. It seemed as if he was trying to make up his mind about something. Molly thought how difficult it must be for him to be betraying his own father.

Then, as if the same subject was troubling Sinclair, he said, "You know, Primo Cell isn't my real dad. He adopted me. And my sister, Sally, too." He opened a cabinet below the glove compartment. Inside was a tiny refrigerator. He reached for some drinks.

"Adopted?" Molly and Rocky said in surprised unison.

"You got it," said Sinclair, handing Rocky a bottle of water. "Sally and I aren't real brother and sister."

Molly and Rocky were fascinated. Being orphans themselves, the subject of adoption was very close to their hearts. What was more, neither had ever before met a person outside the orphanage who'd been adopted, so both listened intently to Sinclair as he told them his life story.

It turned out that he and Sally had first been adopted

at the ages of four and five by a ringmaster and his wife, who had owned a circus. It was, Sinclair said, as if a huge family had taken them in. He and Sally had been extremely happy. The ringmaster was also a performing hypnotist. Unfortunately, he was such a good one that when he came to Primo Cell's attention, Cell thought he was a threat and so got rid of him. He hypnotized the circus couple. They were now gardeners at Magpie Manor.

The young Sinclair and Sally came to live with Cell. He seduced them with a new glamorous lifestyle, giving them everything they wanted—miniature cars to drive, fantastic bedrooms, a home with a movie theater and a pool, a country house with horses to ride and vacations by the sea where there were always big boats, Jet Skis, and all the toys they wanted. He got them a home tutor. One day, he said, they'd run his empire. When they were ten and eleven, he began to train them as hypnotists.

"But," said Sinclair, his voice bitter, "from the day he took away my circus parents' freedom, I hated him. I saw he had no heart. I vowed that I would do everything I could to stop him ever needing to hypnotize *me*. I played my part. I pretended I loved him like a son loves a father. But underneath, I didn't. I hated him. Sally made mistakes. She disagreed with him once too often. Primo hypnotized her. But he's never hypno-tized me. He likes to think that there's at least one person out there who likes him not just because they've been hypnotized to. But, as I told you, I don't like him at all. I loathe him."

Molly looked out at the sea and the millions of tiny ripples on the water. She didn't know how to react to Sinclair's life history. At this moment, she just felt bowled over by all the day's surprises. Molly knew she had other questions to ask Sinclair, but she couldn't remember what they were. Instead, overcome by the vibrations of the car and the hum of the engine, she fell asleep. And Petula snuggled up to her, very relieved that the real Molly was back at last.

Thirty-two

Sinclair lived in a house in the Hollywood Hills. The car growled in low gear as it negotiated the steep tree-lined road. On either side, snug buildings hugged the slopes.

"All these houses are seismically safe—that means they're built to withstand earthquakes," said Sinclair. "Mine too."

He turned into a drive. His house was a modern blocky building supported on columns.

They climbed out in a parking court underneath it, where the pillars were covered with tropical ivy and bougainvillea. Sinclair led them toward an elevator door.

"I can see you don't like stairs much," said Molly as they swept upward.

Then, "Wow!" both she and Rocky exclaimed as they stepped into Sinclair's living room.

A panoramic window gave spectacular views of Los Angeles. And the famous Hollywood sign, looking like a giant geography-book label, was stuck on the hillside only a mile or so away. In the window was a long, curved window seat. Petula jumped up and made herself comfortable. Molly looked out. A narrow aqueduct, supported on towers and filled with water, snaked away from the house over trees and the hill and a road. Then it looped back again and entered the building below a gap in the glass window. It curled round the back of the room, where it rejoined its tail before it set off again on its route back toward the trees, hill, and road.

"That's my lap pool," said Sinclair. "I love it. Some days I swim once around—away from the house and back—other days I swim ten loops."

"It's so cool," said Rocky.

"I'd love to have a swim in it," said Molly.

"You can. Let me show you round the rest of the place," invited Sinclair.

His bedroom was circular, and so was the bed in the middle of it.

"Ever slept on a water bed?"

Molly and Rocky tried it out.

"Weird," said Molly. "It must be like sleeping on jelly."

"It's really comfortable," said Sinclair, activating a switch. The water in the bed began to vibrate. "It's very relaxing," he told them, but the wobbling water bed just made Molly and Rocky giggle.

Sinclair lived in style. He had it all.

He showed them his screening room, where he could watch the latest films, his computer room, and his darkroom. Newly developed photographs clipped onto a wire trellis showed what Sinclair had been taking pictures of recently. There were Molly and Rocky rowing a boat, with Petula perched between them. Rocky playing his guitar. Molly holding a conch shell up to her ear, listening to the sea. There were also some photographs of Petula. She was being kissed by Gloria Heelheart.

"I completely forgot!" cried Sinclair. "While you were, um . . . away, Petula starred in a film. It's directed by Gino Pucci. See, that's him in this picture."

"Petula starred in a film?" Molly stared at the photograph. "How come?"

"Gino met her at the Academy Awards. Apparently, so did Gloria Heelheart," Sinclair said.

"Ah yes," admitted Molly. "Petula and I—er—met her in the ladies' room."

"Gloria adored her and so did Gino. He tracked Petula down. Mrs. Trinklebury gave him permission to hire her. The film's called *Thunder Roll*, and it's out in ten days."

"What a pug!" Molly beamed. She felt really proud. "Petula, you're a star! And so clever, to organize it all yourself."

"She got paid a nice fat fee, too," said Sinclair. "She'll be able to eat steak as often as she wants."

Molly gave Petula an extra-specially tight hug. Petula wondered what all the fuss was about. Then Molly noticed a picture of a crystal.

"Where's my crystal?" she asked.

"I had to give it to Primo," said Sinclair. "He wanted me to take it off you once you were dead."

"Great," said Molly.

"I've still got mine." Sinclair pulled his crystal from under his shirt. "You can borrow it if you need it."

"Thanks." Molly felt really annoyed that Primo Cell had her crystal as well as his own.

"Look," said Sinclair, "if ever we get Primo under control, I can get all the crystals back from him, and then you can have two, or three."

"Why, how many has he got?"

"Eighteen, including yours. They've all come from other hypnotists. He sits on them like an old magpie."

"What I want to know," said Rocky, examining the photograph, "is how come so many hypnotists have these? I mean, how did they all know the power that the crystals would give them? Molly didn't know. She just found hers by accident."

"The truth," said Sinclair, "is very mysterious. I don't think that those other hypnotists knew they needed crystals either. I think the crystals found their owners for themselves. It's as if they have minds of their own. They don't, of course, but I believe they are drawn, in a magnetic way, toward hypnotists."

"Do they move by themselves?" asked Molly, aghast.

"No. But it seems that they cause urges in humans to move them. They can manipulate people to put them nearer and nearer to where they want to be."

"Which is where?"

"Near hypnotists."

"But why?"

"So they can be used for their true purpose, maybe. I don't know. It's completely mysterious. They've got a homing instinct—like eels."

"What do eels do?"

"Every year, eels swim out of the rivers of Europe all the way across the Atlantic Ocean to the Sargasso Sea, where they breed. Then the eels' larvae return to the European seas, where they turn into elvers and swim up exactly the same rivers that their parents came from, even though they never met their parents. Then, after about ten years, when those elvers have grown into big eels, they swim to the Sargasso Sea to breed. No one tells the baby elvers what their parents did. They just know to do it. Of course, these crystals aren't alive, but they seem to have some built-in instinct—just like animals. It makes them attracted to hypnotists. I thought scientists might explain the mystery. I've hypnotized some of them. No one has been able to work out how these crystals and hypnotists and stopping the world are connected."

"So Primo has a collection of crystals," said Rocky. "Like his collection of hypnotism books."

"Just like that."

"Horrible," said Molly. "At least he hasn't got his thieving hands on Lucy Logan's copy of the hypnotism book." Her voice leaped. "Lucy Logan! I said I'd call her, and I haven't been in touch for *months*. She must think I'm dead."

Sinclair frowned. It was then that Molly learned some terrible news. Sinclair told her that soon after the magpie episode, he'd overheard Primo Cell talking to someone called Lucy on the phone. After the conversation, Sinclair had traced the call and discovered that the number was in Briersville. At that time he hadn't known about Lucy Logan, so he thought nothing of it. But a few days later, when the hypnotized Molly had talked about Lucy, he'd realized who this telephone caller must be. Sinclair had come to a distressing conclusion. After Molly had disappeared, Lucy must have decided to call Cell to try and hypnotize him over the phone. Not realizing how masterful a long-distance hypnotist Cell was, *she* had been hypnotized instead. She was, Sinclair said, one of the enemy now.

Molly put her head in her hands as she contemplated this dreadful news.

"At least," she said, "at least I suppose she isn't in any more danger. At least being on Cell's side means she won't have any more car accidents." Then the reality of Lucy's being brainwashed by Cell hit Molly. "This is so depressing. Poor Lucy. She knew about Cell, and she hated him." Molly thought about the afternoon she'd spent sitting in Lucy's basement room looking at her videos. "So, Sinclair, was Lucy right about Davina? Did Cell kidnap her?"

"She was completely right," said Sinclair. "Cell was in New York, and he had problems hypnotizing her. I don't know why. Anyway, Davina then suspected what he was up to. Cell felt she had to be removed. He used his crystal and stopped time so no one saw her being taken. Davina's been living at Magpie Manor all year.

He keeps her like a caged bird in very beautiful quarters there. She is given everything she wants, as long as she sings for him. He guards her like a hawk. She's impossible to get near to. It's very strange."

"Poor Davina! And as for Lucy, I can't bear it. I felt lovely down on the beach today, with no worries. Now I'm full of them again."

"Molly, I know how you must feel," said Sinclair, "but you've got to rise above your feelings. We've all got to, because now the most important thing to do is to stop Cell being sworn in as president. To do this, we've got to break his pyramid of power. You've got a job to do, Molly. You've got to do something I've never been able to do. You've to figure out how to find out Primo's passwords so you can dehypnotize everyone."

"But how can I find out his passwords? They're in his head!" hissed Molly.

"Molly, you have an extraordinary gift when it comes to hypnosis. I think it's an instinct in you—you know, like the eels. This instinct might show you how to extract the passwords from Primo."

"I'm not going near him," said Molly, her hackles up.

"You don't have to go near him," said Sinclair. "The person I wanted you to meet is a friend who is going to teach you something so that maybe you can get into

Cell's head without being remotely near him."

Molly looked alarmed. Had Sinclair gone absolutely bananas?

"I've tried enough," she declared. "Look what's happened to Lucy. I told you, Sinclair, I'm not magic."

"You're stressed out," said Rocky.

"The time has come," said Sinclair, "for you to meet Forest."

"Forest? What's that? A country walk under trees?"

"No." Sinclair laughed. "Forest is my yogic meditation teacher."

Thirty-three

Sinclair went to the window and wolf whistled. A few minutes later, in came a tall, very thin guy with gray hair in dreadlocks that fell to his waist and bottle-thick glasses. He wore baggy white sweatpants and a zipper top, with socks and flip-flops on his feet.

"Hi, nice to meet you both, Molly, Rocky. I've heard so much about you."

Forest, it turned out, had been a yogic meditation teacher for ten years. Before that, he'd traveled the world. He'd lived as a hermit in a cave in France for three years, contemplating the meaning of life, eating nothing but nuts and berries, insects and canned soup. Later he'd traveled to the depths of the Amazon jungle with a group of monks who didn't believe in cutting their hair. He'd stayed with a hardy bunch of

Inuits and learned to build igloos. He'd spent eleven months in a tree house in Sri Lanka, hitchhiked across India, and caravaned on a camel across the Kalahari Desert.

Now he lived in L.A., where he was Sinclair's personal yoga teacher. His small apartment was downstairs. He had a yard where he kept chickens and a glass-blowing workshop. He was responsible for all the beautiful mirrored sculptures on the coffee table. Molly wondered whether Sinclair had hypnotized him to stay put.

"What is yogic meditation?" she asked as Forest sat down cross-legged on the floor.

"Well," began Forest in a deep voice that reminded Molly of a rock-filled mountain river, "yogic meditation is making your body comfortable so that you can tune in and pick up the positive vibes of the universe."

Forest suddenly lay back and swung both his feet up to his head, where he hooked them around his neck. His head poked out between his calves, and his arms lay flat on the floor where his legs should have been. He looked like a human knot.

"Mmmmn, so comfortable," he sighed, shutting his eyes. "Now, I concentrate on nothing, and the more I see nothing, the more the light of nothing fills me up until I'm . . ."

Molly and Rocky waited.

"Until you're what?" asked Molly.

"I think he's gone," whispered Rocky.

"He's meditating," said Sinclair.

"How long does he stay like that?" asked Molly.

"An hour. A day. I wish I could do it, but I can't. Sometimes Forest travels long distances in his head. It's called Astral Projection. He can go on a trip to his friends in India, and if they're meditating too, they have a kind of astral meeting."

"Sounds like a good excuse for a quick, I mean long, nap," said Molly.

Sinclair ignored her.

"Sometimes," he said, "Forest focuses his mind so that he can walk on fire."

"Or water?" asked Molly.

"Or air?" suggested Rocky. Sinclair didn't register their cynicism.

"I'm hoping," he went on, "that Forest will help you focus your mind and relax so that you are in the best possible state to surf the cosmic airwaves and telepathically extract Primo's passwords."

"Are you really?" said Molly, as if Sinclair had just asked her to flap her arms and fly. She'd heard about Californian new-age spiritualism, and as far as she could see, it was complete nonsense.

"Don't be negative," said Sinclair. "Forest will put you in touch with your instinct. You wait. You'll be amazed at yourself."

Sinclair left Molly and Rocky to study the knotted-up man on the floor. Forest let out a squeaky fart. Rocky and Molly found themselves stifling mouthfuls of giggles.

"Don't know about getting in touch with my instinct," said Molly quietly, "but his *in* stink is going to be unavoidable."

The next few days were quiet ones. Sinclair left for Washington, D.C., where Primo was organizing his new team of government advisors. It was very important for Sinclair to keep up the pretense of being Primo's loyal son and right-hand man, so he had to help when he was asked. But it also suited his plans to be near to Primo, as he needed to know his movements.

Back in the Hollywood Hills house, as far as Molly could make out, Forest wasn't teaching her anything that would help her extract passwords from Cell's mind. Still, she enjoyed spending time with him.

Next to his studio apartment, Forest had a lovely flower-filled garden. It was a kaleidoscope of color with mosaics underfoot and trellises of herbs along its walls. He introduced Molly and Rocky to his chickens and fed them each a home-laid egg. He showed them how to blow glass. He put a cold lump of it onto a long metal pipe, heated it up on a fierce flame, and carefully blew through the pipe until the hot glass blistered into a bubble.

Forest also taught them to meditate. Rocky tried to concentrate, but he found throwing a Frisbee for Petula was much more fun than sitting with eyes shut beside Forest. Molly, on the other hand, found it was very relaxing. She had always been able to switch off her mind and float up into space, so she was very good at it.

As her mind drifted up like a cloud, bobbing above the Hollywood sign, and climbed farther until Sinclair's house was too small to be visible and Los Angeles disappeared beneath her, Molly pondered on how minuscule she was. Twelve and a half million people lived in Los Angeles, and she was only *one* person in that vast population. As she floated higher in her imaginary universe and considered the *six billion* people in the world, Molly felt even tinier.

For a moment she let herself believe in Forest. If she *could* discover Cell's passwords, if she *could* stop Cell from being sworn in as president, stop him from becoming the most powerful man in the world, then her action would be huge. Huger than huge.

As she floated, Molly felt microscopic and at the same time massive—a giddy combination. But it was good, because the small feeling stopped the big feeling from making Molly believe she was some sort of important, superhuman being.

"How do very famous people feel when they know that so many people in the world know them? Do they think they're superhuman?" she asked Forest as she sat on the floor one day, sorting out good lumps of colored glass from bad ones.

"The stupid ones do," said Forest. "The smart ones realize that they've been lucky to be born who they are—with talents, and lucky to have gotten into situations that catapult them to the top. They know fame doesn't make a well-known person any better than an unknown person. Fame is like a pyramid, with really famous people at the top, less famous people underneath, and completely unknown people at the bottom, but happiness is like an *egg*. You can say that the happiest people are at the top of the egg, the middling happy ones are in the middle, and the unhappy ones at the bottom. There are lots of famous people who are unhappy, at the bottom of that egg. I'd rather be at the top of that egg than the top of the pyramid."

"So," Molly persisted, "why do people think fame is so special?"

"Maybe, wrongly, they think fame is the key to happiness."

"I know lots of people who are always reading about the lives of the stars, and they wish they were famous too."

"Those magazines are full of chicken dung. After a while, readers of those magazines start to feel that their *own* lives are chicken dung. And that's not good, to think that your own life is chicken dung. Chicken dung stinks. I should know."

Molly looked outside at a bantam that seemed to be laying an egg in one of Forest's walking boots.

"Life's like a summer vacation, Molly. It's over in a flash. We're all made of carbon molecules from stars and, in a flash, when we die, we'll be that same stardust again."

"So we may not all be stars," said Molly, "but we *are* all star*dust*."

"You got it." Forest shut his eyes. "There's power to be found when you discover the dust in yourself. Often, then, you find the big side of yourself too."

Molly doubted that these life-probing conversations with Forest were going to lead her to Primo Cell's passwords, but Forest didn't seem to have any specific lessons for this telepathy that Sinclair had talked about.

"I feel your energy is good, Molly," Forest continued.

"You must look for the nanu of small . . ."

"Who's the Nanu of Small?" Molly asked, thinking the Nanu sounded like a wrinkled, billion-year-old person.

"It's not a person. Nanu just means the smallest. If you look for the smallest of small in yourself, Molly, there you will find your true power."

"Er, thanks," said Molly. "I'll remember that." Sometimes, she thought, Forest was bang-out-there weird.

Thirty-four

The few days of relaxing came to an abrupt end.

Primo Cell had decided that his Washington headquarters were now under control. With his new presidential power, all sorts of money-making opportunities had opened up, and he was organizing a big conference for foreign businesspeople back in Los Angeles.

Sinclair arrived home one morning looking rattled. As he put his case down and the elevator door shut behind him, he said to Molly and Rocky, "I told Primo I had to go home to do some meditation with Forest, but he didn't like it."

His countenance was as gloomy as the gray weather outside. It was getting difficult, he explained, for him to escape from Primo Cell at all. Primo wanted him to move into his mansion so that he could be on call day and night. Sinclair didn't know how much longer he could keep up his act. He was finding it more and more of a strain to do what Primo told him. He was sure that Cell would soon smell a rotten haddock, and then, he knew, he'd finally get a dose of Cell's eyes.

Molly and Rocky had been allowed to go for swims in Sinclair's lap pool and for walks in the garden, but now, with his new paranoia, he forbade them to go out at all. Sinclair was worried that Cell might be spying on his house—he had often employed spies in the past, he said. Molly and Rocky had to stay hidden.

A fog descended. Molly wished she could get out of the house. She began a game of chess with Rocky, while Sinclair paced the room, occasionally gazing out at the view, lost in thought. Eventually he spoke.

"There is only one way of dealing with Primo."

"You don't mean kill him?" Molly glanced up from the chessboard. "We can't. We're not murderers."

"How about a good hypnotist?"

Molly put down the pawn she was about to move and shook her head in disbelief. She knew what was going on in Sinclair's mind. "Have *you* ever managed to hypnotize Cell, Sinclair?"

"I tried once," said Sinclair. "When I was younger.

Primo thought it was funny. He knows I could never hypnotize him. My power is nothing to his. He's got that extra something. There's only one other person I've ever met who has it too."

Petula whined. She felt Molly beginning to get agitated.

"Molly, you do have that extra something. You must know you do." Sinclair plowed on. "When I saved you from the magpie, the only reason I was able to hypnotize you was because your strength had been exhausted. Otherwise you would have been able to resist me. When I saw those ads you did in New York, I recognized your true power. Your eyes are as powerful as Cell's."

Molly got up and walked to the far end of the window.

"Don't make me try and hypnotize him, Sinclair," she said, looking out. "Please don't. I wouldn't stand a chance. Not a chicken of a chance."

"You would," insisted Sinclair. "I really believe you could do it."

"You have to say that," Molly said sadly. "Because I'm your last hope." She thought of Primo Cell sucking the memories out of her head and leaving her as empty as a dead packet of ketchup.

"This is so stupid," she said. "There must be someone

other than *me* who can do this. A grown-up hypnotist. I don't *want* to do it."

"All the others have been overcome by Primo," said Sinclair.

"Exactly, so what chance do I have?" cried Molly desperately.

"Sorry, sorry. I'm sorry," said Sinclair. "You don't have to do it. Of course you don't." He put his hands up against the glass of the window and leaned against it. "But please, think about it. It is your decision and I will completely understand if you decide not to risk it." Sinclair swung around. "But listen, Molly, I can get *access* to Primo. He trusts me. We can get him when he's off guard, when he's just woken up or is tired at the end of the day. Just imagine, Molly." Sinclair looked at his watch. "Drat, I have to go now or he'll be wondering where I am. I've got to help him host a dinner. He's got the head of the FBI and the deputy prime minister of Japan coming to meet Suky and Gloria." Sinclair gave Molly and Rocky a grim smile. "I hope tonight's not my last."

Then he patted Petula, took a deep breath, and went off to find his coat.

Molly, Petula, and Rocky were left sitting looking out of the panoramic window.

Great big tears rolled down Molly's cheeks.

"Sorry, Rocky," she managed to say, through sniffs and hiccuping sobs, "but—but I don't know what to do."

Rocky took off a scarf that he'd wrapped around his wrist and gave it to her to wipe her nose on. He watched as his best friend shook with tears, and he felt terrible.

"There's got to be another way," said Molly at last. "I don't want to end up with guacamole for a brain."

"I think there is another way," said Rocky thoughtfully. "And I think I know what it is."

Thirty-five

How, you might ask, could a person of Primo Cell's position and with his immense power be brought down without Molly having to hypnotize him? The answer was, by attacking him from a completely unexpected direction.

The best form of attack is always surprise, and Rocky's solution relied on this. He said that a head-on collision with Cell would never work. When Molly found out what his idea was, she refused to let Rocky risk his life alone and insisted on being the one who carried out the plan. Someone still had to face Cell, but it was in such a surprising way that Molly wanted to be that someone.

Two days later, Sinclair left to oversee the final arrangements for Primo's conference for foreign business leaders. The conference was being held at the Cell Center, but it began with a formal reception and lunch at Primo's house.

Early that morning, a top Hollywood makeup artist and costumer arrived at Sinclair's home. Of course, they had been hypnotized.

The two professionals set to work, and Molly watched with fascination as the tall, long-fingered master of disguise turned Rocky into somebody else.

From eight to nine, he worked on a new nose for him. Using special prosthetic rubber, he molded a majestic, chiseled nose onto his face. From nine to ten, he worked on wrinkles and hair, giving Rocky dense black eyebrows and a short, dark beard. Rocky was put in padded underwear to make him look rotund, and then he was dressed in a black, embroidered robe called a *dishdasha* and a red-and-white head covering tied about with a band. The finished result was fantastic. Rocky looked like an authentic Arab.

"It's hot in here," he complained to Sinclair. "What's my name again?"

"Sheikh Yalaweet. You're one of the richest oil magnates in Saudi Arabia."

"And you're sure the real Yalaweet's not going to turn up?"

"Absolutely sure. I told him the meeting was post-poned."

"How about his size? Are you sure he's as small as me?"

"Once you get these platform shoes on," promised the costumer, "you'll be exactly five foot three, and that's how tall the sheikh is."

"Well, I might get away with it as long as I don't have to say anything," said Rocky nervously.

While the finishing touches were being made on Rocky, Molly paid a visit to Forest's workshop. He was dipping a piece of glass into a bowl of chemicals.

"It's nearly ready," he said. Molly thought how she'd love to stay there all day with him. As if reading her mind, he patted her head and said, "The nanu of small will protect you, Molly, don't you worry." Even though this didn't make sense, for some reason it did make Molly feel better.

Upstairs, Molly took her turn to be transformed. She was dressed as Sheikha Yalaweet, the sheikh's wife. Like Rocky, she had padding to make her bigger, a flowing robe called an *abaya*—Molly's was purple—and platform shoes for height. But she didn't need much makeup, as her head was covered in a veil and her face, except for her eyes, was hidden by a black silk *niqab*. Around her eyes, her skin was tinted a darker hue.

Finally, at midday, feeling very constricted by their new bodies and clothes, Molly and Rocky climbed into a black, chauffeur-driven limousine, looking and trying to feel like Arabs.

They arrived at the guarded gates of Primo Cell's mansion. Their car was smoothly ushered through.

Remembering the torture chamber beneath the house's foundations made Molly feel sick. So instead she tried to think of Davina Nuttel, imprisoned somewhere within these walls, and of Davina's joy when she was freed, if their plan worked. The steel-beast sculptures on the grounds glittered in the lunchtime sun, looking hungry and malevolent. She dreaded having to cross the cobbled courtyard on her platform shoes. Both she and Rocky had walking sticks, as if they were very old, but would these be enough to steady them?

"Cell's going to see through this act," Molly said frantically to Rocky. "I look like something out of the *Arabian Nights*. Maybe we should go home."

"You look completely authentic," Rocky assured her. "Now, let's go." His voice sounded muffled to Molly, because, like him, Molly had stuffed her ears full of wax, to make any verbal hypnotism that Cell might try powerless.

With her mouth as dry as the Sahara Desert and her hands clammy from nerves, Molly took a grip on her silver walking stick and carefully emerged from the car.

The entrance was very busy with other cars arriving and guests making their way toward the house. Through her veil, Molly saw that the place was teeming with guards—security had obviously been increased for these foreign VIPs. Her body seized up. Rocky had to prod her with his gold-plated cane to make her take a step forward.

The courtyard egg shot a burst of flame to welcome them. Even though Molly was expecting it, she lurched sideways.

Sinclair helped his old Arabs down the front stairs. Then, using their age as an excuse, he led them through the marble hall, where the delegates were gathering, and straight to Primo Cell's conference room. This way they avoided any conversations with other guests or, worse still, with Primo himself. They passed a display showing the strength of Cell's biggest businesses: Primospeed, the car manufacturer, Compucell computers, One Cell Medicine, Cell Oil. Huge photographs illustrated his most famous brands: Honey Wheat Pufftas, Timezze watches, Bubblealot, Heaven Bars, In the Groove deodorant, Sumpshus toilet paper, Mightie Lightie diet bars, Fashion House. The picture that made Molly the most nervous was of Shlick Shlack knives.

In an empty galleried room, a huge table was laid with twenty-eight places. Each setting had a glass, a bottle of mineral water in a silver holder, a cut-glass bowl of ice, and a few wrapped chocolates. Sinclair led Molly and Rocky to the side of the room where name cards for Sheikh Yalaweet and Sheikha Yalaweet were placed halfway down the table.

"Okay," said Sinclair quietly. "I'll leave you now. I'll start ushering the guests and their translators in. When everyone is gathered, Primo will make his entrance. Molly, I've put you next to him, on his left. He usually starts with the people opposite him, and then works his way clockwise round the table, until he gets to the person on his immediate right. Then he'll turn to you. Good luck and see you later."

Molly sat down, her legs quivering and her heart beating fast. On the table in front of her was Cell's speech transcribed into Arabic. Molly picked up the paper and pretended to read.

Sitting on cushions that Sinclair had put on their chairs, Molly and Rocky looked convincingly big, especially when two very small Filipino men sat down on the other side of Primo Cell's place. The Filipinos were very jolly. They chatted excitedly, opening their chocolates. They introduced themselves to Molly, who nodded, leaned toward them, shook their hands, and mumbled, "*Sabah alkheir*," in what she hoped was an Arabic accent. Then she fiddled with her veil and prayed that they wouldn't want to talk to her.

Molly peered out through the slit in her *niqab* and watched the room fill up. An elegant Indian woman dressed in a red-and-orange sari arrived with her dark-green-suited partner. Then a Japanese couple sat down. The lady was in a specially creased yellow designer outfit and a peculiar corrugated triangular hat. More and more guests took their seats. Molly had never seen such an array of different-colored skins, or clothes of such colorful variety.

Molly sat quietly, head down, pretending to read, but the writing danced sickeningly in front of her eyes. She tried to relax herself by meditating, but the tense situation was too distracting.

Soon twenty-five businesspeople had taken their places round the great table. The room hummed. Everyone felt enormously privileged and flattered to have been invited to the president elect's own home. They all hoped that their companies were about to receive big contracts from the future president of the United States and that they were going to make lots and lots of money.

All at once there was a loud *cling cling*, as Sinclair hit

the side of a glass with a coffee spoon.

"Ladies and gentlemen!" he called, hushing the excited conversation. "Please welcome the future president, Mr. Primo Cell."

With great aplomb, Primo strode into the room. He smiled, nodded at his guests, and saluted everyone.

He was wearing a black-and-white striped suit, and there was a fiery confidence in his eyes. He looked immaculately poised and calm, but Molly sensed the raging greed that lay beneath the surface of this act.

"Welcome to you all," Cell began. "Good morning! *Bonjour! Hola! Sabah alkheir! Buon giorno!* Hi! *Konnichiwa! Marhaban!* Thank you for traveling thousands of miles to be here today. I am extremely grateful. It is wonderful to see so many nations of the world represented, and I am glad that, as president elect, I can now ensure that America will work with your enterprises."

The translators around the table relayed his words to the guests, who murmured approval and listened intently as Cell continued.

"In business, it is essential that you trust the person you are dealing with. If you look into my eyes, I hope you will see that I am someone you can trust."

Molly was amazed at how quickly Cell was operating. Every person in the room politely and obediently turned their eyes toward him.

"Yes," continued Cell in his beautifully modulated, velvet voice. "If you—look—into my eyes—you will see—that you can trust me—en—tire—ly."

And as he talked, he began to hypnotize the company. The wax in both Molly and Rocky's ears muffled his voice. Both sat motionless, concentrating very hard on not listening. Molly sang the words of the magpie song loudly in her head.

Steel your heart,
Magpie man, ooooh,
Wants the sun and the stars and you, oooooh,
Magpie man.

Now Molly could feel the fusion feeling rising all around her as Primo Cell, the supreme master of hypnotism, went systematically around the table overpowering every single person. As Sinclair had said he would, Cell had started on the guests opposite him. Now he was working on those to his right. He was knocking them down like tenpins.

Molly's moment was nearly upon her. She tried to breathe in the yogic way that Forest had taught her, in one nostril and out through the other. But calm was impossible when her heart thumped like the hind leg of a kicking, terrified rabbit. She raised her head at exactly the right angle to look into Primo Cell's eyes. In a few seconds, he would turn his attention from the Filipino to his right, and face her.

In her hand Molly held a coin-sized plastic counter. It was attached to a thin wire that led up her sleeve and under her veil. Now she pressed its button. A small, concave mirrored plate, perfectly crafted by Forest—which had been held in position under her *niqab* veil—slid down like a little curved door and filled the gap in front of her eyes. The mirror was two-way. Molly could see a black-and-white Cell through it. She would wait until the moment he turned and looked straight at her. Then she would snap her eyes tight shut.

Primo Cell felt supremely confident. As he'd expected, the collection of hopeful entrepreneurs in the room were all dolts. There were just a few more to go. The sheikh and sheikha Yalaweet were next. Primo tilted his head toward the sheikha. It was unusual for an Arab woman to be involved with her husband's business. Perhaps she was especially good at making decisions. He would give her an especially seductive hypnotic look, one that she wouldn't be able to peel herself away from. Primo locked his eyes onto hers.

Her eyes shone out from the slit in her veil, and to his surprise, he saw they were like his own in color.

One was turquoise, the other brown. Cell thought how rare and attractive the combination was.

"It is important to *trust* those you do business with," he insisted smoothly, smiling. Her eyes smiled back at him. Cell flinched in surprise. Was she resisting him?

Primo Cell calmly and slowly repeated the few Arabic words that he knew.

"*Marha—ban dikoum.*" Through the wax in Molly's ears, the words sounded muffled and like a spell.

It was time, Cell decided, to give this Sheikha Yalaweet a final annihilating blast. So, with a force of violent energy summoned from deep within him, he lasered a beam of hugely destructive eye power straight into the woman's eyes.

It happened in a second.

The bullet of his look hit Molly's mirrored visor and ricocheted back.

Primo Cell's head swung sideways as if he'd just been punched by King Moose. With a blow of his own making, Cell knocked himself out. He was left staring at a glass of water on the table.

Molly raised the mirrored plate inside her veil.

"You did it," breathed Rocky, hardly able to believe what he was seeing.

To Molly's left three other guests and their translator looked concernedly at the president elect. Sinclair quickly dealt with them. Now everyone in the room sat staring glassy-eyed at Cell, who continued to gaze blankly at the tumbler of water in front of him. Sinclair edged toward Cell, fascinated—as if he was observing a sleeping tiger.

"It worked," he said, astounded. "I've always wanted to see Primo hypnotized, and you've done it."

"He did it to himself, really," said Molly, pulling the hot veil, the *niqab,* and the mirrored contraption from her head. "And it was Rocky's brilliant idea and Forest's expert craftsmanship." She looked at Cell with satisfaction. "But we'd better not waste time. He might come around."

Molly and Rocky kicked off their platform shoes, and Rocky thankfully peeled off his nose and his headwear. Sinclair threw them a knapsack with their sneakers in it. Then he quickly programmed the translators, so that they could make up stories to tell to the foreign businesspeople, giving everyone a clear idea about what had happened over lunch. He told them that he and Primo had left for a long weekend in the mountains and that they would all come out of their trances in an hour.

Molly approached Primo.

"I'm going to get his crystal," she said, pulling up a chair to stand on.

Primo stood, immobile as a waxwork. But unlike a manmade sculpture, he was breathing. Molly carefully unclipped the platinum chain, pulled the whole necklace from out of his shirt, and placed it around her own neck. It felt very at home there.

"Okay, time to stop the world," she said, putting her hand on Rocky's shoulder. "Are you ready?" He nodded. Then, concentrating on a cut-glass water pitcher, Molly rapidly breathed the cold fusion feeling into herself, and like a practiced professional, she effortlessly stopped time. Instantly, everyone around the table, including Cell, became as still as doorstops.

Sinclair smiled. "All those times Primo's done this to other people. I bet he never expected it would happen to him. I hope I can do this without releasing him from the freeze." He tipped Cell backward and caught him under his arms. "Oooof. He weighs a ton."

With difficulty, he began to drag him out of the dining room, concentrating hard on *not* transmitting any cold fusion down his arms into Cell so he would stay frozen. It was very difficult.

"You okay, Molly? Think you can keep it up till we get out of here?"

Molly nodded. As far as she could see, Sinclair was the one who might have problems. Sinclair heaved the president elect through the marble hall. As he thudded up the oak stairs like a dressmaker's dummy, his suede loafer came off. Molly, keeping a firm grip on Rocky, picked it up. She looked up to the top floors of the house and imagined Davina Nuttel sitting by herself somewhere there. They couldn't rescue her now—they didn't have time. But if all went according to plan, Davina would soon be free.

Sinclair dragged Cell across the courtyard, where a solid flame hung over the giant egg. They reached the Aston Martin, and Sinclair struggled to manhandle Cell into the backseat. Molly and Rocky climbed in next. Wiping the sweat from his forehead, Sinclair jumped quickly into the front and, with a screech, accelerated around the bend of the gravel drive.

Minutes later, they were tearing along Sunset Strip, weaving through the frozen traffic. Where there was a jam, they drove on the hard shoulder or on the sidewalk and shot straight through any red lights. Molly was beginning to shiver with the effort of holding time still.

Suddenly Sinclair pulled over and stopped the car. Molly released the time stop, and the cars on the street were in full motion again. Primo Cell grunted but remained in a trance.

"Was it my imagination or did you feel that too?" Sinclair said quietly.

"What?" said Rocky. "An earth tremor?"

Molly looked nervously out of the window. "It came from the sky."

"It was a way off, but it felt like it was coming closer," Sinclair agreed.

"I didn't feel anything," said Rocky.

"Someone was resisting the freeze," explained Molly.

"*Aliens?*"

Molly felt herself paling. Never in her life had she considered that aliens might really exist, but these days, she'd learned that anything was possible.

Thirty-Six

Molly, Rocky, and Sinclair sat on the long white banquette under the huge picture window in Sinclair's living room. They felt weary, but at the same time an excited satisfaction thrilled them all. Sinclair could hardly contain his delight.

"This is just so cool," he said again—a phrase he'd been repeating ever since they'd finally gotten Cell up the elevator and into his house. The truth was that as well as being pleased, Sinclair was shocked. Seeing Primo, the man who'd dominated his life, now reduced to an empty shell, was more shocking than he'd realized it would be.

Cell sat in a high-backed chair, completely and deeply hypnotized, looking as if he had swallowed a gallon of wet concrete. Petula sniffed at his legs.

"What shall we do now?" asked Rocky quietly.

"We must take away his desire to be president," whispered Sinclair. "We must put an end to all his ambitions to be powerful. Stop him from wanting to control the world, from wanting endless wealth."

"Obviously we must stop him from knowing how to hypnotize people," said Molly.

"Yes," agreed Sinclair. "And then we should do a locked-in hypnosis, with a password, so that he's stuck like that for good."

Molly shifted uncomfortably from foot to foot. She never had liked the idea of anyone being programmed to think a certain way *forever*.

"We don't have to. I mean, we never did a forever hypnosis on Nockman. Just look how much better he is. Can't we make Cell improve himself?"

"Cell isn't small fry like Nockman, Molly. His brain isn't normal. We can't risk it."

"I suppose not," Molly said reluctantly.

"The most important thing," Rocky reminded them, "is to release all his victims. We must find out where they all are and what his passwords have been, so that we can dehypnotize them."

"Okay," said Molly. "Let's do it."

Molly faced the man who, until a short while ago, had

been one of the most powerful people on the planet.

"Primo Cell—you will now answer all my questions," she told him. "Where is Lucy Logan? Is she safe? Is she alive?"

"Logan—is in—California. She is staying in—the Beverly Hills—Hotel."

"Wow!" said Sinclair. "So he's got her nearby to work for him when he needs her."

"That's incredible," said Molly. "But thank goodness for that. We can get to her sooner and dehypnotize her." Then with the burning question of Lucy off her shoulders, Molly dared ask a darker one.

"So, Primo Cell, how many people have you actually hypnotized?"

"Three thousand," said Cell, as easily as if he was telling her how many people he'd beaten playing table tennis. Molly reeled back in horror.

She managed to ask, "Don't you feel sorry for what you've done?"

Sinclair sighed. "Molly, I've told you, he's insane. Of course he won't."

"Sorry?" Cell hesitated. "A—part—of me—some-where—somewhere—deep down—does. But—I don't have access to that—feeling. Davina—Davina Nuttel helped me—contact—my feelings. But otherwise—there's a wall."

"A wall?" said Molly.

"A forbiddance."

"A what?"

"I am forbidden to go to my feelings."

Molly frowned. Rocky and Sinclair sat up. Like a miner of information, Molly had unwittingly chanced upon an unexpected vein of truth.

"Are you saying, Primo, that someone has forbidden you to go to your feelings?" she asked slowly.

"Yes."

"Who has forbidden you?" Molly felt the hairs on the back of her neck prickle with a strange, horrible excitement.

"My master," said Cell.

"Your master? Who is your master?"

Primo Cell shuddered as if he was trying to summon up the name but couldn't. Sinclair and Rocky leaned closer, eyes wide.

"Say it," insisted Molly. Primo began to shake his head as if he was trying to dislodge an earwig from his ear.

"The answer's—imprisoned," he said.

Molly took Primo's hand and stared at her shoes.

"Sinclair," she said, "help Rocky so he doesn't freeze." As easily as pressing a button on a film projector, Molly stopped the world.

"Now," she said to Cell. "You will forget all instructions you have received to keep anything secret. No secrets now. Who is your master?"

Cell began to froth at the mouth as he strained to speak the name. "Slackg Clegg," he spluttered. "Slacgg Cllack." It was as if the name was locked in his voice box and couldn't come out. "Slasss Shhludd." Petula, still as a stuffed dog, stared up at him.

"There's a password," said Sinclair, astonished. "The name's been locked in with a password."

"There must be some way to find out the password," Molly said. She spoke to Cell. "What is the password that has been used to lock in your instructions?"

"I cannot tell—you that," said Cell.

"We're just going to have to guess," said Sinclair.

"But that might take a million years," said Molly. "I mean, there are trillions of possibilities."

"Make the world move again," Sinclair said nervously. "I can feel that resistance feeling again. And it's getting closer." He looked out of the window at the horizon, from where the strange electric, tingling feeling was once more coming.

Molly nodded, and she released the time freeze. The water in the lap pool began to flow, and outside she heard Forest's deep voice as he sang to his chickens.

"Whoever it is out there," continued Sinclair,

"controls Cell. And they must be looking for him now." His expression was fearful. "If they get here, if there's more than one of them, we're in real trouble. They'll want their president elect back."

Molly's mind whirled. For all they knew, Primo Cell's master or masters might be about to break down the door. She grabbed a pen and paper from the coffee table and urgently turned to Cell.

"Okay, Primo, I want you to quickly tell me *all* the passwords that you have used on other hypnotists, on the stars, on all the people you have hypnotized, so that we can release them."

"There has only—ever been one—password that—I've used," Cell hissed.

"So what is it?" Molly lowered her pen. The air was thick with anticipation as everyone waited, hardly breathing.

"The password I use is 'Perfectly punctually.'"

Molly felt as if she'd been punched in the brain. Perfectly punched.

"Perfectly punctually? But that's . . ." She couldn't speak. Those words. Those two unusually joined words had been used on *her*. Used to wake Molly the first time she had ever been hypnotized. Used by a person whom Molly trusted. And those *very same words* were the ones that Primo Cell used to control his victims. Those weren't Cell's words, they were someone else's.

Molly's brain suddenly added two and two and two. Was "Perfectly punctually" also the password that had been used to keep *Cell* under control?

Without warning, Molly grabbed Rocky and Cell's hands and froze the world again.

"I order you to tell me who your master is," Molly shouted at Primo. *"PERFECTLY PUNCTUALLY."*

Molly's guess had been a bull's-eye. This was not only the password that *Cell used*, it was also the one that had been used on *him*.

At once, Primo melted with obedience, and he said quite simply, "Lo—gan—is my—master."

Thirty-seven

Rocky's mouth opened so wide, someone could have pushed a large wedge of cheese into it. Sinclair looked as if he'd just swallowed a live eel. Petula looked as if she was growling too.

"You mean Lucy Logan is your master?" said Molly, trying to absorb this ghastly fact.

"Lucy Logan—is my master," confirmed Cell. "Almost everything I do is because Lucy—has ordered it so."

Molly felt the resistance to the time freeze again, closer than it had been before. Immediately, she let the cold fusion feeling drain, and outside, a helicopter that had been held in midflight continued on its way.

So Lucy Logan was the enemy. Lucy Logan, the quiet, sweet librarian whom they all thought Cell had hypnotized had actually, all along, been the master of

Cell. And if Sinclair was right, it was Lucy Logan who was creeping through the stopped world, searching for her prize automaton—and getting closer every minute. Molly was overcome with shock. That Lucy was the enemy was almost impossible to comprehend. It was the sourest, most hurtful discovery. She'd thought Lucy was her *friend*.

Everyone felt horribly jumpy. They didn't know what to do. Should they take Primo and make a run for it before Lucy reached the house? But where would they go? They couldn't risk a hypnotized president elect being spotted. Molly could practically hear the sirens blaring if they were caught.

But maybe the librarian wasn't heading toward the Hollywood Hills at all. Maybe she was still completely oblivious to the fact that Primo Cell had been taken. What they did all know was that their best chance of safety lay in finding out as much as they could from Cell.

"How do you know Lucy Logan?" asked Sinclair.

"We met—at college."

Molly was frantically running a series of impossible thoughts through her head. Had *Lucy* invented the magpie killer? Had *Lucy* planned that Molly and Rocky would be killed by it? Surely not. Lucy had wanted to *stop* Primo Cell's plans, hadn't she?

"And where is Lucy Logan from?" Molly asked, hoping madly that there might be two Lucy Logans.

"Lucy is—from Briersville."

Molly's head felt as if it was about to explode. This didn't make sense.

"Why would Lucy send me to destroy Primo Cell if she was behind all his actions?" Molly asked Rocky and Sinclair. "She was the one who made sure I found the hypnotism book and learned how to hypnotize people in the first place. Why would she have bothered letting me find the book if she planned to get rid of me?" Molly turned to Cell. "Do you know why Lucy sent me?"

The hypnotized Cell took a while to think about this; then he speculated, "It may have—been because of the—suspicious circumstances—around Davina—Nuttel. You see—I could not—hypnotize—Davina. And this—was out of the—ordinary. It was—the first—time I had ever failed. Perhaps—Lucy was suspicious—of me then. Perhaps she worried—that her hypnosis over *me*—was wearing off."

"Was it?"

"No."

"Then why couldn't you hypnotize Davina?" asked Molly.

"There was something haunting about her—her age.

Something—that reminded me of—something I had forgotten. I felt—almost—as if—I loved her—like a—daughter. My power was—displaced—by her. I couldn't hypnotize her, and—once she knew about—me, I couldn't have—her telling people—about me. So she—had to—be abducted. All this—I did without—Lucy Logan's orders. Perhaps Lucy sent you to—check that I wasn't doing *other*—things without her orders, too."

"When did you last see Lucy Logan?"

"Eleven and a half—years ago."

This was amazing. Eleven and a half years ago was before Molly was born.

"You mean she never even came to America to see you? She stayed in Briersville all that time?"

"She never came to see me. She traveled to many other parts of the world."

"How did she control you?"

"She spoke to me every week."

"And when did you last speak to her?" asked Molly.

"In—June. Just before I announced—that I was running—for president."

"But that was five months ago," said Rocky. "Why should she talk to him every week for eleven years and then *stop* talking to him in June?"

"Do you know the answers to these questions?"

Primo Cell shrugged.

"Perhaps—she felt—that by June—I could be trusted—and all was safely in—place for the—election campaign—so she felt she could leave me—to it."

"So once you were president, what was Lucy's plan then?" Molly asked.

"Her plan—was to become—first lady."

"First lady? What's that?"

"That's the title given to the president's wife," said Sinclair, letting out a whistle of amazement.

"My wife," said Primo blankly. "She planned—to meet me soon. We were to meet at a Books Build Brilliance—charity event and there—we were to fall in love. The—idea of a romantic—president was one—that she thought—would make me—even more popular with—the American people."

This was such a staggering notion that Molly, Rocky, and Sinclair all sat for a moment looking like their brains had been replaced with molasses.

"She's brilliant," said Sinclair in admiration. "All those years ago she hypnotized Primo to do her dirty work. To get rid of any rival hypnotists who might be a threat to her ambitions . . ."

"Except for you and Sally," Rocky pointed out.

"Well," mused Sinclair, "she must have wanted him to have some trained, tame hypnotists on his side—on her side." He fell glumly silent.

Poor Sinclair, Molly thought. The thought of how his life had been hijacked for one woman's selfish plan must be horrible.

"And then," Rocky continued, "she got Primo to get rich for her."

"He became so rich, he could spend millions more dollars than anyone else on his election campaign, and win," added Sinclair.

"Because," said Molly, "she wants to be the president's wife. She must have reckoned that by the time Primo was president, he'd be so rich and so powerful that it would be safe for her to step in. As first lady, she would travel with him everywhere. She'd be right beside him, breathing down his ear and whispering to him like a snake. It's not Primo who wants to take over the world, it's her!" Molly shook her head determinedly, as if to help it digest all the confusing facts that had suddenly piled up there. "All along," she said incredulously, "Lucy Logan was using me, and in the end she wanted me dead. And"—Molly stuck her tongue out in repugnance—"when I went to visit her in her cottage, everything she told me was lies. Her car crash, her plastered leg, her burned face—she made it all up to persuade me to help her."

Molly remembered that extraordinary Sunday afternoon. She thought about the rooms full of clocks, the secret, locked room with the bonsai trees on the table and the horrible silk shoes in the glass-fronted case—the shoes worn by Chinese girls who'd had their feet bound. They all went with Lucy Logan. She was a mind binder. Molly thought of the meticulously kept topiary hedges. Now, instead of imagining Lucy as a sweet person tending to her garden, Molly saw her as an insane control freak, slicing away at her hedges—to keep them under control and never let them be their own natural wild selves. Molly remembered the big bird bush. Had it been a magpie? Did it stand for Primo Cell? And the other bushy animals. Did they each stand for a person under Lucy's power? Then a horrendous thought struck Molly. Was she herself under Lucy Logan's power? Was she the bush bush baby?

"Do you think I'm hypnotized by Lucy?" she asked Rocky and Sinclair.

"No, I know you're not," said Sinclair. "I would have found out at Dune Beach if you were. But it's amazing that you're not."

"It is, isn't it?" agreed Molly. "I wonder why not."

"Just count your lucky stars. But . . ." Sinclair was suddenly aware of how little time they might have. "We'll think about all that later, Molly. Right now, we'd better concentrate on getting Cell deprogrammed."

This operation took a while, as they had to make

quite sure that there weren't any extra instructions stowed away in him behind different passwords. There weren't. Everything was locked by the "Perfectly punctually" password. It was amazing how much of Primo's life had been controlled. Molly began to feel sorry for him and wondered how he had fallen into Lucy Logan's web.

"But why did Lucy Logan chose *you*?" she asked.

"Because she—loved me once," said Primo. "At the university, she taught me—everything I know about hypnotism. She gave me my crystal. She—had great plans. Plans—to stop the world and to stop—suffering. To bring peace—to the planet. We were happy once."

"What happened? When did she start to go crazy?"

"After she had our baby," said Primo.

"Lucy Logan had a baby?" Molly said. The idea of the murderous new Logan as a mother didn't fit at all. Molly hadn't seen anything in her house that suggested she had a child. There weren't any toys or photographs.

"Poor kid. What a mother to have," said Rocky.

"Has her child grown up and left home?"

"Our baby never—lived at Lucy's house," said Primo. "Lucy took the child—to an orphanage. I never saw—my baby. Lucy—made sure—of that."

"How horrible of her," said Molly. "But which orphanage did she take her to? One in another town?"

Molly's mind had already sieved through every child whom she knew at the orphanage in Briersville. If the child was thirteen, then it might have been Cynthia, but Cynthia was a twin.

"Hardwick House," said Primo Cell.

Hardwick House! That was the name of the orphanage before Molly changed it to Happiness House. "Did she have twins?" Molly asked.

"No. Lucy had one child. One—baby girl."

Molly thought. It couldn't be Hazel. She'd arrived when she was six. Molly's heart suddenly throbbed in a thick, achy way, and she suddenly had the strange feeling she was awake in a dream.

"The child—would be eleven and—a half now," Primo Cell steamrolled on.

Molly felt imaginary arrows pivot all around her. Mentally she tried to dodge them, but however hard she tried, she couldn't get out of the firing line. The truth had arrived, as suddenly and as surprisingly as an exploding bolt of lightning.

"Was it . . . was she . . . delivered in a . . . in a . . . in a . . . in a . . ." Molly couldn't say it. She breathed in and tried again. "In a marshmallow box?"

"Maybe," said Primo matter-of-factly. "Lucy was—very fond of marshmallows—especially when she was pregnant. She ate—boxfuls."

"M . . . Moon's Marshmallows?" Molly didn't want to believe her ears.

"Yes. They were her—favorite brand," said Primo Cell with absolutely no emotion in his voice.

"No. No, it can't be true." Molly looked away.

Inside her head two voices began to vie for dominance.

Don't be an idiot—it's not true, one boomed angrily. *Why trust this man? It's not true.*

Don't be stupid, the other voice yelled. *What more evidence do you need? The truth is staring you in the face.* Molly put her hands up to her head to stop the deafening noise. Rocky put his hand on her arm.

"You've found your parents," he said quietly. Molly gripped his hand.

"But . . . I don't believe it. I don't want to believe it," she said, appalled.

Molly felt totally cheated. Like a person who'd been asking for a certain special thing all her life, and it had suddenly been given to her, but on opening it she'd discovered it was wrong. Molly didn't like her present. Yet she couldn't return it. It was a one-way, you'll-just-have-to-live-with-it present.

"Look who they are, Rocky. I didn't want to find my parents here . . . now . . . like this. I don't want *them* as my parents."

"You've always been looking, Molly," Rocky reminded her. "We both have. You're lucky. Now you know who your parents are."

"But my mother is a maniac!" Molly cried. "I don't *want* her."

Primo stared blankly into space.

"I'm not going to tell him I'm his daughter. I don't want to," said Molly, shuddering at the idea. She clutched Rocky's sleeve. "And I especially don't *ever* want to meet *her* again."

"You don't have to tell him who you are," said Rocky. "You can bring him out of his trance now and he'll never know. But Molly, it's probably the greatest sadness of his life that he never met you. Remember, he was only *hypnotized* not to care." Then he added, "Do you remember what he said about Davina? He said there was something about her that helped him feel things, even though he was forbidden to feel. He said it was something about her—her age—that reminded him of something he'd forgotten. '*I felt almost as if I loved her like a daughter. My power was displaced by her.*' Do you remember him saying that? Even though Lucy Logan hypnotized Primo to forget you, Davina reminded him of you. Do you see that, Molly? He never completely forgot you."

Molly nodded, but she was too upset to speak. She picked up Petula and left the room to think.

★ ★ ★

For the next half hour, Rocky and Sinclair finished deprogramming Cell. They told him that he now had access to all his feelings, that he was completely out of Lucy Logan's grasp, that he was free. Rocky left Primo with all his knowledge of hypnotism. And then they took him to Sinclair's bedroom and told him to sleep.

Sinclair looked at the prone body of Primo collapsed on the circular bed. "He's dog tired because of what's happened to him," he observed. "He probably feels like sleeping for a century. We must let him rest for as long as possible, so that when he wakes, his mind has properly absorbed the deprogramming. And Rocky, as far as the rest of the country goes, Primo Cell is still the president elect. We must keep him hidden in here, because if Lucy Logan was to get to him *before* he announced that he was not going to be president, she'd still have a chance of carrying out her plans. We'll lock him in my room for safety. When he's conscious again, and his head is clear, we'll get him down to Iceberg Studios and he can declare on TV that he no longer wants to be president. As soon as we've done that, Logan's lost."

So they closed the door on Cell and turned the key. Rocky felt sorry for the man. When he woke, he'd have to come to terms with the fact that Lucy Logan had stolen eleven years of his life and used them for herself.

Molly reeled from the succession of shocks that had battered her. That Lucy had betrayed her, that Lucy was behind Primo Cell, was a bad enough shock. The fact that Lucy was her mother, a mother who had wanted her dead, and that Primo was her father, was a shock of such high voltage that Molly wasn't quite sure how to cope. Rocky couldn't help her. She needed to be alone. She went upstairs to sit in the sunlight, on the roof of Sinclair's house.

Thirty-eight

Molly spent the next few hours with Petula, sitting quietly on the warm sun deck on the top of Sinclair's house. She did her best to come to terms with her mammoth discoveries.

She tried to breathe deeply and calmly. She shut her eyes and drifted off, just as Forest had taught her, and in her imagination, she looked down on herself. In her mind, as she floated far above Los Angeles, a thick red line connected her to Primo Cell, and another glowing red line joined her to Lucy Logan, wherever she was. Molly realized that these lines had always been there, but she hadn't seen them before. Molly hated the line that joined her to Logan. But no amount of wishing could make the line go away. Molly was connected to her, whether she liked it or not. That ruthless, evil woman was her mother.

To make herself feel better, Molly imagined special golden lines connecting her to the people whom she knew and loved best: Rocky, Mrs. Trinklebury, Gemma and Gerry, and little Ruby and Jinx. Molly sent silver lines, bronze lines, green, purple, and blue lines swooping away from her. They all helped blot out the horrible red one that shot toward Lucy Logan.

Lucy Logan. Molly hated her very name.

When Logan found out that her plans had been foiled, she would definitely try to pull everything back on track. She'd try to make Primo her puppet again. She'd try to hypnotize him. She'd try to hypnotize all of them. Molly dreaded to think how strong her hypnotic powers were.

Molly let herself fly all the way up into space, until she was aware of her body as a microscopic cell on the surface of the earth. It was as if her mind was drifting, looking down at the spot where her body, her Molly Moon body, was. From her lofty vantage, she imagined where Logan's body might be. She shut her eyes and concentrated hard, but at the same time, she let her mind relax. Molly looked down across to the hazy San Gabriel Mountains, but she had no sense of Logan being there. Molly looked southwest to Santa Monica Beach, but her instinct told her that Logan wasn't there either. Now she swiveled her mind's eye directly below her, to Hollywood. She felt a kind of radarlike certainty that Logan was there. And, as if turning the lens on a telescope, Molly focused her imagination. She zoomed in on the place where she could picture Logan. Her mind became brighter. Sunlight and a bird's-eye view of green trees filled it. Then her mental vision conjured up a view of the top of Logan's head. Molly breathed in and let the strange apparition expand. She saw Logan walking up a path flanked by geranium bushes and pepper trees.

All at once, Molly knew that she had imagined the path to Sinclair's house. And in the next moment, as she opened her eyes, she realized that the vision in her head was not imaginary but true.

The front doorbell rang. Molly could hear Sinclair's voice answering the intercom.

"Hello?"

"Sinclair," came a woman's deep voice. "Sinclair, I wonder whether you might come downstairs. I'm an old friend of your father's, and I'd like to get in touch with him. My name's Lucy Logan."

Molly sat up as if she'd been stung and put her hand around Petula's mouth in case she should bark.

"I'm sorry," she heard Sinclair reply. "But if you'd like to get in touch with Primo Cell, I suggest you make an appointment with his secretary."

"But, Sinclair, I have to speak . . ." The intercom clunked as it disconnected. Molly heard a frustrated sigh from below. Lucy had been left on the doorstep. Molly craned her neck and heard crunching steps walking away from the house. And as soon as she thought there was no risk of being seen, she scuttled through the hatch of the sun deck and bolted it behind her, and she and Petula sped down the steep stairs into the safety of the house.

At the bottom, they bumped straight into Sinclair and Rocky. Molly jumped.

"Molly, I've got—"

"I know. Bad news. She's here, I heard her."

"She must know Primo's here," said Sinclair in a panic, pacing forward and backward on the spot. Molly had never seen him look so scared. "Did you see where she went?"

"It sounded like she was setting off through the garden," said Molly.

"Is Primo's bedroom locked?" asked Sinclair.

Rocky tapped his pocket. "You locked it yourself."

"I've locked the back door too. There's no way she can get in. You two had better keep away from the windows."

"Maybe we should wake Primo up and get him out of

here right now," said Molly.

"Far too risky," Sinclair replied instantly. "He'll still be semiconscious. We might damage the deprogramming. Anyway, who knows what we might meet on the road." Sinclair started rubbing his fingers together as if he was fiddling with a piece of invisible putty.

The minutes passed. They stayed where they were, outside the entrance to the sitting room, all fighting the fear that was crawling up their spines.

"Do you think she's got other people out there?" asked Molly, chewing her sleeve. "I mean, she may have a small army, ready to ambush us."

All at once, Molly and Sinclair felt a coolness on the surface of their skins beneath their crystals, and a chill flickered through their bodies. Molly grabbed Rocky and, as the world froze, she helped him resist it. Outside, the traffic on the road in the valley ceased. The water in the fountain that fed Sinclair's lap pool stopped in midflow. Petula was still. Everywhere was silence.

"What's she up to?" Rocky said.

"The feeling's coming from over there." Molly stepped into the sitting room with Rocky and pointed to where the trees hid the road farther down the hill.

"I think we've got to grab Primo and leave now," said Rocky. "If she's on the far side of the house, we can get him into the car without being seen. Probably."

"Maybe we should risk it," Sinclair agreed.

Just as suddenly, the world started moving again.

"Whatever it was that she needed to stop time for, she's done it now," said Molly. "I'm not sure we should leave. I mean, she doesn't know Primo's here. She doesn't know Rocky and I are here—she thinks we're dead. If we leave now, we might come face to face with her or some cop she's hypnotized. She'd have Primo taken from us. And who knows what she'll do with us? We'll have more of a chance if we wait for her to come to the door. Here, we have the advantage of surprise. I can use my eyes on her."

They all perched uncomfortably at the back of the room on some star-shaped, wire-mesh chairs that weren't really designed to be sat on. Everyone expected the doorbell to ring again at any moment. Rocky picked at a hole in his jeans, making it twice as big. Sinclair scrolled through numbers on his cell phone as if looking at them would give him the answer as to what he should do next. Molly stared at the narrow channel of water that ran along the side of the huge room to the fountain where it was filled. The constant fountain splashed quietly but did nothing to diffuse the tension. Ripples from the opposite direction met the fountain's flow and made the water swish against the edges of the lap pool. Molly's eyes followed the channel as it curved toward the window, and she realized, with a nauseating lurch, that there was an entry to the house they had all overlooked. Then she saw, to her horror, where the ripples were coming from. Someone was swimming in the lap pool. Like a duck in a fairground's shooting gallery, Lucy Logan's head was forging its way through the water, toward them.

Thirty-nine

Slowly, the head started to rise, and like a killing water beast, Lucy Logan rose, dripping, from the water, a silver pistol clenched between her teeth. She no longer wore the bandages and the plaster cast that had covered her in Briersville. Petula began to bark and bark.

Lucy fixed Sinclair, Molly, and Rocky with a cold, petrifying glare. She looked very unlike the Briersville librarian whom Molly had known. She was still dressed in a tweed skirt and sensible cardigan—these were now sopping wet—and her blond hair was styled, as it had always been, into a bun on top of her head, but she looked disturbingly different. Her eyes had lost all their kindness, and her nose looked more hooked.

"Don't look at her eyes," gasped Sinclair. No one

needed to be reminded. Molly had already fixed her eyes on the gun, now in Lucy Logan's hand.

"And don't listen to her."

"But she's got a gun," Molly said, as if no one else had noticed it.

"And it's loaded," said Lucy, as calmly as if she was about to start a guided tour of the house. She pointed the pistol at Petula. "Stop that dog barking or I'll shoot it." Molly snatched up Petula and silenced her, instinctively stepping away from Lucy. Sinclair and Rocky moved with her.

"Where is he?" Logan asked, raising her weapon. "You might as well let me have him, or I'll kill you and find him anyway."

"You'll kill us whatever happens," said Sinclair.

Molly gulped. The idea of a bullet, a hard steel bullet puncturing her body at lightning speed, was terrifying. But mixed with this fear was a thought that tantalized her. The madwoman standing in front of her was her mother.

Logan raised the gun.

"If you shoot, then you'll *never* find out where Cell is," Molly lied. "We've deprogrammed him and he's somewhere so safe that even *you* won't be able to find him."

Lucy Logan lowered the revolver. She glanced

toward the kitchen and the other door that led off the room. Sinclair's bedroom. She walked toward it, keeping her gun aimed at everyone. She tried the door handle, which held fast. Loudly, but as nicely as if she was about to tell him his lunch was ready, she called, "Primo?"

"What is it?" came Primo's groggy reply. Logan smiled slyly.

"No doubt one of you has the key," she said politely. Molly stared at her. It was amazing how now, because she hated her, Lucy seemed far uglier than she had remembered her.

"He's deprogrammed," said Molly. "You won't ever have power over him again."

"You underestimate my influence," said Lucy coolly. "Just as I underestimated your luck."

"You thought the magpie killed me and Rocky ages ago, didn't you?" said Molly.

"Yes. I should have taken the precaution of leaving some hypnotic instruction in you, just in case you did survive."

"You *never* could have hypnotized me that day at your cottage. I was too alert," said Molly defiantly.

"Oh, I could have, if I'd tried," said Lucy. "I should have. It would have been a lot less tiresome now if you were still under my thumb. But the chances of a specimen like you surviving Cell were so slim." Petula growled.

"Slim in your eyes, but your microscope's obviously broken," said Molly. Logan ignored her and pointed her gun at Sinclair.

"And I suppose you had something to do with their escape. I remember seeing pictures of you, Sinclair, when you were a ragged little circus boy. Primo and I were wrong about you. I thought you had potential. I thought you were trustworthy. And you," she said, looking at Rocky. "Perhaps you were more talented than I realized." Lucy's hard blue eyes scanned them all contemptuously.

"You do realize that I have to dispose of you all, one way or another. So which is it to be? My eyes or the bullet? It's your decision."

No one spoke. Patience certainly wasn't one of her virtues, for fed up with no answer, Logan said abruptly, "Actually, I'm sick of the lot of you. I'm going to shoot you all. Good-bye." She pointed her gun at Rocky.

Molly saw Lucy's finger moving to squeeze the revolver's trigger. In the same instant she realized that this was no game. Lucy Logan was about to shoot Rocky. With a speed that Molly didn't know she had, she drew the cold fusion feeling from the air itself and instantaneously stopped the world. In that slice of time, the first nanosecond of a loud bang hit her ears.

Everything stood still. Except for Logan, Molly, Petula, and Sinclair. A bullet three inches from Rocky's throat hung like a frozen missile in the air. Logan smiled and pointed her gun at Molly.

"Good timing," she said. "Try to stop this one."

Molly was confused. She was already holding the world still. Could she stop it again? She watched Lucy's wrist, trying to sense when she would squeeze the trigger again. Sinclair dived behind a chair.

Molly saw the tendon on Lucy's thick wrist rise slightly, and she chose her moment. Again, time stopped. Molly had judged it perfectly. This time, a bullet hung in the air midway between her and Lucy. This bullet was on its way to Molly's chest.

"Hhhmmm," commented Lucy. "That one would have hit you in the heart."

Molly couldn't give in to her numbing fear. She had to remain lucid, or she would be dead. She hadn't known until now that time could be stopped on top of already frozen time. She looked at Sinclair to see his reaction, but now he was a statue too, like Rocky. Molly quickly put Petula down behind the sofa, where she also went rigid.

Molly wondered how many times she would be able to

stop the world. But there wasn't long to wonder, because Lucy was about to kill her. She fired her third bullet. Again Molly froze time. For a moment Logan and Molly were both distracted as they resisted the freeze.

Logan took a moment to adjust to the new time; then she snarled, "You're waning, Moon." She fired again.

A fourth bullet. A fifth bullet. Terror swept through Molly as Logan pointed the gun at her head, at her heart, at her stomach. Molly trembled as she stopped the world for the eighth time. She was almost too late. A bullet hung suspended in the air, an inch from her forehead. Molly threw herself behind the sofa.

"You've only got a few more bullets," she shouted through the icy fog that was beginning to rise from the water and fill the room.

"You've been watching too many films. I've just reloaded," said Logan. Molly glanced around the side of her hiding place. Logan saw her and another shot rang out, the sound cut off instantly as Molly froze everything once more. Molly shivered. Logan shivered. The room was starting to feel very, very cold.

"You're a coward," said Molly, panting. "This would be fair only if I had a gun too."

"I'm not a coward," said Logan. "I just like to have an unfair advantage, that's all. After all, I have to win, Molly."

Logan frowned. She really didn't want to play cat and mouse with this girl. She wanted this business over. All this time stopping was very tiring. She had never suspected that Molly might be this good. To stop the world over and over required extreme focus of mind. Logan had never thought a child would be able to do it. But she also knew that, like folding a piece of paper over and over again, eventually folding time would become impossible. Logan knew that, in the end, Molly would have no way to dodge her bullets. So, although Logan's strength was being tested to the fullest, she also knew that she would win. She raised her gun.

Molly's teeth were chattering. Each time she forced the cold fusion feeling outward, it was as if the world sucked heat out of her body. Now the icy mist was shrouding everything in the room. Lucy Logan's body was just visible, but Molly could barely detect the movement of her finger against the trigger of the gun. She was *sensing* as much as seeing when Logan was about to fire.

Lucy Logan's vision was becoming blurred too. Her hearing was fuzzy. It was as if she was in a cold airplane at a very high altitude. She fired at Molly but, on stumbling toward her, found that the shape she'd shot at was a coat on a chair and not Molly at all. She saw an indistinct figure move to her left.

The world froze again—froze this time before Logan

had fired. As Logan resisted it, her legs went numb with cold. She grabbed at something to steady herself. They must be nearing the impossible fold now. If she was weakening, the child must surely be about to collapse. Lucy had the advantage. She had trained her mind for years. She would win this contest—she knew she would. She felt for her crystal under her wet cardigan—colder than ice. With great effort she spoke.

"So, Molly, orphan Molly, how would you feel if I told you that I know who your mother and father are?"

From behind a chair near the window, Molly replied, "I'd say the news was out of date. You're too late, Logan. I know . . . I know that you are my mother and I know that Cell is my father, and don't worry, I've already disowned you."

Molly was fighting for her life. Her backbone felt cold as an icicle. As if it might snap. The chill of the crystal against her neck bored into her skin, as if it was freezing her very soul. Molly thought how much she hated Lucy Logan. She couldn't believe a person could be so crazy, so bad. But what made it all a thousand times worse was that the foul human being brandishing the pistol was Molly's flesh and blood. All Molly's life she'd wanted to know who her mother was. She'd dreamed of a kind, intelligent, funny person. The reality was this megalomaniac killer. Molly hated her for ruining her dreams. She would not let Logan end her life, too. But she was so cold . . . so very cold . . . and so tired.

Molly shut her eyes. Behind the lids, she saw herself in the room with Lucy. Then, as was so natural to her, she imagined herself shooting away from her body like a rocket into space. In a millisecond she was there.

This time, space was different. Molly saw the whole world, still, below her. She saw the planets around her stopped in their orbits, the stars in the solar systems halted for a moment in time.

Molly sensed space around her stretching forever, for an eternity. In this frozen vastness, she felt herself tinier than tiny, like a speck of dust, smaller than that. She felt herself so small that she was practically nothing. She had found inside herself the nanu of small.

And yet . . .

Molly's feelings of smallness switched. Suddenly Molly was impressed by how big she was. Because of her, the universe was held up. Because of her, all the elements—earth, air, fire, and water—were stilled. Molly felt small, then very, very big, and again, nanu small and gigantically big. Molly felt completely at one with the universe, and an enormous feeling of love for everything in it filled her.

She sensed, far, far below her, Lucy Logan's movement

on the world. Then the world seemed to make an offering to Molly—an idea—the idea of the North Pole. Ice, she realized, didn't feel cold. If she zoned into the essence of ice, perhaps then she too wouldn't feel cold anymore. She let her mind relax, she let her body relax into the ice. And suddenly Molly didn't feel cold at all. The crystal round her neck felt warm. Molly knew that she could stop time again.

With her eyes shut, and as easily as if she was blowing out a candle, Molly stopped time for the eighteenth time. Now, with every breath she took, she drew time to a standstill. For the nineteenth time, breathe out, breathe in. For the twentieth time, breathe out, breathe in . . . for the twenty-first time.

Molly felt no more resistance. Molly was the only moving thing in the universe. Life everywhere was still. Molly felt as alone as if she was dead, except she wasn't dead, she was alive. For a second she wondered whether she *was* alone. Was she the only conscious creature in the realms of space and time? Molly felt that although everywhere was still, the essence of life, the force inside and outside her, was watching her. And the mysterious force seemed to be thanking her.

Molly opened her eyes. Now, instead of being misty and cold, the room was full of color. It was clear and still. And Lucy Logan was frozen with a look of hatred on her face.

Molly walked around the room and carefully picked each frozen bullet from its hovering position. She threw them all out of the window. Then she took the gun out of Lucy Logan's hand and checked her clothes for any more weapons. And she took the crystal from Lucy's neck.

Satisfied that her enemy was no longer armed, Molly brought her eyes up to their hypnotic peak. She positioned herself so that Logan's eyes were looking straight into hers. Then, touching her shoulder, she let movement flow into her again.

If Lucy Logan had any energy left to combat Molly's, it was sapped in a second. Before she even became conscious of being alert, before she realized that she had frozen and started moving again, Molly's eyes had overpowered hers.

Lucy Logan was hypnotized.

Forty

"You are now completely under my power," said Molly. "Is that understood?"

Lucy Logan nodded, and Molly looked at her face, trying to see whether there was any likeness between herself and this horrible creature. Logan's jaw was much heavier and her face was much bonier than Molly had remembered. Her body was wiry. Molly hoped this wasn't how she would turn out when she grew up.

"From now on," she declared, "you will accept that all the plans that you had before this meeting will never be carried out. You now have everything you need. You will not remember how to hypnotize anyone or anything. You will not remember how to stop the world. When you come out of this trance, you will behave as nicely as . . ." Molly tried to think of something that was always sweet-tempered. ". . . as a lamb." Molly paused. The next step would be essential for someone as dangerous as Lucy Logan. "And these instructions will be locked inside you forever by some words that you won't remember. These words will be . . ." Molly glanced at the coffee table. "Moon's Marshmallows." Then she added, "And when I clap my hands, you will wake up."

Molly let go of Lucy's shoulder, and immediately the librarian froze again. At last, she stood still with her arms by her side and she relaxed. She let the cold fusion feeling flow out of her fingertips, out of her body. The layers of freeze that she had forced onto time melted, until the time stop that had captured Rocky and Sinclair and Petula released them and the whole world, too. Molly collapsed on the sofa.

Rocky and Sinclair took a second to register where everyone was.

"It's okay," said Molly. "She didn't shoot any of us. And she's safe now."

Logan smiled benignly at them all and said, "Baa, baaaaa, baaaaaaaaa."

Rocky threw a cushion up in the air.

"Whooooa, Molly, you've done it!"

Molly laid her head on the back of the sofa. "Yup, I

sure have. But wow, that was tiring."

Sinclair picked up Logan's silver pistol from the table and examined it. Then he took it away to lock it in a cupboard.

Rocky sat next to Molly and put his hand on her arm.

"Thanks, Molly," he said.

Primo began to knock on the bedroom door.

"Is that Lucy?" he said. "What's going on out there?"

"We can let him out now," said Molly. Rocky opened the door.

"Is Lucy Logan here?" Primo said, stepping out. "Where is she?" He glanced at Lucy and then all round the room. "Where?"

Molly looked at the woman who had hypnotized Cell for all these years. Obviously he hadn't seen her for so long that he didn't recognize her.

"There she is," said Molly. "She's got older."

"Don't be ridiculous," said Primo Cell. "This isn't Lucy. This person is . . . an imposter." And marching over to her, he grabbed her by the arm.

"Who are you? Where is the real Lucy Logan?" he demanded aggressively.

In a lamb's voice, the person baaed, "She's at Briersville Park."

Molly was stunned. She studied the woman in front of her, and it was suddenly completely clear that this wasn't the Lucy Logan Molly knew at all. This person bore a very strong resemblance to her, but her features were much rougher. Her nose was bigger. Her build was wirier. Molly had thought Lucy had looked uglier than the kind woman she had met in the library, but she hadn't questioned it. Now, as she scanned this face and body, it was obvious that they weren't Lucy's. *And so this person was not her mother.*

"Is the real Lucy safe?" Molly asked.

"Yes, she's locked up nice and safe."

"And so who are you?"

"I," said the person sweetly, and then, as if finding the words difficult to utter, stated, "I am C-Corn . . . elius Logan."

"C-Cornelius? But—but that's a man's name," Molly stammered.

"Yes, that is true." The person's voice suddenly dropped to a low, male tone. "Of course it is a ram's name. I am a ram."

Forty-one

"A what?" asked Rocky, his eyebrows nearly shooting off his forehead. "You're kidding.

Cornelius Logan nodded. "It's true. I am a ram," he said, and he began to skip around the room, as if telling everyone was a great relief to him. "Baaaa," he bleated as he trotted past the panoramic window seat. Petula growled at him.

"A man? But why?"

"Because that was how I was when I was born," declared Cornelius Logan, cantering around the sofa.

"Cornelius Logan!" said Primo Cell. "I haven't heard that name in years." He turned to the others. "He's Lucy Logan's twin brother. That's why he looks like her—like a badly drawn version of Lucy."

Everyone stared at the strange creature who now pawed at the ground with an imaginary hoof. His Lucy Logan disguise, which for the last twenty minutes had convinced them—the hair in a bun, the sensible librarian's skirt, and the sweater set and pearls—was now starting to come apart. As he shook his head, his wig slipped sideways. Then, as he began galloping along the edge of the lap pool, he hitched up his wet skirt and everyone saw that the legs underneath were hairy and sinewy and not female legs at all. When he tore off his cardigan, to reveal a short-sleeved sweater, he also uncovered his muscly arms.

Molly's mind zoomed back to that afternoon in March—to Cornelius dressed as Lucy Logan in the Briersville cottage.

Suddenly she saw how brilliantly this man had fooled her. The plaster cast on his leg and the bandages had been a clever distraction. Cornelius had known that children are taught not to stare at anyone with something wrong with them. And, of course, Molly hadn't wanted to stare at his injured face. Instead, she'd looked at the pink nail-polished toenails sticking out of the end of his plaster cast, and she'd been duped. Molly thought hard. There *must* have been some clue. Suddenly she remembered how *low* Cornelius's voice had been that night she'd called him from the hotel—she'd caught him unawares.

"Do you normally wear *men's* clothes?" she asked him.

"Of course I do. Do you think I *like* dressing as a woman?" brayed Cornelius. "Do you think I *liked* putting on that stupid high voice?" He laughed with mad relief. "Baa baaaaaah! I *had* to become Lucy, I had to do it to get Molly Moon out here to investigate Cell. It was very necessary to investigate Cell, you see. He was behaving so oddly—not being able to hypnotize Davina—and then there was the kidnaping that I never authorized. And, of course, I had to stay behind to weaken Lucy again." Cornelius pawed the ground.

"Again? What do you mean?"

"The real Lucy Logan," explained Cornelius with a bleat, "my sister Lucy, was under my power for years. For eleven and a half years. The same time as Cell. I had Cell *and* her under my power. It was genius. It was wonderful. I was planning to send Lucy out to marry him. She was going to be the president's wife. And *I*, Cornelius, would have controlled them both. Baaaaha ha ha."

At this point, Primo Cell sat down. He had turned a pale shade of olive green. "I think I'm going to be sick," he said. And with that, he lurched toward Sinclair's bathroom.

"Poor man," said Rocky.

"This must all be a horrible shock for him," said Molly.

Cornelius, oblivious of Cell's troubles, continued, "All was going well—until Lucy met that Molly Moon in the library."

Molly thought of their first ever meeting. "What happened then?" she demanded.

"Well, something that I had not counted on," brayed Cornelius. "Even though I'd hypnotized—her to forget—her daughter, and even though I'd done a—permanent hypnosis on Lucy, when she—met her daughter, Molly Moon, and talked to her, the—locked-in hypnosis for some reason started to *unlock* itself. Can you imaha ha ha gine?"

Molly felt a lump in her throat.

"As soon as she remembered the bah bah baby," said Cornelius, "Lucy challenged me—which was foolish—of her—as I, of course, was in a position to overpower her. She—always was led by her heart. Such a stupid woman. She should—have used her head."

"What did you do with her and when was that?" asked Molly.

"I locked her in a room—at Briersville Park. That was at the beginning of January. Ever since then—I've been trying—to weaken her—and then hypnotize her again so that—my plans could be put—back on track. Do you think I wanted to wear—women's clothes—forever?" Cornelius laughed madly and ripped at his pearls. The string broke, and they flew all over the floor like spilled beans. "I should never—have let that—bah, Molly Moon—find the hypnotism book."

"Why did you let her find it?"

"Because I was impatient to see—what her power as a hypnotist—was. I put her in that orphanage all those years ago—bah—so that she wouldn't grow up—normally. I wanted her—hard. I waited eleven years until—baaaah—her powers would be starting to grow. Then I let her find the book. Baaaah. What—a fool I was. She was too like—her mother to—ever be of—use to me. And, of course, she was more powerful than me—I was a twin—so my powers were diluted with my—sister's, but Molly Moon's were concentrated. How blind I was—I never should have used her to check on—Cell. I never thought her powers would be so strong—so soon." Violently Cornelius began pulling at his sweater.

"I think you'd better give him something to wear," Molly said to Sinclair. "He's so eager to get back to his real self that he'll have nothing on in a minute." Indeed, Cornelius Logan had already peeled off his sweater to reveal a strange bodysuit underneath. It was stuffed to make him look as if he had breasts.

"Incredible!" said Rocky. "He didn't half go to town on his disguise."

"He had to," said Sinclair, who was by now laughing with relief. "Here, Cornelius, go into my room and help yourself to some of my clothes. There's a blue tracksuit hanging up in the wardrobe that will fit you."

Cornelius made a beeline for Sinclair's bedroom. As he disappeared, Molly looked at Rocky and both of them started to laugh. The sight of Cornelius charging round the room taking his clothes off had been very unexpected and a bit shocking, but now it was so funny, they couldn't stop giggling.

After five minutes they were still in stitches.

"It's not *that* funny," said Sinclair. But Molly and Rocky didn't even hear him, and when Cornelius came out dressed in a tracksuit with his wig and makeup still on and began to nibble at a potted fern by the TV set, they started laughing all over again.

Finally they got a grip on themselves.

"Phew," said Molly. "I mean, for a while I thought that guy was my mother."

"Yeah, it was bad news," Rocky said. "At least this way, he's only your uncle." And they began giggling again.

Their hysteria was really their way of letting off a lot

of steam. Ever since they'd arrived in Los Angeles, Molly and Rocky had been under pressure. It was really good to feel free at last.

When they'd got their laughter out of their systems, Molly went to the kitchen and fixed herself a ketchup sandwich and half a glass of concentrated grenadine. Rocky made himself a potato-chip sandwich and poured himself a Qube. When they came back, Sinclair was questioning Cornelius, and relaxing on the sofa, they listened to the truth as it tumbled from Cornelius's lipstick-stained mouth.

Cornelius Logan had gotten into the lap pool from the road that ran under Sinclair's aqueduct. He stopped the world in order to position a truck so that it was the perfect platform from which to climb up. That small question dealt with, Sinclair demanded answers to much bigger questions.

Although the real Lucy Logan had lived in the Briersville cottage, from where, in her hypnotized state, she'd done research work for Cornelius, *he* lived in Briersville Park, an enormous stately home outside the town. From there, he'd masterminded his operations. He'd spent years laying the foundations of his power, so that in many other countries he already controlled the heads of police, the heads of armies, the editors of newspapers, and the owners of TV stations.

But the hub of his ingenious strategy was in America. Cornelius planned that Primo Cell, his hypnotized president, would marry the quiet, unassuming librarian, the hypnotized Lucy Logan. As soon as she had moved into the White House as first lady, then he, Cornelius, would move in too. From that moment on, Cornelius would have traveled the world with his twin sister and her husband, President Cell.

"We would have been—an invincible—baaaah—threesome. I would have been supremely powerful. Other countries would have, bahhh, bound themselves to— America, and one day—it would have been—re—bah— named Logania."

They heard how Cornelius had been insanely jealous of his twin. Indeed, when, all those years ago, Lucy Logan had been expecting a baby, Cornelius had been so jealous of her happiness that he'd hypnotized her future husband, the young American Primo Cell, and after Lucy had given birth to the baby, he'd taken advantage of her exhausted mind and hypnotized her, too.

He'd got rid of the baby girl, putting her in an old marshmallow box and leaving her on the doorstep of Hardwick House orphanage. And that was how it all started.

When he'd finished his story, Cornelius's eyes were fluttering, exhausted, and his head kept lolling on his shoulders.

"I was never any good with people, bahhhh."

Molly was sick of hearing his voice. She loathed this cruel person who had shaped her whole life.

"Well, from now on, you will forget your past," she said suddenly, "and you will be happy to do that. And now you will have a long sleep. When you wake up, I don't want to hear another word about your horrible life, unless I ask it of you."

Cornelius Logan nodded and, curling up on the floor by the fire, he slumped into a deep sleep. Molly pulled a blanket over herself and stared at the flames, her thoughts broken only by Cornelius's incoherent mutterings.

"Baaaah," he brayed. "Nooooo," he begged. And "Please don't eat me," he bleated.

Forty-two

When Molly woke up, the light outside was
dusky. She had slept so heavily that one side
of her face was hot and red. As she opened
her eyes, she saw Cornelius Logan still in a pile on the
floor. Rocky and Primo were sitting at the coffee table
drinking something from mugs, and behind them Los
Angeles glittered, electric. Primo looked weary. He was
telling Rocky about things that he had done under
Cornelius's spell. Molly wrapped her blanket around
her and shuffled over to sit down beside them. For a
moment she wondered whether Rocky had told Primo
that Molly was his daughter. Then, knowing that of
course Rocky wouldn't have done this, she relaxed.

"Hi, you're up," said Primo, smiling. He pointed at
Cornelius. "I expect he's got jet lag."

"Hypno lag," suggested Molly.

"He was a bit of a hypno *hag*, wasn't he?" said Rocky, and everyone laughed.

"And what a hag," said Primo more seriously. "It's going to take me a long time to come to terms with the fact that I have lived like a radio-controlled robot for eleven years. I would have lived my life a lot differently if I hadn't been on Cornelius Logan's string."

Molly and Rocky didn't know what to say to make him feel better. They both knew how cheated they had felt to have someone take away their time and choose how they should spend it. Primo, they supposed, would have enjoyed himself some of the time, but unlike them, he had been forced to behave really badly.

"Try and think of the nice things that have happened to you," suggested Molly. "I mean, you've made lots of friends. Now you can *really* make friends with them."

"They were hypnotized to like me, Molly. When I release them, they won't see me as successful and amusing and brilliant anymore."

"Some of them might."

"Maybe."

"And look, you've got lots of good businesses that you still own and you can still run them. You still have your TV stations. And you can do lots of stuff that Cornelius Logan never allowed you to do."

"That's true."

"And you're very, very rich," said Rocky. "At least you've got tons of money."

"You can't buy time," said Primo morosely. "I've had eleven years ripped away from me. And worse than that, you can't buy love. Nobody loves me. Nobody. I haven't even got a dog or a goldfish that loves me."

Molly felt very sorry for Primo, because what he said was true. She didn't know how to cheer him up. She certainly wasn't going to tell him that she was his long-lost daughter. She didn't want a big soppy scene.

"Listen, Primo," she tried. "I feel sorry for you, and you know what? I don't think I could feel sorry for you if I didn't love you *a bit*."

"Same here," said Rocky.

"Love has to start somewhere, and as you can see, it's started in both of us, for you, if you see what I mean. So you're not alone. You've got us." Petula made a little comforting *woof* noise, as if she loved Primo just a bit too.

"Thanks, you three," said Primo. "But I don't deserve it." His face darkened and he shuddered involuntarily. "I'm sorry. I keep remembering things that have happened and suddenly they fill me up with horrible feelings and, oh . . ." Primo shut his eyes in pain.

"It's because you weren't allowed to feel anything for

years," said Molly. "Cornelius barred you from feeling anything. So now the feelings are all tumbling out of the cages they've been kept in."

Primo sighed sorrowfully. "They sure are," he said. "I can't believe what I've done."

Molly looked at her father. For the next few years, she realized, he was going to be a basket case. There was no way that she, Rocky, and Sinclair could handle him on their own. Then she remembered Forest.

Molly found Forest downstairs eating alfalfa sprouts and unwrapping some healing crystals that he'd bought.

"Hey, Molly," he said. "Glad you're here. You can help hang up this body map. Look, if you have a headache, you can get rid of it by pressing the ball of your big toe."

It turned out that Forest knew all about Primo Cell and hypnotism. In fact it was he who had encouraged Sinclair to break away from his father. When Forest learned how Cornelius had stolen years of Cell's life away, he rolled his eyes and chuckled.

"Whooooa. Some people are crazy as headless chickens." And when Molly asked him to help Primo recover, he replied, "Molly, that would be my cosmic pleasure."

"Of course, it won't all be nice," said Molly. "He has done lots of bad things. He even tried to kill us."

"Killin' people's not good," said Forest, "But don't forget, Cell was not in control of himself when he did that. I can handle it, Molly, don't you worry. Remember—I've lived with cannibals."

Molly gave Forest a hug.

"And will you help sort out Davina Nuttel, too? Work out how we can put her back without her knowing where she's been and all that?"

"If you'd like me to," said Forest.

"And Forest," she asked, "would you do me one last favor? Please don't tell Primo that I'm his daughter. I just don't want all that heavy stuff right now. I'm kind of happy the way I am."

"You bet you are," said Forest, passing her a piece of ginger tofu turnip. "You, Molly, are one cool kid."

"Thanks, Forest," said Molly, taking a lump of the gunky vegetable. "That looks . . . *interesting*. I'll take it upstairs and eat it there."

Forty-three

Molly and Rocky were dying to be reunited with all their friends from the orphanage as soon as possible. And the following day, the perfect opportunity offered itself.

Thunder Roll, the film that Petula had costarred in, directed by Gino Pucci and starring Gloria Heelheart, was having its premiere that night. The evening promised to be full of stars, glamour, and excitement. Primo hadn't yet *de*hypnotized any of his celebrities, and at Molly's request, he had invited most of them to come. Molly knew that everyone from Happiness House would love this, especially Mrs. Trinklebury and Hazel. She wanted to give them a night they would always remember.

So the next day, as Primo Cell tackled the serious task of informing Congress and the world that he didn't want to be president, Molly handled the more pleasurable job of taking Petula to Bella's Poodle Salon. Then she made sure that she and Rocky had some nice clothes to wear.

At six that evening, Cell parked his favorite Rolls-Royce next to Sinclair's Aston Martin underneath the hill house. Rocky, Molly, Petula, Sinclair, and Forest came down the elevator all spruced up and ready to hit the town. Forest was in his usual socks and flip-flops, but because it was a special occasion, he was wearing his brown cheesecloth suit and his favorite T-shirt, which said RECYCLE, DUDES. Unfortunately, Cornelius had to come with them, as no one was entirely happy about leaving him behind. Dressed in a gray tracksuit and with a stubbly beard, he looked reasonably normal, although as they drove along he stuck his head out of the window and bleated with excitement. Everyone ignored him.

They drove to Hollywood Boulevard, where they all climbed out and headed toward the movie theater.

As they neared the crowded, spotlit entrance, Molly's heart fluttered. She couldn't wait to see her old orphanage family.

And suddenly, there they were, standing on the sidewalk, all dressed up and obviously just as excited as Molly and Rocky.

"Oooooh, they're here!" shrieked Mrs. Trinklebury, launching herself toward them like a violet chiffon rocket. "I c-can't believe how much I've missed you both," she said, practically knocking their heads together and suffocating them with her embrace.

Molly and Rocky breathed in Mrs. Trinklebury's familiar smell. It was a country-cottage smell, of cakes and rose water, of vanilla and lavender honey and butter. A smell that reminded them of her nursery rhymes and games of hide-and-seek.

"Oh, Mrs. T.," said Molly, her eyes filling with tears. "Oh, it's just lovely to see you again."

"Same here, chick," said Mrs. Trinklebury, giving her a squeeze that made her know she'd come home at last.

"And congratulations . . . you know, being engaged and all that."

"Thank you, s-sweetheart. We won't be m-married for a little while, but look at my ring." Mrs. Trinklebury showed Molly a bright-yellow buttercup that girdled her fat finger.

"It's lovely!"

Molly felt a tug at her dress. Ruby and Jinx were staring up at her.

"I can read now, Molly," Ruby said. "And I can

write. Look." She ripped open an envelope that said
"*Welcum bac*," and inside was a card with a picture of
Petula painted on it.

"It's for you two," she said, thrusting it into Molly's
hands.

Then everyone wanted to say hello.

What Molly found amazing was how all the children
had changed. Everyone was taller, especially Gemma
and Gerry. Gordon, Cynthia, and Hazel had slimmed
down a lot. Craig was muscly. Hazel was the most
difficult to recognize, as she'd dyed her hair platinum
blond. And everyone looked healthy, as though they'd
had a lovely summer in the sun.

"Hi, guys," Hazel said, kissing them.

"What's happened to your accent? You sound
American," Molly observed.

"I'm practicing for a walk-on part I got in a film,"
said Hazel. "I've got loads to tell you."

"Hello, you two, nice to see you," said Nockman,
smiling from behind Hazel. He was wearing a green
velvet suit and a Hawaiian shirt with a red parrot on it.
Molly was amazed—his German accent had worn off, so
now he spoke in his original Chicago accent.

The only person missing from the Happiness
House crowd was Roger. Molly saw him thirty feet

away, talking to a palm tree. He seemed completely oblivious of Cornelius, who was bleating madly and cantering around and around him, shouting, "Bah mine, baaaah mine, baaaah mine."

Sinclair went over to quiet him down.

Cameras flashed as everyone stepped onto the short red carpet in front of the theater. Already the stars were arriving. Hercules Stone kissed Mrs. Trinklebury's hand and escorted her past the barriers lined with cheering fans. Mrs. Trinklebury batted her eyelashes and waved at them as if she was the queen. Cosmo Ace introduced himself to Hazel. King Moose went in with Cynthia, and Stephanie Goulash took a blushing Mr. Nockman and Gordon by the hand. Dusty Goldman led in Jinx and Ruby, Sinclair dealt with Cornelius, Rocky found himself making friends with Billy Bob Bimble, and Molly was very happy to accompany Gemma, Gerry, and Primo Cell in.

Petula and Gloria Heelheart behaved like the true professionals they were. Petula barked at the applauding crowds, twirled on her hind legs for the photographers, and let Gloria smother her with perfumed caresses. Everyone loved her.

The film was Gino Pucci's best work to date. And without doubt, the most entertaining bits in it were Petula's. Everyone clapped and cheered—especially when she had to parachute with Gloria from a burning airplane.

After the premiere, they all went out with the hypnotized stars for a celebratory supper.

Los Angeles is a great city for restaurants. There's Japanese, Chinese, Thai, Spanish, English, Mexican, Indian, Moroccan, Persian, and, of course, always, American. But the restaurant that Primo Cell picked for the party was French. It was called the Orangerie and had a very famous chef. This was the home of lobster bisque and snails in garlic, of complicated sauces and dishes that took hours to prepare, of *frites*, not French fries, and of towering soufflés and oozing desserts.

It was a lovely evening. The ordering was chaotic, as no one understood the French menu, but everything was delicious and all the guests got fuller and fuller and fuller. Molly and Rocky were eager to hear what the others had been doing.

"Craig can surf really well," said Jinx, stuffing *frites* into his mouth. "But he said to start with, it was like being a fly flushed down the toilet. Soon I'm gonna learn too. Except I don't know if we'll be here." Jinx turned to Mrs. Trinklebury. "Are we going to stay in California for a long time?"

The chatter round the table subsided as the ears of the orphanage children responded like radar scanners to Jinx's shrill question. The room went quiet.

"Well, ch-chuck," Mrs. Trinklebury stammered, halfway through a mouthful of salad. "I really don't know. I mean, what d-do you all think? Molly and Rocky are b-back now. Maybe the time has come for us to go h-home. You know we c-can't expect Mr. Sinclair to pay our rent f-f-forever. And Simon will b-be able to make a living if he finishes his locksmith exams back in Briersville."

Primo Cell interrupted. "You can all come and live at my place," he said.

Mrs. Trinklebury coughed as a piece of lettuce went down the wrong way. Mr. Nockman patted her on the back.

"Of course, you and Mr. Nockman are invited, too," said Primo. "Unless you'd prefer to be somewhere else, but I think the children would miss you if you lived farther away than the gatehouse."

"Well, it's a lovely idea," said Mrs. Trinklebury. "Isn't it, Simon, dear?"

"The only problem is that we have a lot of animals and birds," Nockman said.

"Yeah, I've got thirty-three mice now," said Gerry. "Actually, I think Scrunchball might be having her babies right this minute."

"My house is huge. We could start a zoo there," said Primo.

And so it was decided that a vote should be taken. Everyone wanted to come to stay at Primo's. And the matter seemed final, until Molly remembered Roger, who was sitting under an orange tree in the restaurant's hallway.

Roger was eating a bowl of pecan nuts.

"How are you, Roger?" Molly asked quietly. Roger looked shifty and threw a blue paper dart at her.

Molly opened it up. Inside, the scrawled writing said:

Sorry about this, but I know too much.

"Know too much about what, Roger?"

Roger looked up at her sadly. "Too much about the she-he," he said mournfully.

Memories of the words in other paper messages that Roger had written filled Molly's head: *"Send help quick!*

Aliens have eaten my brain!" "Watch out! The brain centipedes are here!" "Don't judge your body by its skin."

Molly thought of the topiary hare in Cornelius's collection of clipped bushes. Was it a mad March hare? Did it represent Roger?

In a moment of pure instinct, Molly stopped the world. She took Roger's hand and sent a shaft of coldness into it so that he could move, and she looked deeply into his confused eyes.

"From now on," she said, "you, Roger, will no longer be under anyone else's power. You will be yourself." Then she added the old, useful password, "Perfectly punctually!"

And with that, Roger blinked and the glazed look in his eyes fell away.

Molly let the world move. Roger stared around him and seized Molly's hand as if he was finding it difficult to balance. He looked completely disoriented, as though everything in the room was upside down. Then he put his hand on his chest as if checking he was alive. In a moment he'd absorbed what had happened.

"Oh, thank you, Molly. Molly, you've saved me," he cried. He threw his arms around Molly's neck and hugged her tightly. He smelled of leaves and bark and grass.

"I've been trapped inside myself—it's been horrible,"

he sobbed. "All the time I was trying to tell everyone, but I couldn't communicate. Cornelius did it. And he made me have hallucinations. He hypnotized me to think that voices were hunting me. It's been so frightening. I can't tell you how frightening."

"Don't worry, Roger, it's going to be all right now," said Molly, hugging him back.

"Thank you, Molly," Roger sobbed. "You've freed me. Thank you, thank you, thank you." For a moment Roger clung to Molly. Then he let go and put his head in his hands.

"So, you found out too much about Cornelius Logan?" guessed Molly. "How?"

"You remember how I liked to go through garbage cans," said Roger. "Well, I went through the cans at the library, Lucy Logan's cans. I found instructions that Cornelius Logan had written. I saw Lucy Logan arguing with him. They looked so alike. It was weird. I saw him push her into a car. She was driven away. Cornelius saw me. I knew too much. He hypnotized me. I've been crazy for months."

"Well, not anymore, Roger," said Molly.

Molly thought of Forest. He was going to have two basket cases on his hands this winter. Roger, like Primo, would need to stay here with Forest until he had recovered. And the decision that everyone must stay in L.A. became clear.

Except for Molly. Molly had to leave. For Molly knew that soon Primo Cell would learn that she was his daughter, and she really wasn't ready for that yet. She wanted to live with the idea of having a father before she introduced herself to him properly. Besides, she had something much more important to do.

Much later that night, as everyone else arrived at Primo Cell's gray stone mansion, thrilled that this was to be their new home, Molly, Petula, and Rocky stood on the tarmac of Los Angeles airport. A private jet, a black-and-golden symbol painted on its tail fin, awaited its single passenger.

"I'll miss you," said Molly.

"I'll miss you," said Rocky. "Are you sure you don't want me to come?"

"No, Rocky. This is something I need to figure out. It won't be any fun for you. You need a vacation. And Billy Bob Bimble seems to be very interested in doing some music with you. You've got to go for it. I'll be back soon."

"As long as you think you'll be all right, Molly. But if you need me for anything, at any time, even in the middle of the night, call me."

"I will."

The two friends hugged, and then Molly gave a whistle. "Come on, Petula."

Rocky watched his best friend climb the plane's steps. The engines started, Molly waved once more, and then she was gone.

Forty-four

Flying home in Primo Cell's luxurious private jet was fabulous. Its main cabin was laid out like a sitting room, with cream-colored carpets, small tables, and green leather armchairs.

The flight attendant was very welcoming, and soon Molly was belted up, with a grenadine in her hand and Petula beside her. The engines roared and Los Angeles, lit up with a billion bulbs and a million wannabe stars, slipped away beneath them.

Molly spent most of the eleven-hour flight asleep in a comfortable full-sized bed. She touched down feeling wide-awake.

At the airport a car was waiting for her, and soon she was sitting in the back of a spacious Mercedes, rolling down country roads.

★ ★ ★

It was a fifty-minute journey to Cornelius Logan's house.

Cornelius hadn't lived all these years in a humble cottage like his sister. He'd had access to as much money as he'd wanted—money made by Primo Cell. So, fond of luxury and excess, Cornelius had bought himself an astonishingly grand house in the country.

Briersville Park had a four-mile-long drive. Once Molly had hypnotized the gatekeeper, the car purred smoothly along it. She and Petula stared out of the window at the herd of llamas grazing under old oak trees. Then the llama paddocks came to an end, and now the parkland was full of dark-green bushes. They were all topiary hedges. And each one was of a different creature. A horse hedge, an elephant bush, a cat, a mouse, a monkey. Here and there, Molly saw people in yellow suits on ladders with shears in their hands, clipping the leafy sculptures. Molly felt sure that every one of the bush animals stood for a person Cornelius Logan had hypnotized.

Eventually, the car turned a wide bend, and before them was the house. White, stately, and splendid, it had four tall columns supporting its palatial porch and steps leading down to a circular gravel drive. Topiary animals stood on the lawns in front of it, looking as if they wanted to walk in. A giant magpie bush, shaped to look as if it was flying, grew in the center of the circle of gravel.

Molly picked up Petula and stopped the world.

She climbed out of the car and up the broad steps. She walked straight past the frozen butler at the front door and into the hall. Animal heads—of bison, tigers, leopards, antelope, and deer—stared down from the walls. Petula growled at them. A display of antique shears reminded Molly of exactly where they were.

She looked at the map that Cornelius had drawn her and went up the main stairs. Here the walls were covered with clocks. At the top stood a maid, still as a statue. Molly started to run. She ran down a corridor lined with tables. On each one sat a tiny bonsai tree in a pot. She picked her way up another flight of stairs.

Now they were at the top of the house. These rooms were the servants' quarters. Molly squeezed Petula for comfort and started down the long passage.

At the end there was a motionless guard sitting by a red door.

For a moment, Molly caught her breath. Then slowly she lifted the latch.

Inside, Lucy Logan stood motionless, still as the window that she was staring out of. She was dressed in a white dressing gown, and she looked thin and tired. But she was, at last, the real Lucy Logan—the Lucy with the sky-blue eyes.

Molly stepped toward her. As she did, her eyes fell on a piece of paper on the windowsill. On the paper were handwritten words, a verse. Molly couldn't help reading them. They went:

Sitting on an island in the ocean
May seem kinda free.
Lying on a beach of golden sand
May sound as life should be.
Sounds like heaven,
But it ain't heaven,
No siree.
A billion waves of sea, you see,
Divide you from me.
Only you can make my world
Heavenly.

They sounded like the words of an old-fashioned song.

Molly paused, suddenly aware that an uncertain future was before her. She wondered how old-fashioned Lucy Logan would be. She hoped they would like each other.

In fact, now that she was about to wake her mother,

Molly wasn't really sure that she wanted one. It was one thing knowing who her mother was, and quite another actually having one. Would Molly suddenly find herself being told to do things? She didn't like this idea at all. She was used to being her own boss. For a few seconds, Molly's eyes lingered on the song as she pondered her predicament. Well, she thought, she would have to make her feelings very, very clear to Lucy Logan as soon as she could. That was all.

Molly was just about ready now. Then another fear reared its head.

If Molly was now Lucy Logan and Primo Cell's daughter, would she have to change her name? The thought that she might have to become Molly Cell or Molly Logan was extremely unsavory. Molly could already feel herself digging in her heels to refuse.

But worse than that was the notion that Molly might be made to be someone else in *other* ways. She didn't want to become a person her new parents might like her to be. She wanted to always be herself, Molly Moon.

Molly sat down on a chair. She looked at her mother's slippered feet and then at the sneakers on her own. In an instant she realized that it made no difference who her parents were. They were themselves and she was herself, if she chose to be. What had she been thinking? That she might be brainwashed by her new parents? Of course she wouldn't be. Her mind was a free place, wasn't it?

It was then, in the silence of the turret room, that Molly made a secret oath. She promised that *whatever* happened, she would always make up her own mind about things. However the dice fell, she would always be true to her Molly Moon self.

Her changing self. Molly looked out the window at an autumn leaf that hung in the air, and she considered how much she'd changed since she'd last seen Lucy Logan. Nearly a year had passed, and in that time she'd almost been blown away. There had been brilliant moments, but some dreadful ones, too.

As Molly held the world still, she felt scared by the future—worried by its uncertainty. She was nervous of letting it come. Who knew what other nasty surprises her life held in store for her?

But life was always unpredictable, she realized. That was what made it exciting. No one ever knew what was around the corner. Of course there might be bad situations, but life was so full of interesting things and beauty and clever people and lovely animals and funny friends that there really was nothing to fear. Life was there to be lived, not to be held captive like a genie in a bottle.

Outside the window, the sky was irresistibly blue.

Molly felt her spirit inside like a fiery bird longing to fly. She was ready for both sunlight and rainstorms. So, seizing the moment, Molly popped the cork and bravely unleashed time.

In the Hollywood Hills, a girl sat cross-legged on the ground in a scruffy chicken yard. She was wearing purple pajamas and dark sunglasses. Beside her hand, a chicken pecked the ground for grain, and in front of her sat a tall old hippie. His eyes were big and swirling behind his bottle-glass spectacles. His hair was long and gray.

"More tofu turnip, Davina?"

"Yes, please. And Forest, can we eat it standing on our heads again?"

"Sure thing. That would be my cosmic pleasure."

Georgia Byng

grew up by the River Itchen in Hampshire, England, in a large family. After leaving school, she studied drama and worked as an actor and children's entertainer. Ms. Byng lives in London with the artist Marc Quinn, her daughter, Tiger, and son, Lucas. She is also the author of *Molly Moon's Incredible Book of Hypnotism*.